Days Like
Shadows Pass

A Yorkshire Murder Mystery

Tom Raven Book 5

M S MORRIS

PROLOGUE

The sea fret enfolded the town of Whitby like a shroud, draping the streets with a cold, grey mist, snaking into alleyways, rolling up the River Esk and obscuring the abbey perched on top of the East Cliff.

Mia Munroe locked the door of her terraced cottage in Silver Street and descended the stone steps to the road, lifting the hem of her dress so as not to step on the delicate fabric. In her heeled, satin pumps, the skirt just skimmed the ground.

The ivory silk gown hung a little loose on the bodice – she'd lost weight in the year since it had been tailor-made for her. As she walked down the narrow street, the multi-layered net petticoat beneath her skirt rustled against her bare legs. Behind her, the veil of embroidered tulle attached to the tiara of silver flowers and butterflies billowed in the light breeze.

She didn't feel the cold.

She passed her local fish and chip shop where a man in overalls and Wellington boots was unloading crates of ice-packed cod and haddock from the back of his van. As Mia walked past, he stopped his work, setting a heavy crate down on the ground and straightening up to stare at her. His mouth fell open as if he had something to say, but no words emerged. Mia continued on her way, feeling his eyes boring into her back. She was used to being stared at. She'd endured a year of such reactions, and of receiving unkind comments, even outright mockery. She no longer cared what people thought. Today was her special day. Let them look.

A bride was supposed to be the centre of attention, wasn't she?

No doubt the fishmonger was surprised to see her in white. After all, she'd spent a whole year wearing nothing but black. A living spectre haunting the quaint seaside town.

It was a year and a day since her fiancé, Nathan, had drowned after being washed from the East Pier during a ferocious storm. Since then, Mia had donned traditional Victorian mourning attire, entombing her grief in a long-sleeved, floor-length black crepe dress, her milk-white skin adorned with jet jewellery. The colour had mirrored the feelings of her heart. The light had gone out of her world and she had clothed herself in darkness.

The Victorians had displayed a healthy respect for death. You might say they'd been a little obsessed with it. But death came to all of us. It was folly to pretend otherwise. Queen Victoria had led the way, donning black from the day of Albert's death until her own death years later. The nation had followed suit, following strict rules and observing a specified mourning period following the passing of a loved one. In those days, everyone had understood the need for grief, and those in mourning were treated with respect.

In the modern world, things were different. Inevitably, Mia's elaborate black gowns had drawn the attention of the locals. She had seen the curiosity and pity in their eyes; had heard the whispers behind her back. Yet she had remained steadfast and true, honouring the memory of the man she had loved and lost.

She turned left into Flowergate and paused briefly outside the shop where she worked: Vivienne's Vamp & Victoriana. It was still early morning and the shop hadn't yet opened. The windows were filled with beautiful clothing, some new, some vintage. Floor-length frocks in black and purple; lacy blood-red bodices; leather corsets; velvet jackets. Each one exquisite and unique. The distinctive look of the shop's wares attracted visitors in search of anything from vampire mini-dresses to steampunk crinolines.

Of all the townsfolk, Vivienne had been most kind to her. Before the accident, Mia had appreciated the older woman's words of wisdom on the subject of love and marriage. Together they had designed and made her wedding dress, spending countless hours in a back room of the shop after closing time. After Nathan's death, Vivienne had kept her counsel when Mia started dressing in ever more elaborate mourning costumes. And she would surely understand why Mia had chosen to wear her bridal gown on this day. The dress she should have worn eight months earlier on her wedding day at St Mary's Church.

Mia turned away from the shop and continued along Flowergate. The cobbled street narrowed and veered to the right, descending steeply. She held the railing at the side of the road to avoid tripping over her dress. At the bottom of the hill she emerged onto St Ann's Staith, the road that ran along the west bank of the Esk. She crossed the river by the swing bridge and turned into Church Street, the heart of the old town. Here the shops, cafés, bars and inns that lined the street were beginning to come to life. At one of the many jet jewellery stores, the owner stared at her in surprise as he rolled up the shutters to reveal sparkling silver-and-black necklaces and earrings on their display stands. Mia touched the jet necklace that embellished her own neck – a gift from Nathan. At the White Horse & Griffin two cleaners who were arriving for work looked up at her. One whispered something to the other, and they giggled.

Mia walked on, her head held high.

At the foot of the one hundred and ninety-nine steps that led up the hillside she paused for a moment. This was the route she would have taken on her wedding day. A long trek for a bride, but not for one as determined as Mia. In olden times, the faithful had seen the journey up to the church as a test of their commitment, and Mia was resolved to pass that test now. With a renewed sense of purpose, she began the long climb to the top.

The steps were broad and shallow, a winding path that led from sea level to St Mary's on the clifftop. Her heart beat faster as she climbed, and yet the burden she carried in her soul felt lighter with every step. Halfway up, she stopped by a bench and looked back down. The sea fret still clung to the town, reluctant to let go, but she knew that if she continued she would eventually rise above it. Breathing steadily, she made her way to the top.

Beyond the final step, the square-towered church sat solidly amid the gravestones that surrounded it. Beyond the church, through veils of grey mist, she glimpsed the skeletal remains of Whitby Abbey.

She wandered freely among the graves, inhaling the smell of damp earth. With each step the heels of her satin pumps sank into the soft ground, leaving a trail of small indentations behind her. The hem of her dress swept the wet grass, soaking up morning dew.

On the south side of the church she lingered to read the words inscribed on the stone sundial. *Our days pass like a shadow.* This last year had been a half-life, a shadowy existence, a poor reflection of the life she should have led. But now her period of mourning was over. It was time for a new beginning.

As she reached the edge of the graveyard, the sea mist finally released its grasp on the town and a tentative ray of sunlight pierced the greyness. Mia turned her face to the light and felt its warmth lift her spirits. The clouds parted, revealing a dazzling blue sky. She felt a flicker of hope, a growing sense of freedom. Here was the promise of a new life awaiting her. She knew she had come to the right place. The universe was waiting to embrace her.

Far below, the waves broke against the rocks, spitting flecks of white foam into the air. These were the very rocks that had claimed Nathan's life. The sea was calm today, only a gentle swell disturbing its stillness, but just as grey and cold as the day it had stolen him away from her.

Mia shivered as she gazed down upon its silvery, treacherous surface. She moved to the very edge of the cliff and lifted her arms wide. She felt weightless, the sky itself seeming to hold her in its embrace. 'I'm coming, Nathan,' she whispered.

And then she was falling.

For a moment she thought she was flying. Her wedding dress billowed behind her like a parachute. A seagull shrieked in alarm, just inches from her face, at the sight of this white apparition invading its space. A cry escaped Mia's lips, whether of joy or terror she couldn't tell. For a moment she felt free of the grief that had been her constant companion for a year and a day.

And then the darkness reclaimed her.

CHAPTER 1

Three months later

DCI Tom Raven hated waiting. He checked his watch for the umpteenth time as he paced up and down the concourse at Scarborough railway station, anxiety twisting his gut into knots. It was a Thursday morning in late April – the end of the Easter holidays – and the station was filled with bustling crowds of suitcase-wheeling tourists, business people on their mobile phones and shoppers heading to York for the day. Raven scowled at them all as he passed.

Relax, he told himself, taking a deep breath. *This is supposed to be a holiday*. The problem was, Raven wasn't good with holidays.

This was the first proper leave he'd taken from work since his father's funeral back in October and that certainly hadn't been an enjoyable experience. It had turned into an existential crisis, with Raven resigning from his job in London, transferring to Scarborough CID, and ultimately divorcing his wife of twenty-three years, Lisa.

So much for holidays.

Now he'd been living in Scarborough, his birth town, for six whole months and his life had changed beyond recognition. A new job, a new house, and a chance to do things better this time round. Which shouldn't be hard, given the way he'd messed up so badly in the past.

Where had the years gone? Two weeks ago, while attending a media awareness course, he had turned forty-eight, a fact that made him acutely aware of the ticking clock, nudging him ever closer to the half-century mark. On some mornings, when he woke before first light with the Yorkshire cold in his bones and his leg stiff and aching, he felt as if he'd already crossed "over the hill" and was descending the other side without having enjoyed the view from the top.

But perhaps there was still something worth seeing on the way down.

His phone buzzed, pulling him back to his present concerns. It was a message from Hannah, his daughter. She'd been texting him all morning, updating him on the progress of her journey. She'd caught the 08:00 departure from King's Cross – she'd been staying with her mother in London during the university holidays – and was now on the 10:03 from York, due to arrive in Scarborough at 10:53. Raven scoured the digital board overhead to verify the information. The trains, for once, were running like clockwork. A minor miracle, given the normally unpredictable nature of the British rail network.

He texted back to say he was waiting to meet her, then decided he had time for a quick coffee before she arrived. It might help to calm him down. Not the coffee itself, obviously; that would only add fuel to the fire. But the simple act of making himself sit still and drink it. It would be good for his leg too, which was never happy when forced to move too quickly or for extended periods. He ordered a double espresso from the station buffet and took up residence at the last unoccupied table to await the arrival of the train.

There were many reasons for Raven's anxiety, not

simply his inability to successfully navigate days off work. He had never enjoyed a close relationship with Hannah. It was one of his greatest regrets that he had allowed his dedication to his job to keep him away from his daughter while she was growing up. Now, since his separation from Lisa and his move to Scarborough, along with Hannah being away at university, he hadn't seen her in person for almost a year. What would they find to talk about?

And then there was the state of his house in Quay Street. In recent months, the old townhouse, which Raven had inherited in a dilapidated state from his father, had undergone a transformation. But even though Raven had repeatedly insisted on having the last of the work finished before Hannah's arrival, he had left home that morning with Barry Hardcastle, the builder who had become a mainstay in Raven's life, in the midst of a last-minute scramble to complete the final touches to the kitchen.

To his credit, even Barry, despite his usual casual approach to deadlines, seemed to understand the importance of Raven's need. He had begun work at the crack of dawn and promised to pull out all the stops to get the last tasks done. 'It's a team effort, Raven,' he had assured him. 'All sides pulling together. Isn't that right, Reggie?' he had asked his assistant. Raven could only hope that it was.

His phone buzzed again and he scrutinised it apprehensively. This time it was, in fact, a text from his builder. Raven's heart sank, expecting some new calamity.

Nearly there, mate. Just the sink to sort out.

He sighed, relieved, just counting on Barry's definition of "nearly there" being less elastic than usual. He checked his watch again. 10:50. He could only trust that the sink, the last piece of his newly renovated kitchen puzzle, would be in place by the time he brought Hannah home.

Born in London and now in her final year of studying Law at Exeter University, this would be the first time she had ever visited Raven's home town of Scarborough. She'd never known her paternal grandmother who had died when Raven himself was just sixteen – a tragedy that had kept him from returning to Scarborough for thirty-one years. The idea of introducing Hannah to her late grandfather, the alcoholic and violent Alan Raven, had been unthinkable.

She was a confirmed southerner, conditioned by Lisa's disdain for all things northern into thinking of Yorkshire as a backward, ignorant place inhabited by stubborn folk who wore flat caps and kept whippets. Raven wondered what she would make of the North Yorkshire coast, and whether it might persuade her that civilisation didn't end north of the M25 motorway that separated London from the great unwashed. He mentally drew up a list of places he might take her. The ancient castle, overlooking the town from its hilltop eyrie; the North and South Bays, even though it was only April and hardly sunbathing weather; the Rotunda museum, which he had only recently visited for the first time himself. He hoped she wouldn't find these dull and provincial.

The station intercom crackled into life as a woman's pre-recorded voice announced the imminent arrival of the train from York. Raven downed the last of his coffee and clambered to his feet, heading to the ticket barriers and feeling a sudden surge of anticipation and last-minute nerves. He longed to hold his daughter in his arms. Between the demands of her studies and the renovations on his house, their relationship had been reduced to Skype calls and text messages. He realised now just how much emotional energy he had invested in this visit. It was a chance – perhaps one final chance – for them to rebuild their relationship, as two adults.

The train pulled into the station and the first passengers started to appear at the ticket barriers. Raven scanned the faces of the new arrivals. Strangers, every one. Where was Hannah? The crowds milled about chaotically and there was an inevitable delay when someone's ticket wouldn't scan and the guard on duty had to open the accessible gate. Raven's jaw clenched with a mixture of annoyance and concern. Still no sign of his daughter.

And then there she was.

He almost didn't recognise her for an instant. She was taller than he remembered. More beautiful than ever, her long blonde hair streaming over her shoulders. A grown woman. Her mother's fair features, but with his own dark eyes looking out.

She spotted him as soon as she was through the ticket barrier. 'Dad!' she called, her face breaking into a wide grin as she saw him. She rushed over, her heavy backpack bouncing against her shoulders.

'Hannah!' Raven opened his arms, embracing her tightly. He could feel her laughing against his chest, a sound that filled him with a warmth that had been missing in his empty house.

'Missed you, Dad.' She pulled away and looked up at him.

'I've missed you too, sweetheart. Come on, let's go home. Do you have any luggage?'

'Just my rucksack.'

They strolled to his car, chatting about her journey. Easy, neutral small talk. Even Raven could manage that.

'Still driving this?' said Hannah, indicating the silver BMW M6 standing in the far corner of the car park.

'Of course,' answered Raven, leaping automatically to the defence of his ageing car. 'It still goes.'

But there was no need for him to justify his love of the impractical gas-guzzler with its cramped rear seats. Whereas Lisa would have infused her remark with derision, Hannah's question betrayed genuine fondness for the old car. She deposited her rucksack in the boot and settled herself in the passenger seat. 'Ah, the smell of this car takes me back.'

Raven smiled. Now that the family home was sold and the family itself broken into its constituent parts – himself, Lisa, and Hannah, each following their own separate path through life – perhaps the old coupé was one of the few objects that still tied them together. It was more than a car, it was a vault of shared memories, a piece of history. He would tell Lisa that if ever she was rude about it again.

He was just about to start the engine when his phone rang. If this was Barry calling to say he needed an extra half an hour then Raven wouldn't complain. Instead, he would take Hannah for a spin up Oliver's Mount and show her the stunning views over Scarborough's South Bay. He was feeling in a generous mood, even towards his builder. But when he glanced at the screen he saw that it wasn't Barry. It was his boss, Detective Superintendent Gillian Ellis. What on earth did she want, today of all days? She, of all people, had encouraged him to take some time off, warning him that if he didn't use his annual leave in the allotted time, he risked losing it. He considered letting it go to voicemail then thought better of it.

'Sorry,' he told Hannah. 'I'd better take this.' He accepted the call and pressed the phone to his ear. 'Gillian, this had better be good.'

'Tom, I need you in Whitby. Urgently.' She offered no apology for interrupting his holiday. Maybe she had forgotten he was on leave. Come to think of it, he'd never known her take a day off herself. But that didn't mean she could ride rough-shod over his own meticulously-laid plans.

'Sorry, Gillian. I've booked a few days off. I've just collected my daughter from the train station.' He grimaced at Hannah and mouthed the words *my boss* at her. Hannah raised her eyebrows in response.

'I know that, Tom, but hear me out.' There was an odd inflection in Gillian's voice that Raven hadn't heard before. It took him a moment to identify it. Then with a start he realised: it was a pleading tone. Gillian was appealing for his help. 'There's been a murder, Tom. Not just a routine kind of crime. When you see how the victim was killed you'll understand...' Her voice faltered. 'The fact is, I need my most senior detective on this.'

Although flattered, Raven knew he had to refuse. His dedication to his job was the reason he had never truly bonded with his daughter. Now of all times was his chance to prove he had chosen the right priorities at last. 'Couldn't DI Dinsdale...' He hated suggesting his rival for the job. Dinsdale was lazy, incompetent and unimaginative. But he would have to do.

'No,' insisted Gillian. 'Dinsdale is not the person to take the lead on this. You're the only person who will do.'

Raven glanced across at Hannah who had clearly caught onto the gist of the conversation. She looked resigned. Maybe Lisa had warned her that something like this might happen. Maybe it was exactly what she'd been expecting all along.

'Look,' he heard himself saying. 'Send me the details. I'll drive over to Whitby and take a look. But it had better be as serious as you say.' He ended the call and turned to Hannah, feeling dread in the pit of his stomach at the prospect of letting her down once again. 'I'm really sorry, sweetheart, but something major has come up. But once I get my team started on this, I'm sure I'll be able to hand over to my sergeant for a few days. Then we can spend some time together as we planned.'

Hannah looked glum for a second, then she quickly rallied. 'Don't worry about it, Dad, I'm sure I can find things to do in Scarborough. I'm a big girl now.'

'I know.' Raven sighed, feeling his last-ditch opportunity to bridge the gap with his daughter slipping from his grasp. He drove back to Quay Street, wracked by guilt. Barry had better have finished that kitchen sink, or there would be hell to pay.

CHAPTER 2

'This had better be good,' moaned Raven. 'Or bad. This had better be seriously bad, or else I'll be cross.'

The M6 gobbled up the miles to Whitby, Raven taking the journey at his usual speed. Fast. Probably even faster than usual. Beside him in the passenger seat sat DS Becca Shawcross, one hand firmly clenching the handle of the door to brace herself against the twists and turns, the hills and valleys, the sudden changes in speed as Raven pushed his foot to the floor or stamped hard on the brake in annoyance. The roar and whine of the car's engine helped to vent some of his frustration.

'You're not already cross, then?' Becca enquired mildly.

'I'm already *quite* cross,' he conceded. 'But if I get there and it turns out that I'm not really required' – he paused as he pressed his foot on the accelerator and twitched the wheel to overtake a car hauling a caravan up an incline – 'then I'll be really cross.'

'I'll wait to see what that looks like, then.'

Raven had collected her from Scarborough police

station immediately after dropping Hannah off at the house in Quay Street and making sure once again that she would be okay without him. 'As long as you tell me the wi-fi password,' she'd assured him with a grin. 'Honestly, there's no need to worry, Dad.'

He was glad she was proving to be so understanding. If Lisa found out about this, she'd be kicking up a storm soon enough. Lisa was always looking for an excuse to berate him.

Becca had greeted his arrival at the station with raised eyebrows. 'Back so soon?'

'Not my choice,' he'd grumbled at her. 'Come on, you'd better get your coat on. We're off to Whitby.'

He'd spent a surprisingly large part of the journey telling her about Hannah and how glad he was to have her visiting him, and how bad he felt at having to leave her behind, with only Barry and Reg for company. Inevitably, Barry had still "not quite finished, mate, any minute now" which had earned him a dark look and a stern rebuke from Raven. Still, Hannah hadn't seemed to mind. 'At least I'll have someone to talk to,' she'd informed him.

Raven didn't usually reveal so much about himself and his family, but today, perhaps because he was supposed to be on leave, he had opened up to Becca, who had proved to be an attentive and sympathetic listener. She had done her best to assuage his feelings of guilt.

'Don't worry,' she reassured him. 'Hannah sounds like a resourceful person. I'm sure she'll be able to entertain herself in Scarborough for a day or two while you get the investigation started. With any luck you'll be able to spend the weekend with her.'

'Yes,' agreed Raven, 'especially if you deputise for me.' It would do Becca good to take on more responsibility, and she was more than capable of supervising the day-to-day tasks of a murder inquiry once everything was up to speed. In a few years she might even be ready to start thinking about promotion to detective inspector.

'I'd be happy to,' she said, sounding pleased.

Raven turned right off the A171, following the sign for Whitby Abbey. The road soon narrowed almost to a single track bordered by a dry stone wall with fields beyond. The abbey stood on the eastern headland high above the town, and the terrain here was bleak. Gusts of wind blasting in from the sea buffeted the car from side to side. A few caravans and mobile holiday homes dotted the landscape, but he didn't fancy spending a week in one of them this early in the season.

'Nicer in the summer months, I expect,' remarked Becca.

Before long, the sea came into view on their right and then the ruins of the abbey itself began to loom steadily before them, all broken arches and shattered towers. They passed a small brewery and the road veered left into the visitors' car park. Raven pulled up next to an ice-cream van which was offering a special deal on ninety-nines. Unfortunately it didn't look as if it was doing much business today, despite the undeniable attractiveness of its offer. The car park was closed, and uniformed police officers were ushering disappointed and bemused visitors away.

'Let's find out what the circus is all about, then,' he said.

A rotund, middle-aged sergeant ambled over to them as they got out of the car. He extended a hand. 'Sergeant Mike Fields, pleased to make your acquaintance, sir. You must be DCI Raven and DS Shawcross. I was told to expect you.'

Whitby didn't have its own Criminal Investigation Department, so it was normal for Scarborough-based detectives to be called to the scene of any major incident in the town. Even so, Raven was sensitive to the fact that he was the outsider here, and Sergeant Fields was the local with intimate knowledge of the location and its inhabitants. Fields would want to feel respected and valued.

He grasped the man's hand and shook it warmly.

'Pleased to meet you, Sergeant. We're in your hands. Lead the way.' They set off across the car park, Fields moving at a relaxed pace, Raven eager to get going yet privately relieved that he wouldn't be obliged to hurry. His leg never responded well to that. 'How and when was the body discovered?'

'First thing this morning,' said Fields. 'One of the English Heritage staff was just checking the place over before opening the abbey to visitors. Gave her quite a shock, I can tell you.' His face turned to Raven, revealing a shadow of unease. 'Gave me a shock too when I saw it, I don't mind telling you. Thirty years in the job and I've never seen the like.'

The sergeant seemed to want to leave them in suspense, and Raven didn't press him for more information. He would be able to view the scene for himself very shortly.

At the ticket office, Fields lifted the crime-scene tape cordoning off the area and Raven ducked beneath it, entering the abbey grounds via a flight of stone stairs. The remains of the building stood before him amid neatly-clipped grass and he glanced up at the massive stone walls and archways, rising grey in the pewter sky. Vague images of a school trip tickled the edges of his memory, but he'd been more interested then in the hemline of Donna Craven's skirt than in the history of an old ruin. Not for the first time he wished he'd paid more attention to what he'd been told. What he did recall was that for some reason Yorkshire possessed more than its fair share of monasteries, all of them now ruined, thanks to Henry VIII, whose dedication to flattening them had been impressive. Fountains Abbey and Rievaulx Abbey might be better preserved, but Whitby enjoyed the most dramatic location, high on the East Cliff, overlooking the harbour that faced the battering waves of the North Sea.

Apart from the police presence, the place was deserted and felt quite desolate. As Raven approached the abbey, his coat flapped wildly in the wind, and a murder of crows took flight from the gothic arches, circling overhead and cawing like a bad omen. It was easy to understand why Bram Stoker had chosen Whitby as the fictional location for Dracula to first set foot on English soil.

'That Bram Stoker's got a lot to answer for, if you ask me,' remarked Fields, as if reading Raven's mind. 'The Whitby Goth Weekend starts tomorrow and the whole town will be swarming with incomers,' he grumbled. 'That's the last thing we need with this happening.'

It didn't sound as if Fields was a fan of the goths. Raven was aware of the goth festival that drew crowds from all over the country. He'd been a bit of a goth himself, back in his teen years. Still was, if being goth meant wearing black and being generally miserable. An image of Donna clad in a short black dress, her smoky eyes heavy with mascara and eyeshadow floated into his consciousness. He brushed it aside reluctantly. Those days were long gone.

'You just can't keep away from a gruesome murder, can you, DCI Raven?' The CSI team leader, Holly Chang, was zipping up her white coverall at the entrance to the abbey. 'And they don't come much more gruesome than this.'

He acknowledged her greeting with a wry smile. 'Holly. I should have known you'd be here before me.' He was growing used to her blunt manner and dark humour and liked to think they were developing a mutual respect. He was sure they'd get on, just as long as he didn't make unreasonable demands on her time. 'What have we got?' he asked, his curiosity starting to overcome his guilt at leaving Hannah to her own devices.

'Blood,' said Holly. 'Or in this case, not so much. I hope you've got the stomach for it.' Raven frowned, his sense of unease growing. 'This is a weird one,' warned Holly. 'Come and take a look.'

Raven, Becca and Fields followed her up the ruined nave, now completely grassed over, passing stumps of stone columns to either side. One wall was entirely gone; the other stood teetering, the roof open to the sky and the birds. Of the four huge piers that had once supported the transepts, only one remained. Grooves in the grass marked the places where other walls may once have stood.

At the far end of the building, they halted. 'According to the site map,' said Holly, 'This is where the presbytery would have been. The holiest place in the abbey.'

The body was arranged with eerie precision. A man in his late twenties or early thirties, dressed as a Victorian undertaker in a black waistcoat, black trousers and black tails. A black top hat was placed neatly beside his head. His arms lay folded across his chest as if he'd been prepared for burial. But what shocked Raven most was the colour of the man's skin. Or rather, the lack of any colour. He was startlingly pale, almost translucent, as if the life had been drained out of him.

'Now take a look at this,' said Holly, holding a gloved finger to the man's neck.

Raven knelt on the wet grass and peered closely. Just above the starched white collar of the victim's shirt, in the vicinity of the carotid artery, were two tiny puncture marks, flecked with red. Raven shook his head in disbelief.

'His skin's been pierced by something sharp,' said Fields, 'but there's not a drop of blood on his collar or his clothes.'

'So, are you thinking what I'm thinking?' asked Holly.

Raven glanced to Becca, who gave a small shake of her head, unwilling to comment.

'We're all thinking the same,' said Fields brusquely. 'Might as well come out and say it.'

And even though the idea was absurd, Raven couldn't help himself. 'A vampire,' he whispered aloud. 'He looks like he was killed by a vampire.'

CHAPTER 3

Hannah Raven unpacked her rucksack in the guest room and sat down on the bed, doing her best to stifle the inevitable sense of disappointment she felt at her father's hasty and unscheduled departure. He'd barely stayed five minutes to show her around the house and introduce her to Barry the builder and his skinny assistant, Reg, before dashing off to attend whatever crisis had cropped up.

Was he really so indispensable? Didn't Scarborough have other detectives? They must surely have managed perfectly well without him before he moved here from London.

Frustratingly, her feeling of being let down wasn't the least bit unfamiliar. It had been a constant companion throughout her childhood. School concerts, sports days, parents' evenings. So often her dad had arrived late or left early or simply failed to appear at all because of some emergency at work. She recalled one time when she'd been in the school play and had waited for him to show up. Peering out at the audience as the seats filled up, hoping right until the last minute, certain that he'd arrive just in the nick of time. He hadn't.

'Your dad's important,' her mum had told her soothingly afterwards. 'People need him.'

But Hannah had already known that. Her dad was important to her. *She* needed him.

In later years, her mum's tone had changed. She no longer tried to defend his behaviour, but condemned it, leading to angry rows. Her mother's fury had been even worse than her father's absence. Whenever the arguments had started, Hannah had closed her bedroom door and blocked out the sound of her bickering parents with the help of music on her headphones. The solitude had made her feel more alone than ever.

A tear came to the corner of her eye now and she brushed it away, annoyed with herself. She shouldn't have allowed herself to believe that her father had somehow changed. It was obvious that he never would.

Anyway, she wasn't a child anymore. She didn't need a father.

She pulled out her phone and sent a quick message to her mum, saying that the journey had been good and she'd arrived on time. Immediately she resented the fact that her mum had made her promise to send such a message. Sometimes Lisa still treated her as if she were a child.

Straightaway her phone buzzed with a reply, as if Lisa had been waiting anxiously for her to get in touch.

What are you and your dad up to now? her mum wanted to know.

Dad's gone out, typed Hannah, aggrieved by how quickly she'd been coerced into betraying him. She hated being used as a pawn in her parents' divorce drama.

The phone buzzed again with an incoming message. *Let me guess, he's gone off somewhere on police business? Bloody typical!*

Hannah sighed at her mother's bitterness. If anything, it made her more sympathetic to her father. She chose not to respond to the message. She'd spent years being a flashpoint in the ongoing war between her mum and dad.

She was done with that.

She slipped her phone into her jeans pocket and got up. She and her dad had precious little time together and she didn't want to spend it embroiled in a domestic dispute. She decided to explore the house instead.

The three-storey Georgian terrace was far more charming than she'd been led to believe from Lisa's description of the "horrible old wreck your father's inherited." Occasional Skype calls had given her a limited view of the rooms, usually with a ladder and other building paraphernalia in the background, and had tended to reinforce the negatives. But now that most of the work was finished, Hannah could understand what had led her father to make this his new home. The bedrooms were cosy and inviting, and the living room was stylish and calming. The new bathroom was state-of-the-art, boasting a power shower that Hannah couldn't wait to try. It was even nicer than Lisa's house in London, and Hannah was impressed by the job Barry had done with the renovation.

Yet there was something missing from the house.

As she wandered around the rooms, taking in the glossy new paintwork and polished wood, she slowly realised what it was: a distinct lack of personal touches. There was just one framed photograph of herself, taken years ago, together with a black-and-white image of an older woman, her kindly features etched with deep lines. Hannah picked it up and studied it, noticing a family resemblance around the eyes and mouth. Was this her grandmother?

Her father had scarcely ever spoken about his mother, and never about his father. In fact he'd hardly ever mentioned his life in Scarborough at all, and it had come as a complete surprise to Hannah when he'd suddenly announced that he'd inherited the old family home and was moving back to Yorkshire. Hannah recalled that her grandmother had died young, but knew nothing else about her. She replaced the photograph on the mantelpiece, making a mental note to ask about it later.

The sound of hammering burst from the kitchen where

Barry was still hard at work, whistling tunelessly through his teeth. Hannah was already accustomed to the idea that the builder produced a lot of noise while working. His assistant, Reg, by contrast never seemed to make a sound.

Hannah drifted through to the kitchen to see how they were getting on. As soon as she appeared in the doorway, Barry paused in his task. 'Sorry about all the racket, love. Just got this one last job to finish.'

Hannah gave him a smile. 'Don't worry. I was thinking of going out for a walk anyway.'

'The old man's scarpered off and left you on your own, has he?' said Barry. 'No matter. There's loads to see and do in Scarborough. Go and fill your lungs with some invigorating sea air. Peasholm Park's worth a look. And if you're feeling a bit peckish, there's a little café just round the corner from here. Best scones in town. Tell 'em Barry sent you.'

Hannah thanked the builder for his recommendation and headed out to explore the delights on offer. The house on Quay Street was certainly well located, just yards from the harbour. Even as she stepped out of the front door the cries of seagulls assaulted her ears, and she could smell the salty tang on the air. A fresh breeze gently ruffled her hair and she immediately felt invigorated. She just hoped the town had enough to keep her occupied for more than one afternoon.

*

Raven squeezed the M6 into a tight parking spot opposite a crescent of elegant Victorian townhouses. From here, the ruins of the abbey were clearly visible on top of the headland beyond the harbour. Yet although the distance from the abbey was only a few hundred metres as the crow flew, the journey by car had involved a detour of some two miles, driving back inland to cross the bridge that spanned the River Esk. The river made a watery divide, splitting the town of Whitby firmly into two halves. On the East Cliff stood the abbey, while the greater part of the town, including the Royal Crescent where Raven and Becca now were, occupied the West Cliff.

They had left Holly Chang back at the abbey, scouring the site for evidence and arranging for the body to be removed to the mortuary in Scarborough where the post-mortem would be conducted. The sooner a pathologist could examine the body and ascertain the precise cause of death and the nature of the two pinpricks on the man's neck, the happier Raven would be.

Yet while the manner of the murder may have been bizarre, tracking down the victim was proving to be quite straightforward. A search of the man's pockets had uncovered a driving licence giving his name as Reynard Blackthorn. A key with *Northview Guest House* engraved on its wooden fob had also been found. A quick internet search had revealed the guest house's address.

'There it is,' said Becca, pointing to a brightly-painted plaque that advertised the guest house.

Stepping out of the car, Raven glanced up at the imposing façade of the crescent, a curving row of five-storey houses. Stone steps led up to the front door of each house and an ornate iron balcony ran along the tall first-floor windows. The crescent overlooked a semi-circular green ornamented with flower beds. Beyond it lay the sea, a stripe of dull grey metal on this overcast morning.

As Raven rang the bell of the guest house, his phone buzzed. He glanced at the screen and saw it was an angry message from Lisa berating him for abandoning Hannah in Scarborough. He swiped the message away. One problem at a time.

The door opened to reveal a middle-aged woman bearing an apologetic smile. She glanced at the "No Vacancies" sign displayed in the window. 'I'm sorry, but we're full at the moment. It's the goth weekend, you know? All the hotels and guest houses get booked up well in advance.'

Raven presented his warrant card. 'We're not looking

for accommodation. We understand that you have a Mr Reynard Blackthorn staying with you?'

The landlady's eyes widened in surprise. 'Well, yes, that's right.'

'Perhaps we could come in,' Raven suggested.

'Of course.' The landlady retreated into the hallway, beckoning them inside with a welcoming gesture.

'Thank you,' said Raven. 'It's Mrs...?'

'Harker.' She led them into a hallway painted in shades of blue and green, hung with watercolours of Whitby Abbey and the harbour. The banister was polished to a mirror shine and the place appeared spotlessly clean and well-kept, if a little fussy in style. A smell of grilled bacon wafted temptingly from the dining room at the back of the house.

'The lounge is empty,' said Mrs Harker, leading them into the front room. 'Will this do?'

'Perfect,' said Raven, taking a seat on a sofa covered in bright chintz fabric. His gaze wandered around the room, taking in the many pictures, lamps, clocks, figurines and vases on display. It was far too overdecorated for his taste, to the point of being cluttered. If the intention was to include a painting or photograph of every well-known Whitby landmark and an ornament from as many different historical periods as possible, then it could be regarded as a success. His examination of the room ended abruptly at the fireplace as he registered the presence of a stuffed animal, a black cat, stretched out on the hearth, its back arched and its paws extended before it. The animal regarded him haughtily through glass eyes. No wonder the guests avoided this room.

Becca sat down next to him and Mrs Harker took an armchair next to the fireplace. 'What's this about Reynard?' she asked anxiously. 'I do hope he's not in any kind of trouble.' Her hand dropped down absently as if to stroke the dead cat.

Raven noted the use of the victim's first name. The landlady seemed to be on familiar terms with her guest and her concern struck him as genuine. With some effort he dragged his attention away from the cat and fixed it on Mrs Harker. 'Can I first confirm that Mr Blackthorn was staying here?' he asked. 'Is this his key?' He showed her the key to room number eight in its clear evidence bag but declined to give it to her when she held out her hand to take it.

'Why, yes, that's his key. He always stays in the same room.' She wrung her hands together as her concern deepened. 'What on earth has happened to him?'

'Is he a regular visitor to your guest house?'

'Oh, yes, he comes twice a year, every year, in April and October for the goth weekends. He always has a stall at the bazaar. He's a taxidermist, you see.' She gestured to the cat, as if Raven might have failed to notice it. 'I was heartbroken when Milo died. Reynard stuffed him for me as a favour. He's such a nice, kind person.'

'How lovely,' said Becca.

Raven glanced sideways at his sergeant, searching her face for traces of sarcasm, but she was beaming warmly at the landlady, and pointedly ignored Raven's enquiring stare.

'How long had Mr Blackthorn been staying here, Mrs Harker?' Raven asked.

'Well, he arrived yesterday morning. He always likes to come a day or two before the weekend begins properly.'

'And when did you last see him?'

'He had dinner here last night and then went out at about eight o'clock. He said he was going to meet some friends.'

'Did he say who?'

'No.'

The poor woman was looking quite distressed by now, probably imagining the worst. But the reality, Raven reflected, was almost certainly far worse than anything Mrs Harker might envision. It was time to break the bad news.

'I'm afraid I have to tell you that Mr Blackthorn's body was found this morning. The circumstances of his death are suspicious.'

Mrs Harker's hand flew to her mouth and she let out a strangled cry.

Raven remained in his seat while Becca administered consolation and paper tissues. She always seemed to have a ready supply of both to hand.

After a minute the distraught landlady recovered some composure. 'Was it definitely Reynard?' she asked. 'Are you sure there isn't a mistake?'

'There will need to be a formal identification,' said Raven, 'but his face matches the photo on his driving licence.'

'Oh dear.' Mrs Harker blew her nose and reached for the cat, stroking its back with one hand and dabbing her eyes with the other.

'Did Reynard have any family?' Becca asked.

Mrs Harker shook her head. 'No, I don't think so. At least, he never mentioned anyone. He wasn't married and he always came to Whitby on his own.'

'The friends he was going to see – do you have any idea who they might be?'

'Sorry, no. Reynard was always quite a private man. He liked to talk about his work, and about the goth festival, but he kept personal matters to himself. And I'm not the kind to pry.'

'I'm sure you're not, Mrs Harker,' said Raven, rising to his feet. 'Unfortunately, I'm going to have to ask if we can search his room.'

'What for?' she asked.

'In case there's anything there that might shed light on why he met his death.'

He wondered if she might burst into tears again, but she nodded in a resigned way. 'Of course. I'll let you in right away. Anything to help catch the killer.'

She led them up the stairs to the second floor of the house. The door to room eight was locked, but Mrs Harker used her own key to unlock it. The door opened easily.

'If you don't mind waiting downstairs…' said Raven.

'Of course.' The landlady withdrew and went back down to the ground floor.

Raven and Becca pulled on blue nitrile gloves and stepped inside.

The room was small but tidy and showed no signs of a struggle. The bed was made with the sort of precision employed by hotel staff and had obviously not been slept in. A suitcase on the stand at the foot of the bed was empty. On the bedside locker lay a pile of flyers advertising Reynard Blackthorn's taxidermy business. Raven pushed open the door to an ensuite bathroom, but apart from a shaving kit, some men's toiletries and some black eyeliner, the room appeared empty.

Becca opened a large wooden wardrobe. 'Look at this.'

Inside hung a couple of long-tailed black suits and half a dozen white shirts with wing-neck collars. It appeared that the outfit Reynard had been wearing when he met his death was his everyday attire.

Becca searched the pockets of the clothing but came away empty-handed. 'Seems like our man travelled light.'

'It certainly looks that way.'

Becca picked up one of the flyers to study. The flyer featured a gothic-looking image of a rather malevolent black bird perched atop a human skull. The words *Blackthorn Taxidermy* were printed at the top, and at the foot was a website address. Becca handed the flyer to Raven and began thumbing the address of the website into her phone. She moved closer so he could watch over her shoulder.

The website's *About* page featured a photo of Reynard dressed in the now familiar garb of Victorian undertaker. There were also many examples of his work – cats, dogs, birds and Reynard's namesake, a fox. But there was nothing on the website or among his personal possessions to suggest how or why he had met such a gruesome end in the grounds of Whitby Abbey.

On leaving the room, Raven locked the door behind them and pocketed the spare key. Mrs Harker was waiting for them on the ground floor. 'I'll need to keep this until further notice,' he told her. 'There's nothing amiss in the room, but don't let anyone else in there for the time being. The CSI team will need to take a closer look.'

The landlady nodded her understanding.

'Now,' said Raven, 'before we leave, is there anything else you can tell us about Mr Blackthorn? Anything he might have said to you, or any behaviour that struck you as odd?'

'Well...' Mrs Harker hesitated. 'There is just one thing. I don't know if this is relevant or not.'

'Yes?'

'It might be nothing, but I did wake up in the night. I heard the front door opening and closing, but I didn't hear a key turning in the lock, so I think it was someone going out.'

'What time was this?'

'Gone midnight. I always turn the radio off at twelve because that's when the news comes on, and it keeps me awake if I listen to it in bed. Always so much trouble in the world.' She put her hand to her mouth, perhaps recalling afresh the reason why the police were there.

'Do you have any idea who was leaving?' asked Raven.

'No. People come and go at all hours. But this occasion stuck in my mind because... well, it's probably of no interest to you at all...'

'What?'

She gave him a sideways glance as if fearful of being judged foolish. 'It's just that immediately afterwards, I heard a dog barking. It was right outside, in the street below.'

CHAPTER 4

The abbey was windswept, desolate, and to Holly Chang's way of thinking, deeply unsettling. Tar-black crows swept across the sky like dark harbingers, their caws echoing ominously around the stone ruins as they shared secrets and gossip with each other. Those birds on the ground strutted about pompously, as if the place belonged to them, and the humans were intruders.

Holly was no fan of crows. The birds displayed uncanny intelligence and a knowing manner, as if they had already solved the crime and were waiting to see how long it would take the police to catch up.

Smug little buggers.

In Chinese culture, crows were regarded as a symbol of ill fortune, deceit and death. They were supposed to be able to recognise human faces, and be capable of holding grudges. Holly didn't appreciate the way they appeared to be scrutinising her work and finding it wanting.

Dark wings, dark thoughts.

'Go flap your feathers at someone else!' she muttered, gratified at the way the crows cawed in annoyance and took to the sky, circling overhead in a black spiral before settling again further away from the abbey.

She was glad to have the solid, reassuring presence of Sergeant Fields by her side. 'We get a lot of crows here on the headland,' he said when he saw her glancing warily at the birds. 'Ravens too, sometimes.'

'Hah, ravens! The bane of my life. Let's hope none of them show up.' Holly returned her attention to the ground. She wasn't going to find answers in the sky.

Thankfully, apart from the presence of the birds, she and the police team had the abbey grounds to themselves. The area had been cordoned off and English Heritage officials were turning disappointed visitors away from the entrance to the abbey and suggesting they go and look at St Mary's Church instead.

The body still lay at the eastern end of the abbey where it had been found beneath the row of tall gothic windows of the chancel. Jet-black hair, bone-white skin, crooked nose and hooded eyes. A cadaverous look, if ever there was one. And that creepy old-fashioned outfit was doing nothing to calm Holly's nerves. She didn't scare easily, and had encountered plenty of corpses in her time, but the presence of this one filled her with unease. Those crows were carrion birds and she didn't trust them anywhere near the body. She wished the mortuary van would come and take it away.

The victim had been placed with precision, as if for burial, with legs extended and arms folded across the chest. The painstaking care that had been taken in arranging the corpse was disquieting, even before considering the manner of death. This was clearly no routine murder, and no ordinary murderer.

Yet even the most careful of killers left clues.

Holly moved slowly up and down the grassy nave and transepts, examining the ground in minute detail. There were no visible scuff marks, no signs of a struggle. Either the victim had been killed where he lay, or he had been carried there, but not dragged across the ground. That suggested the work of someone strong, or of more than one person.

Holly wondered what message the killer was sending by positioning the body in such a way, in the most sacred part of the church. Was it in mockery of Christian tradition? And if so, why?

But she preferred to leave such speculation to the detectives. Her domain was a more concrete one – the world of hard facts and physical evidence.

'Over here!' The call came from the latest recruit to her team, a young lad called Jamie, his voice snatched away almost immediately by the buffeting wind. Holly plodded over to where he was crouching beside what appeared to be a shallow, open sarcophagus.

'What's this?' she asked. The grave was clearly ancient, carved from a single block of stone. It was too small to accommodate an adult, even one as short as herself. Perhaps it had been intended for a child?

'Dunno what it is, boss,' said Jamie, 'but look what I found in it.' He pointed to a small metal object at the bottom of the coffin, or whatever the damn thing was.

Holly called over the CSI photographer to take a shot of the find before it was moved, then picked it up and turned it over. It was a single brass key, the sort that opened a night latch. One small piece of the puzzle, or not.

'If this key belonged to the victim,' said Jamie excitedly, 'it could have fallen from his pocket.'

'Maybe,' said Holly, slipping the key into an evidence bag. 'But remember what I told you,' she cautioned.

'Accumulate, don't speculate,' said Jamie glumly.

'Dead right,' said Holly. 'Leave it to the detectives to come up with crazy theories.'

A call from another team member brought her back over to the body. It was Erin this time, another youthful member of her team. She held up a plastic evidence bag containing short black hairs. 'I found these on his clothes,' said the girl. 'They look like dog hairs to me.'

Holly peered at the hairs closely. 'Same colour as the

victim's hair. What makes you think they're dog hairs?'

'They're just like the ones our family dog sheds.'

Holly snorted dismissively. 'What am I always telling you?'

'Accumulate, don't speculate.'

'Dead right.' And yet the discovery was an intriguing one, and Erin might well be correct. The lab guys would be able to tell for sure.

Holly turned and looked around the bleak abbey grounds. What had a dog been doing at the scene of the crime? And more to the point, where was it now?

*

Becca could really have done without the sight of a man drained of his blood first thing in the morning. She was no stranger to dead bodies, even to gruesome murders and decomposed corpses. But this one had made her feel quite faint, which wasn't like her at all. She hoped that Raven hadn't noticed her hanging back from the scene.

The reason for her queasiness wasn't difficult to pin down. She'd had a late session at the wine bar the previous night and hadn't managed her usual eight hours of sleep. That bottle of Chardonnay she'd shared with Ellie Earnshaw, her new flatmate, hadn't helped. Skipping breakfast probably hadn't set her up for the day either. She could imagine what her mum would have said about that.

But her mum was no longer on hand to observe and to comment.

Since leaving the family home the previous month and moving in with Ellie, life had certainly shifted up a gear. The two women shared a stylish modern apartment overlooking Scarborough's North Bay and it was all great fun. Ellie was the manager of a brewery and liked to go out partying. She was good at persuading Becca to join her, not that Becca had thrown up a huge amount of resistance. It was good to have a vibrant social life again. But she was beginning to feel the effects of too many late nights fuelled by alcohol.

She was also missing her mother's cooked breakfasts. She may have lost a few pounds in weight (1.6 kilograms to be precise, or three-and-a-half pounds in old money) by cutting back on her daily helping of fried eggs and bacon, but sometimes you needed a plateful of hot food to give you the energy for a day's work.

At Mrs Harker's guest house, the smell of fried bacon had almost driven her mad with hunger, but she could hardly have asked the landlady if there was any going spare. She wondered if there was any chance of calling in at a sandwich shop for a quick bite and a cup of tea, but Raven seemed keen to be on his way. 'Where are we going now?' she asked.

He surprised her by starting to cross the road. Usually he hated having to walk anywhere. 'Let's check out this bazaar where Reynard was going to have his stall.'

'Good idea,' she said. 'You fancy buying a dead cat?'

He gave her a grin. 'Never know when one might be handy.'

She scurried across the road, hurrying to catch him. Raven might have a limp from his old war wound in Bosnia, but he still had a long stride that forced her to put some effort into keeping up.

Exercise. That was another thing she needed to think about. But how was she supposed to fit it in? She barely managed to find time for sleeping these days.

They skirted the edge of the Crescent Gardens and crossed the main road running along the seafront. Ahead of them was a small kiosk selling coffees, teas, pastries and ice-creams. Becca gazed longingly at the muffins on offer, but Raven paid no heed.

The town was already filling up with visitors for the goth weekend. Many of the people ambling up and down the front were dressed as vampires or looked as if they'd just stepped out of a Victorian costume drama. Ladies in elaborate silk gowns with figure-hugging bodices and rear-enhancing bustles sauntered past on the arms of gentlemen in top hats and tails. Pirates and witches mingled with sinister, hooded monks. It seemed as if it was impossible to overdress for the event. There was an abundance of lace and feathers, and black eyeliner was *de rigueur*.

Even the men were wearing more makeup than Becca. She felt downright dowdy in her waterproof coat and sensible trousers, although Raven, in his long black coat and Stygian hair fitted in just fine. 'You'd think a Victorian undertaker would stand out,' she remarked to him, 'but here he'd just be one of the crowd.'

A path sloped downhill to the pavilion, which overlooked the beach. The redbrick Victorian building had a modern extension and when Becca entered it she found an auditorium, a bar and a café in the foyer. Signs pointed to the bazaar which was taking place in a hall downstairs.

'After you,' said Raven.

Becca descended the stairs, aware of Raven hobbling down behind her, clinging tightly to the railing. She did her best not to look at him as he navigated the steps.

The subterranean bazaar in the room beneath the pavilion was one of the strangest fairs that Becca had ever seen. Ellie would have loved it, with its eclectic mix of gothic artwork, new and second-hand costumes and striking handmade jewellery. This was a place where you could find all things goth and alternative. There were stalls displaying weird and wonderful headgear, chocolates in the shape of spiders, creepy-looking black candles and packs of tarot cards, not to mention magic potions and spells. Becca was briefly tempted by a pair of oven gloves featuring skulls and bats, which would have made a perfect gift for her brother, Liam. But she was here to observe, not to buy.

The bazaar was busy, but one of the stalls, perhaps the most striking in the whole room, was doing no trade at all.

On a table in the far corner, an exhibition of taxidermy had been carefully arranged. The collection consisted entirely of stuffed crows staged in a variety of remarkably lifelike poses, perched on small branches or posed ominously over miniature coffins. To Becca's mind, these birds were much more successful examples of Reynard's skill as a taxidermist than Mrs Harker's hapless cat which probably hadn't been such a great specimen even in life.

Though why anyone would want to own a dead crow was a mystery to her.

'If you're hoping to buy one of them birds,' said the man at the next stall selling black-and-white prints of ruined castles, 'Reynard didn't show up today. I dunno what's happened to him.' The man had an accent that marked him out as a native of Birmingham. It was clear that the goth festival drew crowds from all over the country, not just the north.

'When did you last see him?' asked Becca.

'He was here yesterday setting up his stall. Should've been back here before ten when the bazaar opened.'

Becca began speaking to the other stallholders, enquiring about Reynard, but in each case the response was the same – he had last been seen arranging his display the previous day.

'Nothing,' she reported back to Raven. 'Nobody knows what happened to him.'

Raven was busy studying the black-feathered birds on display. 'We need to track down these mysterious friends he said he was going to meet.'

Just then a woman of about Becca's age approached the stall. She was stunningly beautiful and strikingly made up. Her skin was whitened to a ghostly sheen, her lips painted blood-red and her eyes outlined in thick black kohl. She was dressed as a vampire in a slim-fitting black mini-dress adorned with silver chains and a flowing layer of embroidered chiffon over her arms. A choker that matched her black lace gloves encircled her long neck.

But the most extraordinary aspect of her appearance was her hair. Shining gold amid a sea of black-haired goths, it flowed like a golden waterfall, parting in the centre of her forehead, waves and curls cascading over her shoulders and down to her waist. It was thick, standing out from her head like a cloud.

Becca reckoned it must have needed half a can of hairspray to hold it in place. She could smell the fumes from six feet away.

The new arrival made a beeline for Reynard's neighbour and spoke quickly to the Brummie stallholder. 'Where's Reynard today?' she asked. 'Have you seen him?' Her voice was clear and articulate. A southern accent.

'Sorry, love, I was just saying to this lady here that he didn't show up this morning.'

The woman with the startling hair turned to Becca as if only just noticing her. She looked her up and down, a frown gently creasing her smooth forehead, perhaps as she registered Becca's strange – in this place – attire. 'Who on earth are you?' she demanded.

'Detective Sergeant Becca Shawcross. And this' – Becca indicated Raven – 'is Detective Chief Inspector Tom Raven.'

The woman's frown deepened. 'Police? What are you doing here? Do you know what's happened to Reynard?'

'Perhaps we could go upstairs and have a chat?' suggested Raven.

The woman seemed vexed, but allowed Becca to lead the way up to the café in the entrance foyer.

'Can I fetch you a cup of tea?' Becca asked her, once they were installed at a table by the window.

'I think that's the least you can do, since you won't tell me what's going on. I'll have a coffee. Flat white, no sugar.'

Becca was relieved to get away from the overbearing woman for a minute, and equally glad of an opportunity to grab herself a bite to eat. She returned to the table with a cup of tea, two coffees, and three plates of Danish pastries. She'd had to pay for the whole lot out of her own pocket, but it was worth it to get some food inside her.

'What's the nature of your relationship to Reynard Blackthorn?' Raven was asking the woman, whose name, it turned out, was Aurora Highsmith.

'We're friends,' said Aurora, accepting the coffee from

Becca without a word of thanks. 'We met at Leeds University ten years or so ago. Look, what is this about? I insist that you tell me what's happened to Reynard.' Her tone was becoming ever more imperious.

'When did you last see him?' asked Raven, ignoring her demand.

His question seemed to enrage her further. She pushed the plate with the pastry away in a show of petulance. But perhaps she sensed she had met her match, or realised she had little choice but to answer the police questions. 'I saw him at the pub last night,' she conceded grudgingly.

'Which pub?'

'The Elsinore.'

'At what time?'

Raven seemed to be on a roll with his questioning, and Becca took the opportunity to take a large bite out of her Danish. Flakes of pastry showered the table but she didn't care. Never had food tasted so good. She really must stop skipping breakfast from now on.

Aurora glanced sideways at her, then back at Raven, as if trying to decide which one of them was most irritating. 'I met him there at half past eight. We left at eleven.'

'Was it just the two of you?' continued Raven.

'No, there were a couple of other friends with us.'

Raven took out his notebook. 'I'd like their names.'

But it seemed that Aurora's supply of patience had finally been exhausted. 'Not until you tell me what this is about!'

Raven sighed, then nodded to Becca. Perhaps he thought that having successfully consoled Mrs Harker, she had a knack for breaking tragic news.

'I'm very sorry,' she said softly, 'but Mr Blackthorn's body was found this morning in the grounds of Whitby Abbey.'

'*What?!*' Aurora turned paler than ever, if that was possible under her ivory foundation. She opened her handbag – an expensive designer brand – and extracted a black lace-trimmed handkerchief, saving Becca the bother of reaching for her own packet of tissues, which was somewhat depleted after the visit to the guest house. Aurora dabbed at her eyes, trying not to smudge her makeup. When she next spoke, her tone was gentler than before. 'What happened to him? Was it an accident?'

'We're still establishing the facts,' said Becca, 'but we're treating his death as suspicious. You mentioned two other friends who were with you in the pub?'

Aurora was immediately back on guard. 'You can't think that any of his friends would have wanted to harm him?'

'We'll need to interview them and take witness statements,' said Becca. 'We'll want to build up a picture of Reynard, and also trace his movements last night.'

'Maybe you could write down their names and phone numbers.' Raven tore a sheet of paper out of his notebook and slid it across the table with a pen. 'And where they're staying in Whitby.'

'Yes, all right.' Aurora wrote down the details and handed the paper back to Raven.

He read aloud. 'Dr Raj Sandhu, staying at the White Horse & Griffin, and Lucille West, staying at the Black Horse. Where are you staying yourself, Ms Highsmith?'

'I'm at Bagdale Hall.'

'Until when?'

'Sunday.'

Raven pocketed the slip of paper. 'Thanks. Please don't leave Whitby before then without letting us know first. We might need to speak to you again. And by the way, I'd appreciate it if you didn't contact your friends until we've had a chance to speak to them first.'

Becca didn't think there was much chance of Aurora agreeing to that. She would probably be on the phone as soon as they finished speaking to her. 'Perhaps you could tell us a little more about yourself?' she suggested. 'Do you usually come to Whitby for the goth weekend?'

Aurora nodded. 'Yes, every time. It's held twice a year, once in Spring and again at Halloween. It makes a change from my day job.'

'Which is what?'

'I work in the City of London. I'm the PA for a hedge fund manager. Boring, but it pays the bills.'

So that explained the expensive handbag. Plus the fact that Aurora was staying at one of the town's premier hotels. 'And are your other friends regulars at the festival too? Including Reynard?'

'That's right.' She nodded enthusiastically. 'We were all goths at uni together. That's when we got to know each other, and we've been meeting here twice a year ever since.'

'And are you all on good terms?'

She scowled. 'Of course. I already told you, none of Reynard's friends would ever hurt him.'

'Then did Reynard have any enemies?' asked Raven.

'Enemies?' Aurora snorted derisively. 'This isn't a book or a movie. What normal person has enemies?'

Becca looked her up and down again. It was hard to picture this white-skinned, black-clad woman with her blood-red lips and amazing hair as a "normal" person. And equally hard to imagine that a man who dressed as an undertaker and who stuffed crows for a living led a particularly conventional life either. 'So tell me,' she said, finally overcome by her curiosity, 'what exactly is the attraction of dressing as a vampire?'

Aurora's eyes narrowed with disdain. 'Seriously? What's not to like about vampires? Power, allure, eternal youth. Who wouldn't want to be one?' She stared at Becca as if daring her to suggest otherwise.

Becca declined to rise to the challenge. In her opinion, there were obvious disadvantages to being a vampire, not least the whole undead business. The part about sleeping in a coffin wasn't too appealing. Becca preferred a nice, soft bed at night. But she found it intriguing that Aurora had answered the question as if she believed vampires were real. She filed that piece of information away for later.

'So, are we done now?' asked Aurora, turning back to

Raven.

'I think so. Thanks for your cooperation.'

'No worries.'

She rose from her chair and stalked out of the pavilion, leaving her coffee half-drunk and her Danish pastry untouched.

Raven eyed it with interest, but Becca reached out and took it before he could make a grab for it. 'Just as well vampires don't eat sugary snacks,' she remarked, sinking her teeth into the sweet crispy dessert.

CHAPTER 5

Fishing boats bobbed in Scarborough harbour as Hannah emerged onto the seafront between a café and a shop selling beachballs, buckets, spades and other seaside paraphernalia. Enormous seagulls wheeled in the sky, making an infernal racket. They swooped low to snatch scraps of food from unsuspecting tourists and seemed to laugh as Hannah took in the heady sights, smells and sounds of the harbourside. There was certainly plenty going on. The noise from the gulls, the cries of excited children, and the stench of fish from the nets and lobster baskets was overwhelming. Was this the "invigorating sea air" that Barry had mentioned? She wondered if the café she'd just passed was the one with the famous scones the builder had recommended, but there were several other cafés nearby and no way of telling. Anyway, she'd had a snack on the train and wasn't hungry just yet.

She crossed the road, stopping at the harbourside to get her bearings. Behind her rose the headland, steep and inaccessible, the castle just visible on top. She would try climbing up there later. A small funfair nestled at the foot of the headland, and a breakwater with a lighthouse at its far end enclosed the harbour. Beyond it, the bay swept in a wide arc of yellow sand. After sitting on trains all morning she felt an urge to move her legs, so she set off along the seafront at a brisk pace.

It certainly wasn't warm enough to go paddling in the sea on a day like this, let alone go swimming. The overcast sky mirrored the grey gloom of the water beneath it. Her mother had warned her that Scarborough was bracing and had advised her to pack a warm coat. But it seemed clear to Hannah that Lisa's jaundiced view of the seaside town was tainted by the fact that her own visit here just before Christmas had failed to save her marriage to Raven and had, in fact, precipitated their divorce. Hannah doubted her mum would ever set foot in Yorkshire again, never mind Scarborough.

She was determined not to be influenced by her mother's negative opinions and prejudices. The fact was, Lisa was a bit of a snob. Hannah had grown up listening to her mum constantly moaning about all kinds of places and people, and preferred to make up her own mind about things. So far, the vibrant buzz of the town was making a good impression.

The place was far busier and livelier than she'd expected. The seafront was packed with a lively array of amusement arcades, ice-cream parlours and colourful souvenir shops, not to mention fish and chip shops, pubs and yet more cafés. There was certainly no shortage of places to eat, and the aroma of battered fish drowned in vinegar assaulted her nostrils at every step. Walking along the seafront, she felt a new sense of freedom. Her mother was far away, and the memories of her unhappy visit needn't cloud Hannah's own experience.

About halfway along the bay, a huge Victorian hotel towered above the foreshore. Easily the largest building in Scarborough, it seemed to rise from the cliffs like a giant fortress. As she approached it, she spotted a quaint funicular railway chugging up and down the steep hillside. She would try a ride on that later if her legs got tired.

At the far end of the beach she reached the spa, an impressive Victorian edifice with a balconied façade in the classical style. An open-air arena and bandstand overlooked the sea. The timeless grandeur of the building made a stark contrast to the hubbub along the seafront. Curiosity piqued, she ventured inside.

The main part of the spa featured a theatre with a bar and restaurant. Poster boards in the box office advertised the usual kind of seaside entertainments – Elvis and Abba tribute nights as well as comedy shows and variety performances. They all seemed a bit tame and family-orientated, but browsing through a rack of leaflets, Hannah's eyes were drawn to a flyer for a music festival at the Whitby Goth Weekend. She checked the dates and found that it was taking place during the next couple of days.

Hannah was no goth – her musical tastes were more mainstream – but the thought of attending a live rock concert excited her. It would fill an evening and would be something to tell her friends about when she returned to university the following week. Hannah was keen on meeting new people and making her own memories, and the festival seemed like the perfect opportunity for that.

As her father had apparently dumped her, she hardly needed to consult with him before making her decision. She took out her phone and booked a ticket online. Then she pocketed the leaflet and started back along the seafront, wondering if the funicular railway might get her any closer to the castle. Even if it didn't, it looked like a fun ride.

*

The White Horse & Griffin was a charming seventeenth-century coaching inn on Church Street in the heart of the town. Raven and Becca hadn't yet managed to make contact with Lucille West, the other person whose name Aurora had given them, but Dr Raj Sandhu had agreed to meet them in the wood-panelled bar of the hotel.

A worn wooden sign over the archway leading to the rear courtyard of the building offered the weary traveller "Good Stabling" but unfortunately there was no "Good Parking" to be had. The town centre had been closed to traffic, obliging Raven and Becca to leave the BMW on the West Cliff and walk across to the east side of Whitby, crossing the river once again, but on foot. This time they had taken a swing bridge, rubbing shoulders with a surreal blend of Victorian ruffles, vampire wannabees and Edwardian inventors making their way through the old cobbled streets. It seemed that the main activity for those attending the goth weekend, apart from shopping, was to see and be seen. A small flock of photographers had also descended on the town, and were busy snapping away as the black-clad visitors strolled past.

Raven regarded the goths surreptitiously as he went. Although his music collection consisted almost entirely of gothic rock and he had dressed almost exclusively in black since his teenage years, he had never taken the trend as seriously as the people who frequented the goth weekend. He was a casual adherent to the movement, scarcely even conscious of identifying himself in that way. Happy to throw on his black woollen coat and declare himself dressed, he had never once flirted with makeup, never had his ears pierced, never considered getting a tattoo. Looking around him now, it felt like he had never fully embraced his potential.

It came as no surprise to him to find that Raj Sandhu wasn't wearing normal clothes. The doctor had gone for the steampunk look, with patterned leather waistcoat, checked jacket and oversized bow tie. The gold chain of a fob watch dangled from his waistcoat pocket and his top hat was adorned with a pair of old-fashioned goggles, as if he'd travelled to Whitby by hot air balloon. His black beard was elegantly tapered at the chin, and the tips of his moustache oiled into dramatic twirls.

He rose to greet them as they entered the bar, signs of

distress evident in the lines on his forehead and the pinching of his eyes. 'Aurora just phoned to tell me what's happened,' he said, reaching out a trembling hand to grasp Raven's own. 'It's shocking news.'

Raven suppressed a sigh. He'd asked Aurora not to contact her friends but aware that in reality his request was destined to be ignored. His worry was that if Raj or Lucille were in some way involved in Reynard's death, it was a chance for them to "get their stories straight." Well, it seemed that horse had well and truly bolted, good stabling or not.

'I'm sorry for the loss of your friend.'

'Thank you,' said Raj. 'That's kind of you to say so.'

He had a measured, precise way of talking, with just a hint of a Yorkshire accent. Raven wondered if he had been born locally then moved away as he himself had done, or was an outsider who had come to the area as an adult. He was keen to find out if Raj was a medical doctor or if his qualification was in some other subject.

Raj tugged at the tip of his beard. 'Do you want to talk here, or should we go up to my room?'

Raven glanced around the oak-beamed lounge. It seemed they were alone for now. The rest of the hotel's guests were probably out and about, either dressed in outlandish costumes or watching those who were. 'I think this will do.'

Raj returned to his seat, gesturing for Raven and Becca to join him at his table. 'As a doctor, you probably imagine that I'm used to people dying, but nothing prepares you for a shock like this.'

'No,' said Raven. His first question had been answered without him even having to ask it. Raj was clearly a medical doctor of some kind.

He seemed eager to talk, as people so often did when confronted with such terrible news. 'It's the personal aspect, you see. As a professional you learn to distance yourself from death, then suddenly it comes right up and smacks you in the face. How did Reynard die? Aurora was

45

a bit vague about the details.'

Raven deflected the question with one of his own. 'Perhaps you could tell me a little more about yourself?'

'Yes, all right' said Raj. 'What is it you'd like to know? I live in Leeds. I work as a junior doctor at St James's University Hospital.'

Raven recalled Aurora saying that the group of friends had first met at university in Leeds a decade earlier. If Raven recalled correctly, doctors spent five years studying followed by up to ten more years working as a junior doctor in a hospital, putting Raj in his late twenties to early thirties. 'Where are you from originally?'

'Leicester.'

'You're a regular at these goth weekends?'

'Yes, we all are. It's a good way to stay in touch with friends from university days. You have to make an effort to keep up with people, otherwise... well, it's easy to lose contact.' His face sank, perhaps as he realised that he would never see Reynard again.

Raven nodded his understanding. The list of people he'd lost touch with over the years was lengthy. School friends; army pals; officers he'd worked alongside in the Met. He'd left them all behind, moved on and never looked back. Perhaps he was too afraid to look behind him, or maybe they'd never been true friends at all. The lads he'd hung out with at school had been rivals as much as mates, and his army and police contacts had been work colleagues. Now he'd moved to Scarborough he'd acquired a new set of colleagues, but still no real friends. The closest was Barry, but he supposed that once the work on the house was finally finished, Barry would disappear from his life just like all the rest. The thought wasn't exactly a cheerful one.

And then there was Lisa. He wished he could leave his ex-wife firmly behind, but she had a way of tagging along, irritating him almost as much as when they were still living together.

'Dr Sandhu,' said Becca, stepping in to plug the gap

caused by Raven's introspection, 'this is a routine question, but please could you tell us where you were last night?'

Raj blinked. 'I met up with the others in the pub. Reynard, Aurora and Lucille, I mean. It's a bit of a tradition, going for a drink at the Elsinore on Flowergate. It's where the goth weekend started years ago.'

'Did you see anyone else you knew there?'

'I recognised a few faces, but no one I knew to speak to.'

'And what time did you leave?'

Raj's fingers clasped around the gold chain of his pocket watch, as if that might provide an answer. 'About eleven o'clock.'

The time and venue Raj had given matched Aurora's account of the evening, Raven noted. That must indicate truth – or else that the pair really had colluded.

'And then what did you do?' asked Becca.

'I walked Lucille back to her hotel. She's staying at the Black Horse. That's just down the road from here. Reynard always stays – I mean stayed – at a guest house on the Royal Crescent. Aurora prefers the comfort of Bagdale Hall.'

It seemed strange to Raven that although the four friends made a point of meeting up in Whitby twice a year, they chose to stay in different places 'Let me ask you about Reynard,' he said. 'How did he seem last night?'

'Just his usual self.'

'He didn't seem in any way preoccupied or worried?'

A ghost of a smile touched Raj's lips, bringing animation to his long moustache. 'Reynard always seemed preoccupied and worried. That was his normal state of being.'

'And why was that?'

'He was just a bit paranoid. He always had been. He was an outsider, with his taxidermy business and the way he dressed as a goth all the time. I mean, it's not exactly conventional, is it?' He smiled ruefully. 'I suppose we were all a bit odd. We didn't easily fit into conventional society. That's what drew us together in the first place.'

'I have to say, Dr Sandhu,' said Becca, 'that you appear quite normal to me.'

He smiled. 'Thank you. Perhaps I've mellowed over the years, become more adept at fitting into polite society.' He tipped his top hat, reinforcing the impression of a gentleman, albeit one a century or more adrift. 'Reynard, on the other hand, tended in the opposite direction. He was drawn more and more to the dark side.'

Raven leaned forward. 'His landlady described him as a "kind" person.'

Raj seemed rather taken aback by the description. His lips thinned. 'I suppose he could be kind when it suited his purposes.'

'Would you care to elaborate?'

'Well, I'd say that Reynard wasn't so much kind as clever. He certainly had a charisma, a sort of beguiling glamour that women in particular found hard to resist. He could turn that on when he wanted something. But at other times… he could be quite difficult.'

'I'm getting the impression you didn't like him much.'

'No, I wouldn't say that,' said Raj. 'It's just that he wasn't always an easy person to get along with.'

'Was there anyone who wished him harm?'

Raj hesitated. 'You're treating his death as murder?'

'Let's say that we're treating it as suspicious.'

'Well, I don't suppose I'm being disloyal if I tell you this now he's dead. There was some trouble a few years ago.'

'What sort of trouble?'

Raj looked embarrassed.

'Please,' urged Raven, 'it might be important.'

Raj lowered his gaze, unwilling to meet Raven's. 'He got into trouble with his taxidermy business. Reynard wasn't good at following rules. In fact, he seemed to delight in breaking them. And it would seem there's money to be made on the black market dealing in protected species.'

'What kind of protected species?'

'Long-eared bats. Reynard should have known better, but like I said, he thought he could evade the law.'

'But he couldn't.'

'No. He was prosecuted and had to serve a short prison sentence. But the worst thing was all the hate he received online. It nearly broke his business.' Raj looked up at Raven. 'You still haven't told me how he died.'

Just then, the door flew open and a woman burst into the bar, her face flushed with anguish. She was dressed from head to toe in rock goth style, with a black leather jacket over a figure-hugging corset and ripped black jeans. Her eyes were green, but heavily made up with kohl, and her lips were the colour of midnight. Metal studs glimmered in her jacket, mirroring the piercings in her nose and eyebrows.

She rushed across the room and almost threw herself to her knees at Raj's feet. 'Raj, Raj, tell me it's not true! Tell me it's just Aurora being a mean bitch! Tell me –' She broke off, suddenly registering the presence of Raven and Becca. 'Oh! Who are you?'

'It's all right,' said Raj, 'these people are from the police. They're here to ask about Reynard.'

The newcomer's eyes opened wide. 'Then it's true!' She broke down in hysterical sobs. Becca reached for her packet of tissues, but Raven thought it would take more than mere tissues to calm this woman down.

Fortunately, Raj seemed to know exactly what to do. He leaned forwards and wrapped his arms around her, speaking in low, soothing tones. The woman shook like a leaf in his grasp, but gradually her sobs subsided. Eventually Raj was able to release her.

He turned to Raven and Becca and gave a look of regret. 'DCI Raven, this is Lucille West, the fourth member of our little circle of friends.'

CHAPTER 6

DC Jess Barraclough had joined the police force in order to avoid being stuck behind a desk all day. She liked to be on her feet as much as possible, preferably outdoors and close to nature. But although she was on her feet right now, she couldn't have been anywhere further removed from nature.

The mortuary at Scarborough Hospital was the most clinical place she had ever been. White tiles, scrubbed surfaces, a sharp chill in the air, and the smell of formaldehyde to mask the stink of decomposition. She was already feeling a little sick, and the body hadn't yet been brought in. Suddenly, the idea of a boring desk job didn't seem too bad at all. But with Raven and Becca tied up in Whitby, she had been asked to get herself over to the mortuary as quickly as possible.

Due to the unexplained and frankly bizarre nature of the death, Raven wanted answers sooner rather than later, and the senior pathologist, Dr Felicity Wainwright, had readily agreed to rejig her schedule to fast-track "the body from the Abbey" as she called it.

Indeed, Dr Wainwright was showing a somewhat

ghoulish interest in the case, as if she were about to open a particularly nicely-wrapped birthday present. 'Ready to begin?' she asked, and Jess nodded glumly. She wondered what she was dreading most – the procedure itself, or the woman who would conduct it. Dr Wainwright had a reputation for being prickly and difficult to work with. At least a corpse didn't argue or make sarcastic comments.

An assistant opened the stainless-steel door of one of the refrigerated units and, with the aid of Dr Wainwright, slid the dead man's body onto a metal trolley. Jess watched as the two women brought the trolley into position ready for the examination to begin.

'Well then,' said Dr Wainwright, 'let's get started.'

Her assistant wheeled over a smaller trolley, this one revealing a row of surgical instruments. They gleamed in the cool lighting, resembling medieval instruments of torture. Scissors, scalpels, knives and saws. Was there any difference between the tools of a pathologist and those of a serial killer?

With effort, Jess dragged her eyes away from the polished steel blades to the central character in this morbid drama. The lifeless body lay on the gurney, draped in a white sheet like a shroud. She found herself staring at it the way she did in TV dramas, searching for the faintest sign that the actor playing the part of the corpse was still breathing. It must be quite difficult to play a dead body.

But in this scene there was no playing.

The mortuary assistant drew back the sheet to reveal the naked corpse. White LED lighting starkly illuminated the contours of flesh, showing every detail and casting no shadows.

Jess felt her skin crawl, and was glad of the protective apron, gloves and mask that provided some separation between herself and the dead man.

Behind her surgical mask, Dr Wainwright peered at the body with interest. 'This one's a beauty, isn't he?'

That wasn't exactly how Jess would have described the man. Although he was youthful and slim in appearance, and in life might have been handsome in a devilish way, with long black hair and a pointed beard, in death his skin was pale and waxen, more like a waxwork from *Madame Tussauds* than a real person.

Dr Wainwright turned her remorseless gaze on Jess. 'Come now, you're not a virgin, are you?'

Jess's mouth formed into a silent 'o', caught off-guard by Felicity's remark. She felt the colour drain from her face to match the pallor of the man on the trolley. 'Sorry?' she stumbled.

A frown spread across Felicity's brow like a bruise. 'To the mortuary, I mean. This isn't your first PM?'

'No, I... I've been to one before.'

'Well, then,' said Felicity. 'Nothing to worry about.'

Yet the post-mortem Jess had previously attended had been a routine one. Death following a fall from a height. There had been nothing... peculiar about that. The corpse laid out before her now had a quite different appearance. There was no hint of violence for one thing, apart from the pair of tiny thorn holes on the man's neck and the purple bruising around them. But that was the only hint of colour on the entire corpse. As for the rest of the skin... Jess had never seen anything like it. It simply had no colour.

She realised with a start that Felicity was talking, recording her findings into a microphone that hung down from the ceiling.

'... male, Caucasian, aged late twenties or early thirties. One point eight metres in height, sixty point five kilograms. The skin is unusually pale in colour. Distinctive dragon tattoo on the right forearm.'

Jess shifted her attention to study the tattoo. There on the man's arm was a small red outline of a dragon. The creature had a sinister appearance, its wings folded along its back, its front claw raised, its jaws open as if about to breathe flames, a malevolent look in its eye. The mortuary assistant leaned in to take a close-up photo.

Felicity waited, then returned to her commentary. 'No signs of physical injury to the body, apart from two puncture marks and associated bruising on the right side of the neck near the carotid artery. Okay, time for the internal examination. Let's cut him open.'

The pathologist's eagerness had a certain ghoulish quality, but Jess was grateful for her briskness of manner. She had no desire to hang around longer than was necessary.

Felicity took up her scalpel and Jess braced herself for the worst. But perhaps because of the bizarre nature of the corpse lying before her, she barely flinched when the pathologist began to slice the skin open. Nothing felt real anymore.

She was expecting a lot of blood, but in fact there was very little.

One by one, Felicity lifted out the organs and handed them to her assistant, who placed them into steel bowls. They resembled lumps of shrivelled meat. 'Just as I thought,' she declared, a look of satisfaction on her sharp features.

'What is it?' asked Jess. She was beginning to feel a little queasy.

'Exsanguination.'

'What does that mean?'

'He's been drained of blood.'

'What, all of it?'

'Not quite,' said Felicity. 'Losing half to two-thirds is fatal and I would estimate that's the case here. We'll be measuring the residual volumes carefully to try to pin it down more accurately. Are you all right, Jess? You're looking a little pale. Do you need to sit down?'

Jess took a deep breath. 'I'm okay,' she said, putting a hand on the gurney to steady herself. 'How was the blood removed?'

'Yes, that's the crux of the matter, isn't it?' said Felicity, and Jess thought she caught a twinkle of excitement in the pathologist's eyes. 'This is certainly an unusual case, perhaps unique. Any ideas?'

'Me?'

'Yes,' said Felicity. 'What do you make of it?'

Jess's gaze returned unwillingly to those two marks near the victim's throat. 'Those puncture wounds, they look like–'

'What?'

The notion seemed too stupid to say out loud. Jess kept her lips sealed, afraid they might betray her.

'They look like a bite from a vampire,' said the pathologist's taciturn assistant.

Felicity clapped her gloved hands together with glee. 'That's right. Are you a fan of vampire fiction, Jess? A lot of women your age seem very taken with Edward Cullen. I'm more of an Anne Rice reader myself... the vampire Lestat. And then there's the original... Count Dracula. A true horror classic.'

Jess stared at her masked face. 'You can't be serious?'

'No, of course not.' Felicity pointed to the marks with one long finger. 'These puncture wounds have a much more mundane explanation. They were made by one or more hypodermic needles. An anti-clotting agent was probably injected first, which might explain why there are two holes. When the results come back from the lab, I expect we'll find that some kind of drug or sedative was first administered to the victim, and then a syringe was used to draw blood from the body.'

Jess had a vague idea that an adult human had about ten pints of blood inside them, but she wasn't entirely sure. 'But that would mean around five or six pints was removed.'

'Roughly speaking,' agreed Felicity. 'And since there was no blood on the clothing, the perpetrator made a remarkably clean job of it. Impressive. Full marks to them.'

The background hum from the refrigeration units seemed to be growing louder. Jess felt the room around her swaying. Her forehead was hot, her palms clammy. 'Then what happened to all that blood?'

'Good question.' A strange expression appeared on Felicity's face. *Concern.* She moved closer. 'Are you sure you're all right, Jess?'

Beads of perspiration covered Jess's hands. Her head felt light, and the room was definitely moving. 'I need some air,' she gasped.

She almost made it as far as the exit before the floor came up and slapped her.

CHAPTER 7

'I need some air,' said Lucille West, 'this is all far too horrible to handle.' Her hysterical initial reaction to learning that Reynard had been murdered had all but subsided, but now she looked as if she were about to be sick. She threw a quick gaze around the low-ceilinged room of the White Horse & Griffin like a trapped animal before rushing out through the front door.

'You stay here,' Raven instructed Raj. 'I'd prefer to speak to Lucille on her own, if you don't mind.' He followed in the woman's wake and found her just outside the hotel, leaning against the white brick wall of the side passage and gasping for breath.

'I'm going to suffocate!' she declared dramatically. 'I really am.'

'Take your time and breathe deeply,' said Raven. 'You've had a nasty shock.' He wondered how much of her behaviour was real and how much for show. People could react in all manner of ways to unexpected bad news. But something made him think that such displays might be all too common for Lucille. The way that Raj had held her silently, waiting for her to calm down, suggested this wasn't the first time he'd had to come to her aid.

Becca joined him and together they waited patiently for the young woman to regain her composure. 'Is it all right to talk now?' he enquired at last.

She tossed her black hair over her shoulder, revealing yet more piercings in her ear, and stood up straight. 'Yes, I think so, but not here. I want to walk somewhere.'

Raven glanced up and down the narrow, cobbled street which was thronged with goths, tourists and professional photographers lugging serious equipment. It was impossible to hold a sensible conversation in this environment.

'Why don't we walk up the steps to the abbey?' suggested Lucille.

'No, I don't think so,' said Raven. The slog back up to the West Cliff to reclaim his car was going to be enough of an ordeal. Whitby's famous one hundred and ninety-nine steps leading up the steep East Cliff presented an almost insurmountable obstacle to a man with a dodgy leg. 'Let's see if we can find somewhere quieter.'

Instead of mounting the steps at the end of Church Street, they turned down an even narrower side alley and made their way to the nearby Tate Hill Sands, a small stretch of beach on the east side of the estuary. Across the river lay the grand terraces up on the West Cliff, and behind them rose the precipitous East Cliff with St Mary's Church perched on top. The two prongs of the West and East Piers, each with their own lighthouse, protruded into the North Sea. Old fishermen's cottages clustered around the edge of the harbour.

Lucille produced a cigarette and lit up as she walked, using a distinctive chrome lighter decorated with a pentagram. Beneath her studded leather jacket, her body was slim and delicate. Her stature was petite, although her platform shoes added several inches of height. Raven's impression was of a woman whose fierce outer appearance was little more than a suit of armour designed to shield a sensitive soul.

She dragged smoke into her lungs and looked out across the smooth grey waters of the harbour. The breeze stole the plume away as she exhaled, bringing a faint hint of pleasure to her darkened lips. 'I love this place!' she proclaimed. 'It's so elemental. I don't know how I'd stay sane if I couldn't come here for the festival. Come on, I want to feel the sand beneath my feet.'

Raven wondered if he was ever going to get a chance to ask any questions, but he was willing to indulge her for a bit longer. They descended a short flight of stone steps and began to trudge slowly along the narrow stretch of beach towards the East Pier, Lucille's platforms sinking into the sand with each step.

She was right about this place having an elemental quality. It was certainly invigorating down here, surrounded by water, sand and stone, the briny scent of the sea filling Raven's nostrils, and the roar of wind and cries of gulls drowning out all other sounds.

'This is the exact place where Dracula arrived in England,' said Lucille, turning back to speak to him, her long hair flapping in the breeze. 'His ship sailed from the port of Varna on the Black Sea coast and came to England bringing the Count and his collection of coffins filled with soil from his native Romania. On the way, he picked off the crew, one by one. The ship landed in a storm that he summoned and he came ashore in the form of an enormous black dog that ran up the steps to St Mary's Church.'

'Is that so?' said Raven.

Lucille nodded. 'Bram Stoker based that part of his story on a real event, the wreck of the *Dmitry*. The ship ran aground right here on this beach carrying a cargo of silver sand. In his book, the *Dmitry* became the *Demeter*. This town is so rich in stories and legends, it's no surprise that Bram Stoker chose it as the setting for his novel.'

They had arrived at a ramp leading up to the East Pier now and Raven had had enough. 'Let's stop here and sit down,' he said, planting himself firmly on a large boulder to circumvent debate.

Reluctantly, Lucille ceased her walking and sat down nearby. Against the mass of grey stone, she seemed impossibly fragile, much younger than her thirty years. With her heavily made-up eyes and lips, she looked like a little girl who had gone wild with her mother's makeup box.

'We need to ask you some questions about Reynard,' said Raven.

It was the first time the dead man's name had been mentioned since they had left the hotel. He wondered if she would break down again, but she nodded her acquiescence. 'What do you want to know about him?'

'Can you think of any reason why someone would wish him harm?'

She shook her head. 'Not really. I mean, he wasn't always the most agreeable of people. He didn't believe in putting on an act to make people happy.'

'He could be offensive?' suggested Becca. It seemed that the glowing character reference that Reynard's landlady had supplied was sounding increasingly biased. Stuffing her cat had obviously endeared Mrs Harker to her regular guest, causing her to overlook his various shortcomings.

Lucille adopted a defiant pose. 'He always spoke the truth. If that made him unpopular, he didn't care.'

'Was there anyone in particular he might have offended?' Raven asked.

'Not that I know of. Reynard wasn't vindictive. He didn't go out of his way to cause trouble. In fact, he much preferred to keep himself to himself.'

'He lived alone?'

'Yes. His parents were dead, and he rented an old house on a farm just outside Whitby. That's where he had his workshop. Really, all he wanted was to be left alone so that he could work on his animals.'

'Tell me exactly what you meant,' said Raven, 'when you asked Raj if Aurora was being a mean bitch.'

Lucille looked away. 'Well, I didn't really mean anything.'

'It sounded as if you meant that Aurora was in the habit of saying unkind things.'

Lucille sniffed. 'I was in shock. People say things they don't mean when they're upset. Reynard's death isn't the first tragedy to come my way.' She stole a look at the cliffs that towered above them and shuddered dramatically. 'This is a place of death! I hate it here!'

Raven and Becca exchanged a glance. Was this just another of Lucille's theatrics, or did she have something more to tell them?

She was back on her feet, pacing about like a cat. She pointed up at the clifftop. 'See up there, at the edge of the churchyard?' Her slim finger trembled. 'That's the exact spot where Mia threw herself over the edge.'

Raven frowned at the new name. 'Mia?'

'Mia Munroe, another member of our group. She jumped from the churchyard of St Mary's.'

Becca pulled out her notebook and wrote the name down. 'When did this happen?'

'Back in January, shortly after New Year.'

'It was suicide?'

Lucille bowed her head. She set off again, walking up the ramp that led to the East Pier.

Reluctantly, Raven followed.

From the vantage of the pier they had a clear view of the cliffs that loomed above them. They rose to a height of some hundred feet, steep, rocky and forbiddingly bleak beneath the leaden sky. At their foot, waves broke against rough rocks, sending up a cold spray. The area was wild and desolate, in contrast to the genteel façade of the West Cliff and its elegant crescent and terraces. Here was nature untamed, in all its might and rugged beauty.

'And why did Mia do that?' asked Becca.

Lucille turned sorrowful eyes to them. 'Because she had lost the love of her life.'

Raven wondered if he would have to cajole an

explanation out of her, possibly trekking halfway along the pier before she was willing to divulge any further details, but it seemed that she was just building up to a full account of her friend's death. She took a deep breath and began to speak.

'Twelve months before Mia took her life, her fiancé, Nathan, drowned right here.' She pointed to the rocks that lay at the base of the cliffs, washed relentlessly by white breakers. 'There was a storm, and for some reason, Nathan ventured all the way to the end of the East Pier onto the walkway beyond the lighthouse. He was washed into the sea by a huge wave. The coastguard was alerted, but it was too late to save him. His body was recovered from the rocks.'

Lucille turned her back on the sea and faced Raven and Becca. 'After his death, Mia began to mourn him in earnest, just as the Victorians would have done. She had always been fascinated by Victoriana but now it became an obsession. We thought it was just a phase, part of the healing process. We hoped she would soon recover and move on with her life. But she didn't. Exactly a year and a day after Nathan's death, she put on her wedding dress, walked through the town and up the steps to the church where she should have been married. Then she threw herself to her death.'

Lucille hugged her thin arms close to her, bowed her head and stalked off back in the direction of the town. In the silence that followed her revelation, gulls shrieked and cried, and the waves continued to batter the rocks.

*

'Mind if we make a short detour?' asked Raven as he drove out of Whitby. He was glad to be nestled again in the comfortable leather seats of the car after the long slog back up to the Royal Crescent. He had done enough walking for one day, much of it spent ascending and descending steep hills, stepping gingerly along cobbled streets or trudging across heavy sand.

The interview with Lucille hadn't revealed a great deal of fresh information as far as Reynard was concerned, only this tragic story of love and loss that had resulted in the deaths of Nathan Rigby and Mia Munroe. They would need to be followed up, but for the moment Raven couldn't see how an accidental drowning and a suicide fitted into the current murder investigation. One thing was becoming clear, however – everyone involved in the case was an eccentric of some sort, whether it was the reclusive and misanthropic Reynard Blackthorn, with his undertaker's garb and his predilection for dead animals, the haughty vampire-obsessed Aurora Highsmith, the misfit doctor, Raj Sandhu, or the highly strung Lucille West.

'Where to?' asked Becca.

'I want to see where Reynard Blackthorn created his works of art.' It was getting late and Raven was conscious that he'd left Hannah on her own all day, but he wanted to see for himself where Reynard had worked. Lucille had given them the address and it was on their way back to Scarborough. Well, kind of.

Littlebeck was a tiny hamlet, located in the heart of the North York Moors. The final approach road was narrow and the BMW took up more than its fair share of space on the road. Raven prayed they wouldn't meet a tractor coming the other way.

A wooden sign pointed to a farm in an isolated spot some distance short of the village. Raven turned the car onto a muddy track, cursing at the condition of the road surface which was filled with watery potholes. The M6 wasn't built for this. But after a short and bumpy drive, the car rumbled over a metal cattle grid and pulled into a farmyard.

Raven peered out at the darkened buildings in the encroaching dusk. 'Doesn't look like anyone's about.'

Lucille had told them that Reynard rented a house and workshop, but hadn't mentioned whether the farm itself was inhabited. From the look of it, the place was deserted.

'Let's go see,' said Becca.

Raven followed her out into the gathering gloom. Old stone buildings stood all around the yard, competing for degrees of dilapidation. The windows of the main house were dark, and no smoke rose from its chimney. A garage stood next to it, its wooden doors closed, and beyond that rose the low shape of a barn, its sides open to the elements and a rusty metal roof arching over the top. The dim shapes of more outbuildings were visible further up an unkept track. The deceased taxidermist had certainly found a secluded spot to run his business.

The sudden sound of footsteps made Raven turn, and he found himself staring into the wrong end of a double-barrelled shotgun.

'Oo the bloody 'ell are tha and what's tha game?' demanded the owner of the gun. Raven took in a ruddy face, its chin grey with stubble, and a flat cap wedged on top. The man was dressed in a pair of worn dungarees and mud-caked Wellington boots. 'Start talkin'!' he bellowed.

Raven began to reach into his coat pocket for his warrant card, and then thought better of it. 'DCI Tom Raven and DS Becca Shawcross, North Yorkshire Police. We understand that Reynard Blackthorn rents some buildings from you.'

The man's pale eyes narrowed in the half-light. 'Might be. What's 'e done?'

Raven gestured at the shotgun. 'Would you mind putting that away, please?'

The man bared his crooked teeth for a moment, as if itching for a chance to unload both barrels into Raven's chest, then lowered it to his side.

'Thank you,' said Raven. 'Do you have a key to Mr Blackthorn's property?'

'Aye.'

'And could we borrow it?'

'If tha must.' The farmer stomped over to his house and emerged a minute later brandishing a ring of keys. He handed them over reluctantly. 'When tha sees Mr Blackthorn, tell 'im 'is rent's due.'

Raven took the keys and followed the man's directions up the overgrown track. Beyond the barn, a small stone cottage was just visible, and next to it an ancient-looking shed with a slate roof.

It was almost dark now, and Becca switched on the light of her phone. Shining into the gloom, the beam quickly found the glint of metal. 'Look,' she said. The heavy wooden door of the shed had been secured with a brass chain and padlock which now hung uselessly open. It had been smashed apart by a heavy object – a sledgehammer perhaps.

Pulling on gloves, Raven gestured for Becca to stay silent. He switched on his own flashlight and gave the door a tentative push. It yielded with a groan, its hinges shrieking in protest. The light from his phone threw a streak of white across a flagstone floor, reaching slowly into the room as he pushed the door wider.

A flurry of wings shattered the quiet as a pigeon, imprisoned within, burst forth, its feathers brushing Raven's face as it made its bid for freedom.

He ducked back in alarm, his heart hammering wildly as the bird flew off into the nearby trees. 'Bloody hell,' he muttered. 'I hope there's not a flock of them cooped up in here.'

Opening the weathered door as wide as it would go, he stepped over the threshold, entering a dark, cavernous space. His torchlight reached only a few yards into the room, revealing hints of worktops covered in strange tools. Over his shoulder, the laboured sound of Becca's breathing echoed in his ears, a noisy counterpoint to the profound stillness within the shed. Her anxiety was palpable in each sharp inhale and shaky exhale.

The interior of the building was as cold as the grave, and the air felt dense. Now that the bird had flown, Raven sensed no life here, only death. There was a cloying sweetness in the air, the scent of decay. He glanced back, catching Becca's wide-eyed gaze, her unease reflected in the wavering torchlight.

'Is there a light in this place?' Raven's hand crept warily across the bare stone wall until his fingers found a metal switch. He flipped it up and was rewarded with a flicker of light. He blinked as bright white flooded the interior of the shed, illuminating every corner. Portable stage lighting had been rigged up around the inside of the building. It threw its cold radiance onto the tops of workbenches and against each wall. Only the dark voids between the rafters remained in shadow.

In the hushed sanctuary of the workshop, industrial shelving units lined the walls, filled with a menagerie of stuffed animals. Raven let his gaze glide across the nearest of them, taking in birds that would never fly again, a sleek fox immobilised mid-stride, a family of squirrels furtively clutching acorns they would never eat. Some were posed with a heavy dash of whimsy: a frog seated in a rowing boat, oars at the ready; a rabbit dressed as a French maid, a feather duster clutched in its paw. All kinds of creatures occupied this place, frozen in death, frozen in time.

The taxidermist's tools were arranged with neat precision, each in its own place. Scalpels gleamed under the unforgiving light, their blades razor-sharp, hungry for their meticulous work. Next to them lay scissors of various sizes. Assorted needles, each with different lengths and gauges, tailored for different tasks, stood at the ready. Jars of preserving chemicals stood on the worktop, their contents holding the promise of a kind of eternity.

Reynard's labours were meticulous and painstaking, and these instruments had been his partners.

Raven's gaze landed on a large plastic container standing on a workbench in the centre of the shed. The clear container held a thick dark liquid.

'Is that...?' asked Becca.

Raven walked towards it, drawn almost against his will. 'Blood?' he queried. The gallon-sized container was about two-thirds full of the rust-red liquid. 'It certainly looks like it.'

CHAPTER 8

'I bought us fresh croissants for breakfast.' Raven held up the paper bag as a peace offering, although to be fair, when he'd returned to the house late the previous night, full of apologies, Hannah hadn't once complained about being abandoned for the day.

He'd come home to find her curled up on the sofa, scrolling through social media on her phone. On the table beside her, a glass of red wine and a half-empty bottle had rubbed shoulders with a takeaway pizza box.

The sight of the wine had triggered his usual emotional response to alcohol – revulsion – and he'd had to fight back the words of criticism that sprang onto the tip of his tongue. Hannah was no longer a child and must make her own choices. He'd been pleased to note how she'd stopped after two glasses and screwed the cap back on the bottle, demonstrating a measure of restraint and self-discipline that his father would never have been capable of. When Alan Raven had started on a bottle, the drinking wouldn't stop until every last drop was drained.

She was sitting at the breakfast bar now, her eyes once more glued to her phone.

'I'm so sorry about leaving you on your own all day yesterday,' Raven told her.

'No probs, Dad.' She laid the phone aside for a second. 'Anyway, I wasn't really alone, not with Barry around. He's quite entertaining once he gets chatting, which is like, all the time. Reg doesn't say a lot though.'

'Did they finish the work?'

'Not quite. Barry said he needed to get some part or other and then come back to fit it. He said not to use the kitchen sink until then.'

A hastily scrawled note on the kitchen worktop confirmed the bad news.

Mate, sink not quite sorted. Need to wait for a part. In stock any day now. Cheers, B.

Raven's brow creased with irritation as he fetched clean plates from the cupboard and arranged the croissants on them. *Any day now.* Was this kitchen ever going to be finished or would Barry and Reg remain constant visitors for the rest of Raven's days? At this rate, by the time they were done, the house would be ready to start redecorating all over again.

He glared at the sink, still with no taps fixed to it. Barry's advice to Hannah about not using it hardly seemed necessary. What use was a sink without taps?

He set the plates out on the breakfast bar, poured two glasses of orange juice and went upstairs to the bathroom to fetch some water for the espresso machine. That was one bit of good news, at least. The longed-for Gaggia now held pride of place in the new kitchen. Raven had already given it a trial run, and it had more than met his expectations. He had almost forgotten how much pleasure could be derived from a perfect cup of coffee.

'Coffee?' he asked Hannah as the Gaggia hissed and spluttered its way towards nirvana.

'Do you have any green tea?'

Raven gazed at her, perplexed. 'Green tea?' Of course he didn't have any. He hadn't even thought to ask her what she liked to drink. 'I'll go back out and buy some,' he said, reaching for his coat.

'No bother, Dad. I'll go and pick some up later.'

'Are you sure?'

'Of course. I expect you'll be needing to head back into work today.'

He turned to her, his guilt no doubt plastered all over his face. 'I'm so sorry, darling. It's just–'

She dismissed his apology with a shake of her head. 'It's okay, Dad. Honestly, I get it. You have a murder to investigate.'

'Well, yes, I do. But I'm going to see if I can hand over to my sergeant by the end of the day. I thought we might go out for dinner tonight.'

'Actually, don't worry about it. I've already made plans for tonight.'

'You have?' Raven felt both surprised and hurt at the news, although he knew he had no right whatsoever to the latter feeling.

'Just a concert I saw advertised in the spa.'

'In the spa?' There was so much he didn't know about his own daughter. Her musical tastes, for instance. He was surprised she'd found something to entertain her in Scarborough. It wasn't exactly London. 'Well, in that case, have fun.'

'I will.' A smile came to her face, illuminating it like a ray of sunshine, and his heart did a somersault. What had he done to deserve such a wonderful daughter? Once again, he was struck by her physical similarity to Lisa. But whereas Lisa could so often be haughty, Hannah was still fresh, untainted. He wanted her to stay that way forever.

Talking of Lisa, his ex-wife had been bombarding him with a steady hail of messages berating him for his latest behaviour. Her most recent directive had been clear enough – *Don't even think about leaving Hannah alone again today* – but he knew already that it wouldn't be her last.

He finished his croissant, swallowed one final taste of heaven from his espresso cup, scowled once again at the unfinished sink, and left the house, pausing only to kiss

Hannah's forehead and grab his coat.

★

'I've gathered everyone together in the incident room,' Becca told Raven when he arrived at the station, slightly later than usual. Nipping out to the bakery to pick up fresh croissants had taken longer than if he'd just grabbed a coffee for himself, but he didn't regret spending a little time with Hannah. He knew he was letting her down spectacularly by coming into work for a second day running. The least he could do was spare ten minutes sharing breakfast with her.

He wondered if Gillian might be on hand to express thanks for showing up at the station on what was supposed to be his day off, but there was no sign of her, and Raven felt quite relieved. His encounters with his boss had a tendency to leave him feeling bruised even when he'd done nothing wrong and had followed every rule in the book. People like Gillian just seemed to enjoy throwing their weight around, and she certainly had plenty to throw.

He was surprised, however, and not best pleased, to find that DI Derek Dinsdale had joined DC Tony Bairstow and DC Jess Barraclough in the incident room. Raven had grudgingly accepted Dinsdale's assistance on his previous investigation. Did Dinsdale now consider himself to be a regular member of the team? Or had Gillian asked him to show his face?

The older man looked up enquiringly as Raven entered. 'Raven?'

'Derek?'

A terse exchange, even by Raven's standards, but he had no appetite for engaging the other detective in further conversation. Dinsdale, too, seemed satisfied with the outcome of the discussion, as if he sensed approval in Raven's one-word response.

Whatever had been communicated, it was too late for Raven to change his mind, because at that instant the door opened again and Gillian bustled in, a wad of files clutched against her bosom. She shouldered her way to the back of the room and manoeuvred her hind quarters onto a desk, from where she could observe the proceedings like a hungry wolf.

'Tom?' she enquired.

'Ma'am?'

Yet another exchange whose precise meaning eluded Raven. For a second time in less than a minute, he suspected he had agreed to something he might later regret. He caught Becca watching him, a glimmer of amusement in her eyes.

'Okay, let's get started,' he said, walking to the front of the room before anyone else could address him. 'We need to crack on. I'll begin by running through yesterday's events to make sure everyone is up to speed.'

He was aware that Becca was the only member of the team who would have all the facts of the case at her disposal. Tony and Jess would have to pick up the ball and start running with it quickly. Dinsdale too, although the notion of the older man going anywhere in a hurry was laughable.

He noted with pleasure that someone had already fixed a photograph of the dead man and a map of Whitby to the whiteboard. He pointed to the map, indicating the location of the abbey and launched into his summary. 'The body of Reynard Blackthorn was discovered early yesterday morning by English Heritage staff at the ruins of Whitby Abbey. He's an IC1 male, twenty-nine years old and a graduate of Leeds University. His body was staged like this' – Raven demonstrated by crossing his forearms over his chest and placing his hands on the opposite shoulders – 'and he was dressed in the style of a Victorian undertaker in black top hat and tails.'

'A theatrical touch,' remarked Gillian from the back of the room.

'Yes ma'am. Yet interestingly, it would appear that those were his regular clothes.'

'One of those bloody goths, was he?' muttered Dinsdale. 'Hordes of them invade Whitby about this time of year.'

Raven shot a sharp look in the man's direction. 'Let's keep our personal prejudices out of this, shall we, Derek?'

'Just saying,' grumbled Dinsdale.

'Reynard was a taxidermist by trade,' continued Raven, 'and had a stall at the bazaar in Whitby Pavilion. It seems that he came to the festival twice every year and always stayed at the same guest house. His landlady, Mrs Harker, described him as a kind and pleasant man, although other accounts suggest that might not be a universally-held view.'

He marked the location of the pavilion and the Royal Crescent on the map, along with the abbey, which he circled in red.

'Reynard appears to have been a bit of a loner. His parents are dead and he had no other family. But the night before his body was found, he met three friends at a local pub, the Elsinore on Flowergate.'

'The Elsinore is a traditional haunt for goths,' supplied Becca.

Raven wrote down the three names on the board. 'Aurora Highsmith, Dr Raj Sandhu and Lucille West first met Reynard at Leeds during their student days and continued to meet up twice every year at the goth weekends in Whitby. They all claim they last saw Reynard when they left the pub at eleven o'clock. Where he went after that, we don't yet know, but Mrs Harker reports that she was disturbed sometime after midnight by the sound of someone leaving the guest house and a dog barking in the street outside.'

Jess raised her hand. 'According to the pathologist, time of death was in the early hours of yesterday morning, probably between three and five o'clock.'

'That fits, then,' acknowledged Raven. 'What else did you get from the post-mortem?' The pathologist's report would no doubt be arriving later that day, but he knew he could depend on Jess to report the findings accurately.

She read from her notes. 'The cause of death was exsanguination, which means loss of blood. According to Dr Felicity Wainwright, the loss of around forty percent of blood volume causes unconsciousness, and losing fifty percent is often fatal.'

'How was the blood removed from the victim?'

'Using a hypodermic needle and a syringe to draw blood from the carotid artery. That's what left the puncture marks on the man's neck.'

It was a relief to hear that there was a rational explanation for the manner of the man's death. Raven pursed his lips in thought. 'How could blood have been removed without the victim struggling to prevent it? I saw nothing to suggest he'd been tied up or restrained.'

'According to Dr Wainwright,' said Jess, 'he may have been sedated or drugged. She sent a blood sample to the lab for analysis.'

'And how long would it take to drain that much blood from an adult male?'

'She estimated several hours.'

Raven did a quick calculation – a time of death between 3am and 5am; perhaps three hours required to subdue, transport and kill the victim – that would mean that Reynard must have been abducted by his killer sometime between midnight and 2am. It matched Mrs Harker's account of being awoken by the barking dog and the sound of the guest house door closing.

'Dr Wainwright also mentioned that an anti-clotting agent had probably been administered,' Jess noted. 'Otherwise it would have been impossible to remove so much of the victim's blood.'

'So whoever did this knew the necessary medical procedure, and they planned it meticulously.' Raven ran the scene through his mind's eye again. The choice of location, the deliberate staging of the body, the lack of any signs of a struggle, the bizarre method of execution – everything pointed to a crime mapped out long in advance and executed with ruthless precision.

'One final thing,' said Jess. 'It might not be important, but the victim had a tattoo of a dragon on his arm.'

'Okay, Jess, thanks. Tony, do you have those photos I emailed you last night?'

'Right here, sir.' Tony reached across his desk to hand Raven a series of printed images, which Raven fixed to the whiteboard. They made for gruesome viewing.

Raven pointed to the first image. 'Last night, Becca and I swung by Reynard's workshop near Littlebeck. The padlock on the workshop door had been forced.' He moved his finger to the second image. 'Inside the building, we found this.'

The photo showed the plastic container of blood that had been left on the workbench. All eyes in the room were fixed on it.

Gillian broke the silence. 'You think that the killer broke into the workshop and left the blood there?'

'That seems the most likely explanation, ma'am.'

'Why would they do that? They must have intended for us to find it.'

Raven shrugged. 'At this stage, it's anyone's guess. But I think we're dealing with a twisted individual, someone who enjoys playing games. This wasn't simply about killing the victim – there would have been easier ways to do that. There's some kind of message here, and the perpetrator took considerable risks to leave that message.'

'A message for whom?'

Raven shook his head. 'At present, we're the only people who know about this. But we'll need to question Reynard's three friends again and try to establish motives and alibis; all the usual avenues of enquiry. Right now, all three of them look suspicious. They were the last known people to see him before he died. Dr Raj Sandhu is an obvious suspect because of his medical knowledge, but both women seem to have something of a vampire fixation. Aurora Highsmith was dressed as a vampire, and Lucille West talked a lot about Dracula, which is an odd subject to bring up when being interviewed by the police about the death of a friend.'

'We're dealing with strange people, Raven,' interjected Dinsdale, apparently unable to keep his mouth shut for longer than a few minutes. 'These goths...' He shook his head in despair. 'Being weird is what they do.'

Raven cast a warning look his way, but said nothing. Why waste words?

'What's the situation at the victim's workshop?' asked Gillian. 'I assume you didn't leave it unattended?'

'Of course not, ma'am. Whitby police have secured Reynard's workshop and house' – Raven recalled the loud complaints of the farmer when uniformed officers had descended on his property in the dead of night – 'and I've asked Holly and her team to head over there this morning. Talking of Holly, has anyone had sight of her report from yesterday?'

'I've got it,' said Tony, holding up a sheaf of printouts. He passed Raven some photos of objects recovered from the scene. The first showed a plain, brass key; the second some thick black hairs. 'This key was found in a stone sarcophagus at the abbey – nothing sinister about that, just a feature of the medieval building. And the hairs have been sent for analysis. Holly suggested they might be dog hairs. If so, the lab should be able to identify the breed.'

Raven pinned the photos to the board. The brass key could have been dropped by anyone, but there was a chance it belonged to the victim. 'Where were the hairs found?'

'On the victim's clothes, sir.'

'A black dog,' Raven ruminated. Dogs kept popping up all over this case. The barking dog, dog hairs, and that story Lucille had told him about Dracula arriving at Whitby in the form of a large dog. 'Let me know as soon as we hear anything from the lab,' he told Tony.

'Right, sir. The CSI team also recovered the victim's mobile phone and that's been sent for analysis.'

'Excellent,' said Raven, 'in the meantime, can I ask you

to check out his phone calls and bank records? Run a next-of-kin check too in case he has some living relatives. You know the routine.'

'No problem, sir. I'll get onto it right away.' Tony never minded being given these nitty-gritty tasks even if they kept him tied to his desk.

'And can you also find out about the deaths of two of Reynard's friends? Nathan Rigby, who died from drowning, and Mia Munroe, a case of suicide. Both deaths occurred at Whitby. There's no reason to believe they're connected to Reynard's murder, but I'd like to know the facts. Oh, and be sure to check Reynard's criminal record. Apparently he has a conviction.'

From the back of the room, Gillian's voice boomed out. 'What for?'

Raven nodded for Becca to fill in the details. 'Offences related to his taxidermy business, ma'am. According to a witness, he was found guilty of killing a protected species. A bat.'

Gillian's face darkened. 'Bats, vampires, blood...' she growled. 'I don't like any of this. We need to move quickly, Tom, and keep this under wraps.'

'Of course, ma'am.' Raven fought back the urge to remark that this was obvious. He needed Gillian on his side, not breathing down his neck.

'So what's your plan of action, Tom?'

It seemed she was determined to keep up the pressure on him. Perhaps there was someone leaning on her, too, from higher up the food chain. A bigger boss, making her own life hell, just as she was doing to him.

He had no choice but to think aloud, on the hoof. 'Well, we'll need to follow up a number of leads. First there's the obvious: talk to Reynard's three friends again. It's possible that the killer was close to the victim, with a personal motive. But we have to keep our minds open, especially given the nature of Reynard's death. The perpetrator may be a person as yet unknown to us, with some other motive entirely. We can't ignore the fact that the killing was staged to look like a vampire attack, and given the close connection between Whitby and the Dracula story, not to mention the goth festival that's taking place…' He caught a spark of displeasure in Gillian's eye and left the thought unfinished.

'So how do you intend to allocate tasks?' asked Dinsdale.

'Given the obvious requirement for the murderer to have some medical knowledge, I'd like to start by re-interviewing Dr Raj Sandhu. Becca, you can come with me again.'

With tasks already assigned to Tony, that just left Jess and Dinsdale.

Raven decided on an unconventional approach, which might just work. 'Derek and Jess, I'd like you two to head over to Reynard's workshop. Holly should be there with her CSI team giving the place the once over. I'd like you to check out his cottage, search for financial records, leads to anyone he might have been in contact with, or anything else that might point us in the right direction. Take the brass key and see if it fits the cottage.'

Jess looked only momentarily fazed at being partnered with the Neanderthal detective inspector but quickly regained her usual enthusiasm. Dinsdale, for his part, yawned openly in reaction to being assigned a task he no doubt felt was beneath him. Raven might live to regret pairing them up, but there was a chance that Jess's eagerness might blend with Dinsdale's experience to produce a satisfactory outcome.

'Any questions? Then let's go.'

From the back of the room, Detective Superintendent Gillian Ellis cleared her throat.

'Tom, stay behind for a moment, would you?'

'Certainly, ma'am.' He waited at the whiteboard while the others filed out, Dinsdale's eyes narrowed, as if he suspected he was being sidelined.

'How did your media awareness course go, Tom?'

The question was the last thing Raven had expected her

to ask. 'It was very...' As far as Raven was concerned, it had been three wasted days away from the field, being briefed about how to deal effectively with journalists and how to get the most out of online social media platforms. As far as he was concerned, the course had been a punishment of sorts, one that Gillian had given him following an unfortunate encounter with a TV news reporter during one of his previous investigations. '...it was very informative, ma'am.'

Her crocodile smile told him she knew exactly how he really felt. 'I'm pleased you feel that way, Tom, because you'll be needing to put those skills into practice on this case. I don't want rumours running wild about vampires in Whitby. If the details of this case leak, I'll want you to put a lid on any speculation right away.'

'I'll be sure to keep any rumours in check, ma'am,' Raven assured her. As if he had any control over what the press might say about anything! Already the abbey grounds had been closed during one of the busiest days of the tourist season. It seemed almost inevitable that someone would let something slip sooner or later. He dreaded the inevitable media circus that would result. And now, it seemed, he would have to deal with that on top of everything else.

How was he ever going to be able to spend time with Hannah?

CHAPTER 9

D I Derek Dinsdale wouldn't have been Jess's first choice of partner. Might as well admit it: the ageing detective with his beer gut sagging over his waistband and coarse grey hairs sticking out of his ears like unruly pipe cleaners would have been at the very bottom of her list. It wasn't just the way he looked, it was his Jurassic-era approach to policing that made him the last doughnut in the box. She would much rather have been with Becca, who she always got on well with, or Raven, who was fun but drove like a lunatic. Or even Tony, who was dependable, if a little dull. But if Dinsdale was to be her co-worker for the day, she was determined to make the best of it.

'Shall I drive, sir?' It was no secret that Dinsdale enjoyed being chauffeured around whenever he got the chance, although whether this was due to his laziness or an inflated sense of self-importance was hotly debated.

'Thank you, Jess. Then I can take the lead when we get there.'

'Of course, sir.'

Jess was always more than happy to take the wheel of

her trusty Land Rover. And even with Dinsdale in the passenger seat, the prospect of a drive across the North York Moors was far preferable to a visit to the mortuary in the company of Dr Felicity Wainwright.

Dinsdale frowned as he approached the ancient vehicle, slowing his pace as if having second thoughts. 'Does this thing have an MOT?' he asked doubtfully.

'Of course it does.' Jess gave the car a friendly slap, taking care not to hit it too hard, just in case. 'It's still got years ahead of it.'

'Looks to me like it's got more years behind it,' grumbled Dinsdale, hauling himself up into the passenger seat with an effort. He grimaced as he shifted his bottom around, seeking comfort on the hard vinyl cushion and not finding it. 'Just drive carefully,' he instructed her. 'Not like that bloody idiot, Raven.'

Jess hid a grin. 'Right you are, sir.' She started the ignition, hoping that the car wouldn't choose today to let her down, but with a little pull of the choke it fired eagerly on the second attempt, and she took it onto the main road leading out of Scarborough without any bother.

Soon they were within the boundaries of the national park, heading north in the direction of Whitby. Home territory, as far as Jess was concerned.

She loved the moors in all kinds of weather and in all seasons. She had walked them many times, from her beloved hometown of Rosedale Abbey, all along the Cleveland Way as it hugged the coast, and up to the half-conical peak of Roseberry Topping. One of her goals was to tackle the famous, or infamous, Lyke Wake Walk later in the year, walking all forty miles from west to east in under twenty-four hours. This morning, a soft mist blanketed the landscape, muting the colours to a hushed earthen palette. But to Jess's way of thinking, the moors held beauty whatever the weather or the time of year.

The Land Rover was the perfect vehicle for the place they were heading – a farm out in the middle of nowhere. As she turned off the main road and bounced along a rutted path, making Dinsdale groan out loud, she smiled to herself, imagining the trouble Raven must have had bringing his BMW this way the previous night.

The cramped space of the farmyard was already filled with CSI vans when Jess pulled up. She felt a stab of heartache at the sight of those white vehicles with the blue and yellow strip down the side and the words "Crime Scene Investigation" emblazoned in capital letters. Her boyfriend, Scott, had been a member of this very team until his untimely and recent death.

She was doing her best to square up to a future without him, yet every time she thought she had turned a corner and come to terms with his death, yet another reminder intruded suddenly into her life, bringing his loss into sharp relief all over again. She brushed her eyes with the back of her hand and switched off the engine, waiting as it coughed and spluttered its way to silence. Scott had always laughed at the way it did that, and the reminder came like another sharp thrust in her side. She blew her nose into a handkerchief to cover her distress.

In the seat next to her, Dinsdale didn't appear to have noticed her emotional upset. He fumbled with his seat belt, pushed open the car door and clambered out of the Land Rover to the muddy courtyard. 'Bloody hell,' she heard him moaning. 'My poor shoes will be ruined.'

She took a moment to steady herself, resolving not to show her vulnerable side. She missed Scott every single day, but was glad she had chosen to ignore her parents' advice and stay in her job. Work was her refuge now; a way to find meaning and make sense of what had happened. Scott had always been a determined investigator, and would have been fascinated by the strangeness of this current case. At times like this, she could almost feel his presence, as if he were peering over her shoulder to check on how she was doing.

She glanced up at the rear-view mirror and imagined his face there, looking on with concern. 'I've got this,' she assured him. 'I'll be okay now.'

Jumping out of the Land Rover, she set off along the rugged track that led to Reynard's cottage and workshop. Dinsdale was making heavy weather of it, muttering to himself as he stumbled along the lane. Jess quickly caught up with him and overtook him in her thick-soled walking boots. She always kept a spare pair in the Land Rover.

At the entrance to the workshop, Holly Chang came out to greet them. Behind her, in the building, white-suited CSIs were crawling everywhere, observed by the glassy eyes of dozens of stuffed animals. A chill ran down Jess's spine at the sight. It was certainly one of the most bizarre crime scenes she had witnessed during her brief time as a detective.

'Found anything yet?' asked Dinsdale.

'And a good morning to you too,' said Holly.

'Morning,' said Jess with a smile. It was good to have Holly around to dilute the wet-blanket effect that Dinsdale brought to every occasion.

'As you can no doubt see for yourself,' said Holly, 'I've got my team hard at work. We'll let you know what we find.'

Dinsdale gave the operation a sceptical glance. 'Is he new?' he asked, pointing to one of the guys examining the floor beneath a workbench. 'Looks like he's barely out of school.'

The young lad was obviously a replacement for Scott, and Jess felt the jolt of the unexpected reminder tear her heart open yet again. She forced back the tears, thrusting her hands angrily into her coat pockets.

Holly glanced at her sympathetically and then turned her ire on Dinsdale. 'I trained Jamie myself, Derek, and I can assure you that he's more than up to the job.'

The CSI team leader was petite in stature but in temperament had often been compared to a Yorkshire Terrier. Dinsdale backed off immediately under her verbal assault. 'Well, I'm sure he is. Let's let them get on with it, shall we?' he suggested to Jess, as if she had been the one to criticise the lad. 'Come on, let's go and take a look at the cottage.'

He trudged past the workshop and on to the house itself, which was really nothing more than a single-storey cottage. It looked as if it had been neglected for many years. Its white stone walls were streaked with dirt, and the window frames were half-rotten. Slates were missing from the roof, and twigs and straw poked through the gap where an enterprising bird had found a place to build a nest.

There were no signs of a break-in. Dinsdale pulled on a pair of forensic gloves and fumbled the brass key from the abbey into the lock. It turned reluctantly and the wooden door opened with a judder. Jess bent down as they entered and scooped up a few letters from the dirty flagstone floor.

It didn't take them long to search the place. The dwelling had just one bedroom and a living room leading into a narrow galley kitchen. A miniscule bathroom had been tacked on at the back. The cottage had no central heating and felt chill and damp now that the fire in the grate had been allowed to go out. There were few personal items and no books. There wasn't even a TV and Jess wondered what Reynard had found to do in his spare time, living so far from civilisation. Perhaps his work had been all-consuming. The only concession to entertainment was an old record player and a stack of vinyl albums. Jess sifted through them, recognising a few of the bands in Reynard's collection, but finding most of them unknown to her. As far as she could make out they were all goth groups.

Dinsdale opened a wardrobe, rummaged through a collection of black clothing and closed the door again in disgust. 'There's nothing here,' he complained. 'What a waste of time!'

Jess returned to the pile of post that she'd put on the kitchen table. Two letters looked like they might be bank statements or unpaid bills. She would give those to Tony. But there was also a postcard of Whitby Abbey.

She turned it over, curious to find out who might have sent Reynard a postcard from somewhere so near. Who, in fact, sent postcards at all in the days of email and instant messaging?

The card was unstamped, so it must have been delivered to the cottage by hand. There was no address, but written in a large and elegant script were the words:

As he took the life from others, so it was drawn from him.

CHAPTER 10

'Did I do the right thing?' Raven wondered aloud as the BMW swallowed the miles between Scarborough and Whitby.

'About what?' asked Becca.

'Pairing Jess with Dinsdale.' Raven tried to picture how the fresh-faced young DC would get along with the older detective. Dinsdale could be a difficult, domineering character, quick to take advantage of weakness.

Becca laughed. 'Jess can handle that old dinosaur. She's tougher than she looks.'

Raven decided to trust her on this. Becca was a good judge of character and was rarely wrong on these things. Besides, he had set the unlikely duo in motion and it was too late to change his mind. He would just have to see how things worked out.

He drummed his fingers on the steering wheel, his gaze steady on the winding road ahead. The moors were coming back to life now that winter's frosty hand had relaxed its grip. Through the pale mist, bright yellow clusters of gorse stood out against the mellow earth tones of faded heather.

'How is Hannah?' asked Becca.

'She's fine. Or at least, I think she is. She's found a concert to go to tonight.'

'You see?' said Becca, sounding smug. 'I said she seemed resourceful.'

'Yes,' said Raven. His daughter was certainly putting on a good display of resourcefulness and independence. He just wished he could see more of her. Perhaps if he could get on top of the investigation today, he could hand over to Becca and spend the weekend with Hannah.

Learning from his mistake the previous day, this time he approached Whitby from the east side of town, driving as close to the centre as possible before parking his car. From his riverside parking spot, he had an unobstructed view of the replica of HMS *Endeavour*, the ship that Captain Cook had sailed on his voyage to Australia, and which had been built at Whitby. It was one of the town's many reminders of its links with the sea.

He and Becca made their way down Church Street, dodging once again around the crowds of tourists and professionally-equipped photographers snapping pictures of any goths willing to pose in their Victorian and vampire finery. The town was even more crowded than the day before, and Raven supposed the numbers would only increase as the weekend festivities gathered pace.

At the White Horse & Griffin they found Dr Raj Sandhu in the restaurant tucking in to a full English breakfast. Raven's eyes landed on the thick slice of black pudding on the doctor's plate, and the memory of the container of blood at the taxidermist's workshop set his stomach churning. He pushed the thought aside, forcing a polite smile as he asked if they might join the doctor at his table.

'Please.' Raj wiped his mouth with a napkin and gestured to the two empty chairs opposite. He caught Raven staring at his plate and gave a guilty look. 'I only indulge in this kind of food when I'm away from home. Normally I have a bowl of muesli. A doctor ought to set a good example, don't you think?'

'Carry on,' said Raven, who never ate muesli and would have enjoyed the same cooked breakfast in Raj's place. Although perhaps not the black pudding under the circumstances.

'Do you have news?' asked Raj, slicing through the juicy black cup of a mushroom.

'Sorry,' said Raven, 'just more questions. Have you been in contact with Aurora and Lucille since we spoke to you?'

'We met again yesterday after you'd finished with Lucille. We had dinner together and went out for a few drinks. As you can imagine, the mood was subdued. There was talk of leaving the goth weekend and travelling home early, but I told the others we should stay to help the police.'

'That's good of you,' said Raven. 'What can you tell us about Mia Munroe and Nathan Rigby? I understand they were friends of yours.'

Raj's fork paused mid-air, loaded with scrambled egg and bacon. 'Did Lucille tell you about them?'

'She did. Now I'd like to hear what you have to say.'

Raj set the fork down and pushed his plate aside, leaving half the food uneaten. When he spoke next, his voice was thick with emotion. 'It's been a terrible couple of years. There were six of us at university: me, Aurora, Lucille, Reynard, Nathan and Mia. We were all outsiders, I guess. It wasn't easy being the only Asian goth in my school. Growing up, I always felt excluded, and my parents made it clear that they expected more conventional behaviour from their firstborn son. So when I met Reynard and the others at university, it felt like I'd found a new family. It was our shared tastes in music and fashion that drew us together, and because we were all loners of one kind or another, we bonded really strongly. Well, you do at that age, don't you?' He gazed wistfully across the room before continuing. 'Nathan and Mia moved to Whitby after finishing university. Nathan was from the town originally – his brother is the owner of a jewellery shop here

– and he and Mia became a couple. They planned to get married, but then Nathan drowned in a tragic accident, and Mia...' He turned away, unable to go on.

'According to Lucille, she took her own life.'

Raj tugged at his checked jacket and straightened his bow tie. 'We should have spotted the signs. A period of mourning would have been normal after Nathan's death, but Mia took it way too far. She wore mourning dress, she lit candles for him, she withdrew from normal life. Looking back, it was obvious that something was badly wrong. We ought to have given her more support, but we weren't around when she needed us most. We were all too wrapped up in our own lives.' He glanced up miserably at Raven. 'I feel particularly responsible for what happened to her. With my background, I really have no excuse for not helping her.'

'Because of your medical training?' Becca queried.

He nodded glumly. 'I'm specialising in Psychiatry.'

Raven thought for a moment. 'But you still had to go through general medical training, before specialising, right?'

'That's correct.'

'What do you know about exsanguination?'

The question caught Raj off guard. 'Exsan–' He blanched visibly as surprise turned to realisation, then horror. Lowering his voice, he leaned across the table. 'Are you telling me that Reynard was exsanguinated?' He glanced around uneasily, but the restaurant was emptying rapidly. Soon they would be the only ones left.

'Just tell us what you know about the procedure,' said Raven.

Raj gave the question some thought. 'Well, to draw a meaningful quantity of blood, you'd need access to a major vein or artery, ideally both. When animals are slaughtered according to *halal* or *kosher* practices, a sharp knife is used to sever the carotid arteries and the jugular veins in the neck. The animals are then bled before their meat is consumed.'

'That's not how it was done,' said Raven. 'A knife wasn't used in this case.'

'Then I suppose you could draw blood directly from an artery or a vein using a syringe, but it wouldn't be easy. Inserting a needle would require some medical knowledge and skill. And the body's natural clotting mechanism would hinder the process.'

Raven's gaze hardened. 'You possess precisely those kind of skills and knowledge, Dr Sandhu. And you also have access to hypodermic needles.'

A look of defiance spread over Raj's face, the colour returning to his cheeks. 'Yes, but I don't bring them with me on holiday!'

'You might do,' retorted Raven, 'if you planned to carry out a murder. Where were you on Wednesday night between the hours of midnight and 5am?'

Raj ran a hand through his thick glossy hair. 'I already told you. I left the pub at eleven o'clock and returned to my hotel room. I was asleep by midnight.'

'Can anyone verify that?'

'No,' said Raj wearily. 'How could they? I was alone in my room.' He jabbed a finger in Raven's direction. 'Frankly, I find it insulting that you could think me capable of doing something so heinous. You might as well accuse Aurora.'

Raven drew his eyebrows together. 'Why Aurora?'

'Well, because she has diabetes. You'll find hypodermic needles in her room if you go looking for them!'

'Really?' said Raven. He recalled the way Aurora had pushed aside the Danish pastry at the pavilion café. 'Interesting.'

Raj looked aghast at what he'd just said. 'I didn't mean... I just...' His words petered out. 'I regret talking to you now,' he said after a moment's reflection. 'I was trying to help, but you keep twisting my words.'

Raven adopted a more conciliatory expression. 'We're simply exploring possibilities, Dr Sandhu. I'm sure you understand that we must investigate every possible avenue.'

Raj seemed to be placated by Raven's response. 'Yes, of course. I do understand that. And I really do want to help.'

'Thank you.' Raven glanced sideways at Becca, indicating she should take over the questioning. If she was going to assume more responsibility, it would be good for her to take the lead.

'Dr Sandhu,' said Becca, in a soothing voice, 'what is your opinion on taxidermy?'

'My opinion?' Raj squirmed in his seat. 'Are you asking me to judge the artistic merit of Reynard's work, or do you want me to comment on the ethics of the practice?'

'You didn't approve?' asked Becca.

'Not really. My duty as a doctor is preservation of life. I can't condone the killing of animals for no good reason. But Reynard was a friend. It's what he did for a living and some people seem to like stuffed animals. I wasn't going to make a big song and dance about it.'

'Not even when he over-stepped the mark?'

Raj sighed. 'You're talking about the incident with the endangered species.'

'The bats, yes,' confirmed Becca.

'Well, what can I say? Reynard broke the law and went to prison. But even I thought that his punishment was a little harsh.'

'You don't think he deserved it?'

'Well...'

'Was it you who reported Reynard to the police?'

Raj bristled at the suggestion. 'Absolutely not. I may not have approved of everything that Reynard did, but I would never betray a friend like that.'

'Then who did?'

'I don't know,' he snapped. 'You're the police. I'd have thought you'd be able to find out.'

'Oh, we will,' Becca assured him.

Just as they seemed to have reached a stalemate, Raven's phone buzzed. It was a message from Jess, telling him what she'd found in Reynard's cottage. A photo of a handwritten postcard was attached. Raven studied the writing in the image. *As he took the life from others, so it was drawn from him.* Raven showed it to Becca who returned his puzzled gaze with a shrug.

'Does this mean anything to you?' asked Raven, showing the photograph to Raj.

'Oh my God, did the murderer leave this behind?'

'Do you recognise the handwriting?'

Raj seemed bemused by the question. 'Nobody writes by hand anymore.'

'Not even doctors?'

He returned Raven's question with an emphatic shake of his head. 'It's not my handwriting.'

'And does the message mean anything to you?'

'No.' Raj inspected his pocket watch, which appeared to be an actual working timepiece, not just a prop. 'Is there anything else? It's just that I arranged to meet the others.'

'Well,' said Raven, 'perhaps you wouldn't mind answering one last question that's been playing on my mind.'

'Yes?'

'I'm curious, what prompted the four of you to come to Whitby for the goth weekend, but decide to stay in different accommodation?' Raven counted them off on his fingers. 'You're here at the White Horse & Griffin, Lucille is down the road at the Black Horse, Aurora is enjoying the luxury of Bagdale Hall, and Reynard stayed where he always did at a guest house on the Royal Crescent. It's almost as if you were trying to avoid each other. Care to explain?'

Raj blinked as if the matter hadn't occurred to him before. 'Well, I suppose we all have – had – different preferences.' He gestured around the cosy restaurant with its low beamed ceiling and exposed brickwork. In the winter, no doubt the fireplace would be roaring with a log fire. 'Personally, I have a great fondness for this place.'

Raven acknowledged the agreeableness of the venue

with a smile. 'And yet it would have been more convenient for you to stay in the same place as the others.'

Raj exhaled a slow breath, nodding in reluctant agreement. 'It's a fair point. But the answer isn't really a great mystery. The simple truth is that we've moved on from our student days.' His voice contained a hint of resignation. 'It's normal, I guess. Life happens, people change. As students we used to stay at the youth hostel next to the abbey, but we outgrew that. Reynard liked Mrs Harker because she looked after him so well. Aurora likes to spend money and is the only one who can afford Bagdale Hall. Lucille and I, well we like these old inns, but we enjoy our own space too. To be honest, Chief Inspector, this will be my final trip to Whitby. If it wasn't for Mia's death, I wouldn't be here now. I only came this one last time to honour her memory.'

CHAPTER 11

It took a whole hour to get from Scarborough to Whitby by bus, but the journey was a scenic one, taking in the rugged beauty of the North York Moors and the charming villages along the way. The names of the stops felt strange but beguiling on Hannah's tongue – Scalby, Burniston, Cloughton, Fylingthorpe – and she couldn't believe she'd never been to Yorkshire before. Peering through the upper deck windows of the bus as it veered around tight corners, her face just a few feet away from old stone cottages, she wondered why her dad had never brought her here when she was younger. It was just the break she needed before heading back to university for her final term.

She got off at Whitby bus station and wandered into town, clueless about where to go, but happy to explore this vibrant town with its seagulls shrieking their noisy welcome. It felt a bit like Scarborough but more compact, and whereas Scarborough was a town ranged along its coastline and beaches, Whitby hugged the river that furrowed a path right through its heart, dividing the town into two.

She passed boats of various shapes and sizes as she walked along the riverside. Fishing boats, pleasure boats, dinghies and yachts. Even a three-masted old sailing ship. And everywhere she looked was yet another reminder of the town's maritime heritage. An old customs house, a pirate flag, a great iron anchor. Not to mention fish and chip shops by the bucketload.

Overlooking everything stood the ruined abbey on the opposite cliff. She would definitely go and take a closer look at that later.

She soon realised something. This Whitby Goth Weekend was much more than a concert. It was a whole way of being. As she moved deeper into the town, she felt like an outsider in a sea of extraordinary individuals. Here was a gothic dreamscape, with men and women strutting about in elaborate Victorian costumes, wreathed in velvet, lace, and satin. Punk goths sported vibrant hair and dark leather, while a group of rock goths stood out in their band tees and ripped denim. Among them, vampires with blood-red lips and pale complexions fitted in effortlessly.

And she realised something else. She couldn't possibly go to the concert that evening wearing her boring old jeans and T-shirt.

Making her way up a steep winding street, a shop sign caught her eye. Vivienne's Vamp & Victoriana. This, she decided, could be her ticket to blending in. Pushing the door open, she stepped into a realm of fantasy. Victorian gowns hung on the racks, an array of colours in rich fabrics that glimmered in the dim shop lighting. Towards the back, seductive vampire outfits clung to mannequins, promising a dangerous allure. Accessories, including lace parasols and feathered hats with veils, were displayed in a corner. She wandered up to the counter where a pile of books was stacked. *Whitby Myths and Legends.* She picked one up, skimming through it. It looked interesting, but she didn't want to be lumbered with a book all day.

'Hi there, my lovely, how can I help you?' Soft fabric rustled, and an older woman emerged from behind a rack of dresses. Draped in black velvet from head to toe, long hair cascaded down her back in waves of midnight black and streaks of purple. Fingerless lace gloves revealed rings of intricate design, and around her slim wrist she wore a silver chain festooned with half-moons and strange talismans. 'I'm Vivienne.'

Hannah hesitated, unsure what to say to this strange woman. But Vivienne's kindly face helped her overcome her nerves. 'I need a goth costume, so that I can blend in.' She glanced again at the huge choice of clothes on offer. 'And I definitely need some help.'

Vivienne eyed Hannah's jeans and T-shirt with a look of sympathetic understanding. Her scarlet lips widened into a smile. 'Then you've come to exactly the right place.'

*

'He feels guilty over Mia's suicide, doesn't he?' said Raven. He and Becca had left Raj staring morosely at the congealed remains of his breakfast, and were back outside the hotel in Church Street. The street was even busier now than before and they ducked inside the courtyard behind the White Horse & Griffin to talk.

'Well, I can understand why,' said Becca. 'He's training to be a psychiatrist and yet he says he didn't spot the signs that his friend was suicidal.'

'Didn't spot them? Or decided not to do anything about them?'

Becca shrugged. 'Perhaps he wishes he'd done more, but at the same time he knows he was too busy getting on with his medical studies in Leeds. That's why he feels so bad about her death.'

'Could he have murdered Reynard?'

Becca made a weighing gesture with her hands as she considered the two possible answers to the question. 'He has access to the medical equipment required, and he might have blamed Reynard for Mia's suicide. Reynard lived close to Whitby and Raj may have felt that Reynard ought to have done more to help.'

'But you're not convinced?'

'We need more than that to bring a charge against him.'

'Certainly.'

Raven's phone rang and he answered, putting it on speakerphone so that Becca could hear the conversation.

It was Tony calling from the station in Scarborough. 'Sir, you asked me to look into Reynard Blackthorn's conviction for illegal taxidermy.'

'I did. What have you found?'

'I've got the name of the person who reported him to the police. It was a Miss Eve Franklin. She's an artist, and according to her website she's currently running a stall at the pavilion in Whitby.'

'Excellent work, Tony. We'll go and speak to her.'

'There's more, sir. I've been looking at Reynard's social media profiles. He's not very active himself, but he gets a lot of hate comments because of his work. Anything from low-level harassment and abuse right up to death threats.'

'Did he ever report it to the police?'

'I can't find any record of a complaint. Perhaps he didn't take it seriously, or he didn't think the police would.'

'Where did the abuse come from? Animal rights activists?'

'His main online enemy was Eve.'

Raven thanked Tony and ended the call.

'Back to the pavilion?' asked Becca.

Raven groaned. The pavilion was on the other side of Whitby, up a steep hill and down the other side. Well, he wasn't walking all that way. 'Back to the car,' he told her.

*

In stark contrast to the rest of the bustling bazaar, Reynard's taxidermy stall stood eerily silent. Lifeless crows perched in mournful solemnity, their glassy eyes seeming to stare accusingly at passersby. A cold wave passed down Raven's back as his gaze lingered on the display. The peculiar artform had always unnerved him, even more so now.

Meanwhile, the other stalls were doing a roaring trade in everything from vibrant artwork to handmade trinkets and chocolates. Raven asked the neighbouring stallholder if Eve Franklin was around. The man pointed him to the opposite side of the hall where a woman swathed in layers of black silk stood behind a display of spooky artwork and scented candles.

Raven and Becca navigated their way through the crowded marketplace to her stall. 'Eve Franklin?' enquired Raven.

'Are you from the Whitby Gazette?' asked Eve, treating him to a broad smile, her ruby lips parting in welcome.

'Afraid not,' said Raven, showing his warrant card. 'We're with North Yorkshire Police. Could we have a word?'

He might as well have presented a silver crucifix to a vampire. Eve's lips closed tight and her eyes flared in anger. 'Who let you in?'

'I didn't see any sign saying police were banned,' said Raven.

'I can't talk to you now,' protested Eve. 'Can't you see I'm busy with my stall?'

'I'll cover for you,' said her neighbour, who was selling gothic jewellery.

Eve shot the woman a look of dark malice, but had little option other than to accept the offer. 'I can spare ten minutes,' she told Raven.

They went upstairs to the foyer and returned to the table where they had sat with Aurora the previous day. Through the window the sea stretched grey and calm.

Eve regarded them sullenly from coal-blackened eyes. 'Is this about Reynard?'

'It is.'

She hesitated for a second before declaring, 'Well, don't expect me to shed any tears. I'm glad he's dead!'

'Are you?'

'Yes. And you can't arrest me for saying so.'

'I wasn't planning to,' said Raven smoothly. Eve exuded rebellion and strength. She was clearly the kind of person who embraced confrontation rather than shying away from it. Raven knew that the best way to handle such characters was to remain calm.

She bit her lip, glaring at him as if disappointed he had failed to rise to her challenge.

'Miss Franklin,' said Becca, 'two years ago you reported Reynard Blackthorn to the police for handling protected species.'

'I did,' said Eve, making no attempt to deny it. 'Do you have a problem with that?'

'Not at all,' said Becca. 'We're grateful to everyone who upholds the law.'

Becca's reply seemed to wrongfoot the stallholder. 'Well, what of it?' she snapped.

'You got Reynard into a lot of trouble. He went to prison for six months.'

'He should have got more. Those animals he killed lost their lives. Not just the bats; all of them. That man was a murderer!'

'Taxidermy isn't illegal,' said Becca. 'At least, not when it's carried out according to the rules. And as far as I know, most taxidermists don't go around killing animals in order to stuff them.'

Eve was unapologetic. 'Well, I'm a vegan, so I disagree with taxidermy as a matter of principle. Exploiting animals is wrong, whether they're dead or alive.'

'You're entitled to your beliefs,' said Raven. 'But that doesn't give you the right to take the law into your own hands.'

'What do you mean?' For the first time, a hint of uncertainty crept into Eve's voice.

'I'm talking about leaving death threats on Reynard's social media accounts.'

Eve averted her gaze, unable to meet his eye. 'Well, he deserved it,' she muttered.

'Where were you on Wednesday night and the early hours of Thursday morning?' Raven asked.

Eve stared up at him in surprise. 'Am I being asked to provide an alibi? You think I killed him?'

'Just answer the question, please.'

Eve pursed her lips. 'I spent Wednesday afternoon setting up my stall, and then I went out in the evening with some friends.'

'We'll need the names and contact details of those friends so that we can verify what you've told us,' said Raven. 'And stay in Whitby until further notice. We might want to speak to you again.'

★

Hannah emerged from Vivienne's shop, reborn. Encouraged by the shopkeeper to go for a daring mix of black lace and faux leather – 'You've got the figure for it, love,' Vivienne had enthused – her new clothes gave her a fresh confidence. Her reflection in a passing shop window was almost unrecognisable – a testament to Vivienne's skill.

As she navigated the crowds in the streets once more, she was met with approving nods and smiles. She was no longer an outsider, but a welcome member of this community with its shared appreciation for self-expression, individualism, and an interest in the darker side of art and culture. It was above all, she realised, an accepting community.

The movement of people through the streets exhibited little pattern that Hannah could discern. Some were drifting across the river in the direction of the abbey perched high on the clifftop; others migrated the opposite way, fanning out through the town or strolling along the harbourside, where waterside pubs and eateries rubbed shoulders with gift shops and assorted entertainments, including a delightfully spooky-looking "Dracula Experience".

She consulted the map on her phone, deciding to check

out the pavilion so she would know where to go later for the concert. A flight of steep steps took her up the rocky West Cliff. She walked through a dramatic arch made from a pair of whalebones and passed a statue of Captain Cook atop a stone plinth. The old sea explorer occupied a commanding position, facing out to sea across the twin piers of the harbour.

Whitby's pavilion was more modest in scale than Scarborough's spa but enjoyed a similar location, nestling beneath the clifftop above the sandy beach. In the foyer, signs pointed downstairs to a bazaar. Hannah had already spent far more at Vivienne's than was wise on her student loan, so she resisted the urge to indulge in more shopping. Instead, she poked her head into the main auditorium where crew members were setting up the stage and running soundchecks ready for the concert.

'Hey. Nice outfit.' A deep male voice behind her made her spin around and she found herself looking up into a pair of mirrored shades. The owner of the sunglasses was tall, slim and slightly older than her, maybe in his mid-twenties. He wore his dark hair long, brushing the shoulders of his black leather jacket. His chin was chiselled, his cheeks hollowed. Dark stubble made a canvas of shadows that added to his dangerous attraction.

'Thanks,' said Hannah.

He nodded toward the auditorium. 'Are you coming to the concert tonight?'

'Yes.' She hoped he wouldn't ask her which goth rock bands she was into. She hadn't recognised a single name in the line-up. This was more her dad's kind of music. Now, she wondered if she'd been missing out.

'Cool,' said the mysterious stranger. 'I'm Dante, by the way. I'm lead singer with Velvet Nocturne.'

He extended a hand and Hannah shook it, feeling a tingle as his strong fingers closed over hers. 'You're one of the bands performing tonight!'

'That's right. We're opening the concert.' He sounded both excited and slightly nervous. 'This is our big break.

Then on Sunday we'll be playing the Abbey Brewery.' He handed her a flyer for that event and gave her a tentative smile. 'Maybe I'll see you there?'

Was that a personal invitation? Hannah accepted the flyer and returned his smile, feeling extra confident in her new persona. 'Sure, why not?' she told him, playing it cool. It wasn't as if her father had anything better planned for the weekend.

CHAPTER 12

'So,' said Becca, 'how have you been enjoying your morning with Dinsdale?'

Jess pulled a face. 'That man's got the charm of a sea slug and all the sensitivity of a hammerhead shark.'

'Yes, but apart from that?'

They burst into laughter. What more was there to say?

The two women were enjoying a breather together while Raven and Dinsdale went in search of food from one of the takeaway restaurants along the harbourside.

A light breeze was blowing in from the sea, ushering away the morning's fret and revealing a brilliant sky in its place. Becca's seat next to the bandstand at the foot of the West Pier gave her a postcard-perfect view of the harbour and town.

In front of her flowed the River Esk, beginning the final leg of its journey as it passed between the sheltering piers and out into the rougher territory of the North Sea where Nathan Rigby had drowned.

Across the estuary, the short stub of Tate Hill Pier jutted out, and beside it lay the smooth golden sands where Becca and Raven had walked with Lucille the previous day.

Above the beach rose the steep headland that sheltered the town from easterly gales. Old fishermen's cottages huddled together in its lee, and at its top, St Mary's Church stood guard. The headland ended at the precipitous cliff face where Mia Munroe had plunged to her death.

The abbey was hidden from view beyond the rise of the land, but Becca felt its brooding presence nonetheless. She shuddered as she recalled the lifeless form of Reynard Blackthorn, skin as white as a shroud, and dressed as if for his own funeral in his undertaker's outfit.

Three violent and tragic deaths. Could they somehow be connected?

'Here they come now,' said Jess, tugging Becca back from her ruminations.

She turned to see Raven and Dinsdale plodding along the waterfront, loaded up with boxes of food and drink. Raven walked ahead, his black coat billowing in the breeze. Dinsdale lumbered in Raven's wake. Neither man was talking to the other and the scowls on their faces indicated fraught affiliations. Jess turned to Becca and they both dissolved into peals of laughter again.

'What's got into you two?' asked Raven grumpily as he trudged up to the bandstand.

'Just admiring your teamwork,' said Becca. 'An excellent display from the senior detectives.'

Raven's scowl deepened. 'Who wanted the mushy peas?'

'Me,' said Becca, holding out her hand to receive the hot carton of food. You couldn't beat good old mushy peas. Some people turned their noses up at the smell of the green Yorkshire nectar, but Becca couldn't understand how anyone could eat garden peas single-handed with a flat wooden fork. It just didn't work.

Raven distributed the rest of the boxes and drinks and they perched together on the edge of the circular bandstand to eat.

It had been a long morning, and the tangy smell of salt and vinegar on battered haddock and succulent chips reminded Becca just how much she was missing her mum's cooked breakfasts. She took a bite and was transported briefly to heaven. Why did fish and chips always taste so much better outside, with the smell of the sea and the cries of gulls in the sky? Perhaps the smells and sounds conjured fond memories from childhood – sunny days on the beach building sandcastles and paddling in freezing water. Or perhaps it was just being close to the sea that made fish taste so good.

'So,' said Raven, holding up a golden wedge of fried potato for inspection. 'Where do you get the best fish and chips – Whitby or Scarborough?' A wicked grin tugged at his lips. Was he determined to stir up trouble by debating such a contentious topic?

Dinsdale groaned at the controversial question, but Becca was a Scarborough lass, born and bred, and answered without hesitation: 'Scarborough.' After all, these Whitby chips weren't bad but...

'I think Whitby might have the edge,' said Jess with a wink. Becca glared at her, unable to hide the dismay she felt at such a low betrayal. Then again, Jess was an outsider, brought up in the middle of the moors, far from the coast. What did she know about fish and chips?

'Derek?' enquired Raven. 'Where do you stand on the matter?'

Dinsdale looked as if he thought he was being mocked, but then he gave a grudging reply: 'I'd put Bridlington in first place.'

'That leaves the casting vote with you, sir,' said Jess.

Raven studied the juicy chip as if it might reveal the truth if he stared hard enough. 'Let's just say we're all in agreement, that the Yorkshire coast has the best fish and chips in the world.'

There was a chorus of consent and they continued their meal in silence, stopping only to swig from bottles of water or cans of fizzy drinks. Becca devoured the food hungrily, licking her fingers after the last piece of fish and savouring the tang of salt on her tongue.

The bandstand was a popular spot for people to stop and take in the view. Today, many of those strolling around the bandstand were dressed in Victorian attire. Gentlemen in frock coats and woollen spatterdashes; ladies in crinolines, corsets and petticoats. Long lace-up boots protruded beneath floor-length gowns, while black parasols swished and swirled overhead. The effect was like stepping back a hundred and fifty years and glimpsing the town as it would have been in Bram Stoker's day.

A crowd had gathered at the railings by the edge of the quay. Two young women were posing against the backdrop of St Mary's Church and the headland on the opposite bank. A photographer with high-tech equipment was encouraging them to turn this way and that, and to look dark-eyed and sultry. Other tourists and day-trippers were making the most of the opportunity to snap pictures on their phones.

'Look who it is,' said Becca, recognising the two models as Aurora Highsmith and Lucille West. For women who were supposed to be in mourning following the death of a friend, they seemed determined to have a good time. In the wind, Aurora's hair was putting on an even more impressive display than before, the thick locks streaming like a silken river on the breeze.

Or writhing like a nest of vipers.

Either way, the shimmering golden veil floated weightlessly in a way that Becca's own flat hair would never manage. Aurora must have brought a whole suitcase of hairspray with her.

Becca wondered idly what would happen if you tried to take pictures of a vampire. Since they had no reflection, presumably you couldn't photograph them either? But the problem didn't seem to be one that worried Aurora.

Probably because vampires weren't real.

Meanwhile, Lucille's elaborate makeup and facial piercings were drawing the attention of the crowds. She was smoking again, puffing away at a cigarette as if her life depended on it.

'Let's go and say hello,' said Raven.

At the sight of the police making their way towards them, Aurora and Lucille stopped posing and the crowd gradually dispersed. The photographer thanked them for their time and gave them his card, then he too disappeared.

'Good afternoon,' said Becca. 'Mind if we talk again?'

They regarded her warily, but Aurora nodded her consent and the pair of them took a seat on a bench where they could speak without being overheard. Dinsdale and Jess came over, gathering around to listen.

'What do you want now?' said Aurora. 'Raj said you were hounding him again this morning.'

'We asked him to provide an alibi for the time of Reynard's death,' said Becca, unperturbed by her hostility, 'and we need the same from you. What did you both do after you last saw Reynard at the pub until the early hours of the following morning?'

Aurora gave a dismissive shrug. 'I walked back to my hotel and went to bed.'

'Can anyone verify that? A night porter perhaps?'

'I didn't see anyone, so no.'

'And what about you, Miss West?'

Lucille shook her head. 'Same here. But why would you need to ask us that? You can't possibly think that either of us might have killed Reynard!'

'I'm afraid we have to ask these questions,' said Raven.

'I understand,' said Becca, speaking to Aurora, 'that you have diabetes. Is that correct?'

Aurora gave her a guarded look. 'Yes.'

'And do you use insulin injections to treat the condition?'

'I do.'

'So you have access to hypodermic needles and syringes?'

'What the hell is this all about?' she demanded. 'You keep asking us questions, treating us like suspects, when our friend has just died.'

'It's because your friend is dead that we need to ask

these questions,' said Becca.

'Well, it sounds to me like you don't have any suspects and are just harassing us because you don't know what else to do.' She folded her arms across her chest.

Through the thin chiffon fabric of her sleeves, Becca caught a glimpse of a red mark on her arm. Jess had spotted it too. 'That tattoo on your arm,' she said. 'It's the same design as the one Reynard had.'

It was plain for all to see now. A small crimson sketch of a dragon. The beast had an evil look to it, its body armoured with scales, its foreclaws lifted as if about to tear flesh. The creature's long tail was wrapped around its neck.

Aurora looked down at her bare arm as if it betrayed her. She hurriedly drew the gauzy material back as best she could, but there was little she could do to hide it. 'Well, what of it?'

'We all have one,' said Lucille.

'Can you show us?'

Lucille gave a shrug of annoyance, then removed her leather jacket. Clearly visible on her bare shoulder was a matching tattoo, the blood-red ink like a gouge in her flesh.

Becca raised an enquiring brow. 'Why do you all have dragon tattoos?'

The two women shared a look of – what? – embarrassment? Shame? Complicity?

'It was just for a laugh,' said Lucille. 'A bit of silliness from our student days.'

'It doesn't sound much like a laugh,' said Becca.

'We formed a group,' said Aurora. 'A secret society, you know? Who wouldn't want to be a part of that?' There was an attempt at lightness in her voice, completely at odds with the sinister symbol on her skin. It didn't fool Becca.

'We called it the Order of the Dragon,' volunteered Lucille. 'That was Reynard's idea. He was big on history, especially form the medieval period.'

'Medieval history?' That didn't give Becca a lot to go on. She didn't recall anything about an Order of the

Dragon from her own school days. She'd done William the Conqueror and Henry VIII, but there'd been no dragons as far as she could remember. Unless that was St George.

Lucille scratched at her arm as if unconsciously trying to rid herself of the strange symbol. 'The Order was a military order of knights, a bit like the Knights Templar. It was founded by the Holy Roman Emperor and its role was to defend Europe against the invading Ottomans. It was most active in Hungary and Romania, the countries that bordered the Ottoman Empire.'

'Why was it called the Order of the Dragon?' asked Becca.

'The dragon was a symbol of evil.'

'So why did you think it would make a good name for your secret club?'

'I knew you wouldn't understand!' said Aurora, a fire blazing in her eyes. 'The Order was dedicated to the *defeat* of evil. That's why the dragon is depicted with its tail looped around its own neck. Nathan designed the emblem, based on the original insignia of the Order.'

'In any case,' added Lucille, 'it was just a bit of fun during our student days. It was nothing.'

Getting identical tattoos didn't sound like nothing to Becca. 'Just to be clear,' she said, 'who were the members of this secret society?'

Lucille and Aurora exchanged glances again. 'There were six of us,' said Aurora. 'Me, Lucille, Raj, Reynard, Nathan and Mia.'

'Six of you,' mused Raven. 'And now three of you are dead.'

CHAPTER 13

There were still hours to fill before the concert in the evening. Hannah left the pavilion and wandered back into town, descending the steeply-sloping streets until she was back at sea level. Then she crossed the bridge to Whitby's east side, stopping to buy a carton of chips which she ate as she went. There was something quite decadent about eating as you walked. She had no plan and simply followed the crowds, turning into a cobbled street called Church Street that seemed to lie at the very heart of the old town.

The buildings here were ancient, and despite being packed together cheek by jowl, each one seemed determined to be as different as possible to its neighbour. Some were wide, some narrow; some of two floors and some of three. Most were built from brick, yet some were made of stone, or else rendered smooth and painted in pastel hues. Between them ran low, narrow passageways, leading to mysterious hidden courtyards or down dark alleyways going who knew where. The place was a network of secret paths, and Hannah pictured smugglers or pirates scurrying down those dark backstreets in days of old.

Most of the houses were now shops, cafés or pubs, and she marvelled at the displays of black and silver jewellery in the many jet shops. She would have loved a pair of jet earrings to go with her new look, but the prices – where they were displayed – were way beyond her budget.

After finishing her food and depositing her empty packaging in a bin, she went inside a museum that explained the history of jet-making in the town. She learned that the gemstone was found in fallen debris from the cliff faces along the coast and that Whitby jet was regarded as the finest in the world. The industry had peaked during the nineteenth century when wealthy Victorian ladies had sought the polished black stones to wear in mourning. These days the striking jewellery was worn for any occasion.

Church Street grew steadily narrower the further Hannah walked. At the very end she found herself at the foot of a wide, shallow flight of steps curving gently up the hill. A sign pointed the way to St Mary's Church and Whitby Abbey. The steps were busy, but there was plenty of room for people to walk up and down at whatever speed they felt comfortable. The top of the steps lay out of view beyond the rise of the headland but undaunted, Hannah embarked on the long climb.

Halfway up, she paused for a rest at a wooden bench beneath an old-fashioned streetlamp. She looked back at the spectacular view of the town and estuary laid out below like a model village. With their red roofs and whitewashed walls, the old cottages ranged along the waterfront were quite charming and she took out her phone to snap some pictures. She even drew attention from some tourists who requested selfies with her, mistaking her for a real goth. She was flattered and happy to oblige.

The steps culminated at the entrance to St Mary's churchyard, which was marked by a huge stone Celtic cross. An inscription on the cross declared it to be dedicated "To the glory of God, and in memory of Caedmon, Father of English sacred song. Fell asleep hard by AD 680." Faintly amused by the idea of falling "hard" asleep, Hannah continued on towards the church.

The building was a sturdy stone structure with a square tower rising from its centre. Topped with battlements like grey teeth against the sky, it looked ready to endure the harshness of winter storms. No doubt it had already survived hundreds of them. The church stood amid a sea of gravestones that leaned and tilted in all directions and Hannah meandered among them, trying to decipher their weather-worn epitaphs. The names and dates on the graves told sad stories of large families with many children dying in infancy, and she shuddered at the thought of all those little bones lying below the cold ground.

On the south side of the church, a sundial was set into the wall. Its white face was etched with markings to record the passage of time as the sun undertook its daily journey. Above it, the words, "Our Days Pass Like a Shadow" were engraved in stone. A metal rod cast a thin line across its face, tentatively indicating the hour. Yet even as Hannah watched, the faint shadow was erased as a cloud passed across the sky and blotted out the milky April sunshine.

A breeze blew up, tugging at her dark clothing and pulling at her long hair. She hugged her arms around herself and set off again, walking around the side of the church and further into the graveyard which extended towards the cliff edge. Out here beyond the shelter of the building, the wind was wilder and the gravestones even more weathered and ancient. One of the gravestones had a skull and crossbones carved into it. She knelt beside it to see if she could read its inscription and discover the name of the grave's occupant, but the letters were too weather-worn to make out.

A man's voice called out from behind her, 'Don't believe owt you read on them stones. Half of 'em tombs are empty.'

She spun around to find an elderly man leaning on a stick. His shock of snow-white hair contrasted with a ruddy complexion, suggesting a life spent out in all weathers. His eyebrows were as coarse and unruly as the tufts of grass that sprang from beneath the gravestones. But his eyes were alive with warmth and humour.

'Why do you say that?' Hannah asked, wondering what on earth he could mean about the graves being empty.

A cheeky smile added to the deep lines on his face. 'Come and sit down on that there bench and keep an old man company, and I'll tell yeh.' He lifted his stick and pointed to a bench looking out to sea.

She guessed he was lonely, maybe a widower, and looking for someone to chat with. He seemed harmless enough and since she was intrigued by his curious statement, she accepted his invitation.

They sat on the wooden bench together, the old man taking a moment to catch his breath. He stared at the horizon for half a minute, seeming lost in thought. Then he pointed his stick at the sea and said, 'She's a cruel mistress!'

'The sea?' asked Hannah.

'Aye, the sea. She takes men's lives without a thought and often keeps ahold of their bodies too. That's why half of 'em tombs are empty. They're the graves of sailors lost at sea. That's why the inscriptions say "in remembrance of" instead of "here lies".'

'Oh, I see,' said Hannah. For a moment she'd thought he was talking about something more sinister.

'Aye, and maybe it's just as well those graves are empty, 'cause in the old days they used t'ave to carry the bodies up the steps! All one hundred and ninety-nine of 'em!'

'That must have been hard work,' said Hannah.

'Oh, aye, it surely was. Rich folk went up in a horse and carriage, but poor sailors and suchlike had to be carried up on foot. That's why the benches were put there, so the pallbearers could lay the coffins down to rest a while.'

Hannah couldn't tell if the old man was joking.

'Have you noticed that some of the graves are carved with skull and crossbones?' he asked.

'Yes,' she said, recalling the strange marks she'd seen

on the gravestone earlier.

He tapped his nose. 'Perhaps they mark pirates' graves.'

'Really?' She thought back to the labyrinth of passageways that criss-crossed Church Street and wondered if pirates or smugglers really had operated there.

'Or the skulls and crossbones might have been put there to frighten graverobbers away.' The old man gave her a wink. 'Or maybe they're just the marks left by freemasons.'

Hannah laughed, realising he had only been teasing her about pirates and graverobbers.

'Shall I tell yeh a story?' asked the old man, a twinkle in his eye.

'Go on,' said Hannah, happy to indulge him further.

He leaned closer to her so she could hear him better above the roar of the wind. 'Whitby's rich in stories, some of them ghost stories. Did yeh ever hear the tale o' poor Mary Clarke?'

'No. I've never been to Whitby before.'

Her reply seemed to please him. 'Well, I'll tell yeh, but it's not a story for the faint-hearted. Mary was a beautiful girl, see? She had this lovely long hair – the longest and loveliest in the whole of Whitby – and she liked to keep it nice, combing it a hundred times every morning and night and brushing it with oil.'

Hannah nodded, encouraging him to go on.

'Now, there was a bakery in town, down below on Church Street, and in those days the baker let people bring their own pies to bake in his oven. One day, Mary took a pie to warm for her father's dinner, and just as she opened the oven door, whoosh' – the old man threw his hands into the air – 'her hair caught fire from the heat of the oven.'

'How horrible,' said Hannah. 'What happened to her?'

'She ran out of the bakery and down the street, but 'er hair was aflame. The baker, he ran after her and tried to put the fire out. She was screaming enough to wake the dead by now. Other people ran to help, but the flames were burning her beautiful hair and the flesh from her scalp. At last they managed to wrap her in a blanket and quench the fire. They took 'er to the infirmary, but she were dead within the hour. And they say her spirit still hasn't found rest. If you ever go down Grape Lane, alone, late at night, you can smell the stench o' burning flesh, and then Mary 'erself appears, her hair all afire and 'er skin crackling in the flames.'

Hannah ran a protective hand over her own hair, shivering at the thought of poor Mary Clarke. She didn't believe in ghosts, but it was quite possible that the story was based on a true event.

'Do you have time for another tale?' the old man asked.

'Sure. I have loads of time.'

'Then let me tell you the story o' the barghest hound.' He cast a wary glance around the gravestones as if afraid of being overheard, and then moved closer to Hannah, shuffling sideways along the bench with the help of his walking stick. 'The hound is a black dog, some say a hell hound. It prowls the streets and alleyways at night and woe betide any who encounter it while out walking the ginnels and snickets of the old town after dark, especially if there's a cold mist in the air.'

The man's voice had become low and husky and Hannah once more felt a shiver in her bones, even though she knew the hound was just another of the man's tall tales.

'The barghest is said to be a kind of spirit, or perhaps a demon in the form of an animal. They say it comes from the moors, or perhaps from hell itself. Some say it has fiery red eyes, and claws as sharp as knives. Some say it has huge fangs and is of monstrous size.' He paused and looked around once more. 'Black dogs have long been thought to be bad omens, and the barghest hound is especially feared. For whenever it is seen or heard, death will surely follow. And most often, it is the one who sees or hears it who will be next to die.'

Hannah must have looked alarmed, because the old man broke into a crooked smile and chuckled. 'Yes, that's what they say, all right. But don't worry, I've lived in this town for nigh on eighty year, and I've not once seen the hound. Reckon my time's not up just yet, and I'm sure you've got many a rosy summer ahead of yeh.' He rose to his feet, pushing on his stick. 'Well, mustn't keep yeh, I'm sure you've got better things to do than listen to an old man ramble on.'

Hannah stood too. 'I've enjoyed talking to you, Mr...?'

'Swales is the name. And the pleasure was all mine, Miss...?'

'Raven. Hannah Raven.'

His eyes sparkled at the mention of her name. 'Raven, eh? You'll have Viking blood in yeh, then?'

'Will I?' Hannah knew nothing about the origin of her surname. Her dad had hardly told her anything about her family history.

'Oh, aye,' said Swales. 'The Vikings came to these shores and left their mark on the land and on the language too. In Norse, the word for raven was "hrafn".'

'Hrafn.' Hannah let the strange word roll off her tongue. 'I didn't know that.'

'Well now you do.' He bowed to her. 'Goodbye, Miss Raven.'

'Goodbye, Mr Swales.' They shook hands and she watched him walk off, leaning on his stick for support. He was quite a character, and he certainly told a good story.

The breeze was picking up, pushing heavy clouds before it, and the air had turned chill. Hannah continued on her way through the graveyard, making a loop around the northern side of the church, walking close to the cliff edge.

Just as she reached the farthest corner of the cemetery, she caught sight of a black dog disappearing behind one of the tombstones. She gasped, not quite sure if she'd imagined it. But a few seconds later, the dog appeared again. It stopped and stared straight at her, one paw raised. Then it barked, a ferocious sound, as loud as a firecracker.

Hannah placed a hand on a stone to steady herself.

And then the hound was off, cutting a path through the

long grass between graves, until only its tail was visible amid the sea of grey stone, and then it was gone.

CHAPTER 14

The car park at Whitby Abbey was abuzz with activity when Raven drove his BMW into it. Despite the police cordon sealing off the abbey, more visitors than ever had turned up, pressing to be allowed in and see for themselves the place where Reynard had met his death.

Raven's breathing quickened as he took in the presence of a large TV broadcasting van and technicians with their oversized microphones, camera and other gear. At the heart of the commotion stood Liz Larkin, the reporter Raven had encountered during a previous investigation. His run-in with her then had resulted in a car-crash interview and landed him in a heap of trouble. It was the reason Gillian had sent him on a media awareness course.

Now she was here again.

Liz Larkin, it seemed, had an uncanny knack for popping up at the least convenient moment.

He'd been alerted to her presence in Whitby by a phone call from Gillian while down at the bandstand. 'Tom, where are you right now?'

'In Whitby, ma'am. Working on the case.'

If she'd detected any sarcasm or annoyance in his voice, she'd chosen to ignore it. 'Good, because BBC Look North have somehow got wind of what's going on. They're broadcasting from outside the abbey. You need to get yourself over there immediately and dampen down any speculation by giving a cool-headed statement. It's a chance for you to put your newly acquired media awareness skills into practice. Do you think you can do that, Tom?'

Raven's heart had sunk. 'Of course, Gillian, I'll handle it.'

He wished now that he'd paid more attention on his course. What had the instructor said? *Tell the truth. Stay calm and stick to the facts. Don't make it personal.* Oh yeah. *And always prepare your answers in advance.* Well, it was a bit too late for that one.

Bracing himself for the worst, he climbed out of the car and marched into the fray.

Liz spotted him instantly, her face lighting up with an excitement that filled him with dismay. She was dressed in a pale blue suit that complemented her blonde hair. Her face was made up to perfection, her skin as smooth as alabaster, and her lips a salmon pink. She made a bee-line in his direction, laying a hand on his arm in an over-familiar gesture. 'DCI Raven, so glad you could come.'

He straightened his tie and smoothed down his suit, suddenly aware that he ought to have checked his appearance before leaving the car. *Look smart.* That was another of the tips he'd been given on his course. What else was there? *Don't forget to smile.*

Damn it, there were so many different things to remember! He plastered the best smile he could summon at short notice onto his face and greeted her with a nod.

She was standing close enough for him to catch the scent of her perfume, something exotic and heady, wafting on the breeze. He took an involuntary step backwards but she only moved closer. 'The viewers are hungry for news of this case. It's all everyone is talking about.'

'Is that so?' How had details of the murder reached the ears of the journalist before any official statement had been released? He wondered how much she knew and how much was fantasy and hearsay.

A man with headphones and a clipboard arrived and threw up a hand in front of Raven's face, his thumb and fingers splayed. 'Five minutes till we roll! Could I ask you to move this way.' He grabbed Raven's upper arm and manoeuvred him to the side. 'Just turn around. That's it, the light's better from this angle.'

Raven knew he had already lost control of the situation. He ought to have been the one taking the initiative here, informing the media only if and when he was ready to issue a statement. Instead he was a puppet being dangled and yanked around on a string. He watched helplessly as the crew went about their preparations, wishing he could be anywhere but here. He wished Gillian had asked someone else to give the interview. He was supposed to be on leave, spending time with Hannah.

He searched around for Becca. She was standing a short distance away, a grim look fixed to her face. He motioned to her and she returned a nervous smile. It wasn't exactly a vote of confidence.

Then the man with the headphones and the clipboard started counting down from ten. The camera lens swivelled in Raven's direction like a cannon on a battlefield. The countdown finished and they were live on air.

Liz Larkin slipped effortlessly into her on-camera persona, poised and professional. 'Good afternoon. Today we're here at Whitby Abbey, following the gruesome discovery yesterday morning of a man's body in what can only be described as bizarre circumstances. I'm joined by Detective Chief Inspector Tom Raven from Scarborough who is heading up the investigation. What can you tell us, Chief Inspector, about this grisly murder?'

Stay calm and stick to the facts.

There were few facts that Raven could divulge about the grotesque nature of Reynard's murder on live TV, yet as the lens of the camera bored into him, he somehow found his voice. 'The victim has been identified as Reynard Blackthorn, a taxidermist who lived in the Whitby area. I can't go into specific details about Mr Blackthorn's death, but this is clearly a serious crime, committed by a dangerous individual.'

Liz, always ready to seize an opportunity, immediately latched onto his words. 'The taxidermy angle is certainly intriguing. Do you attribute any significance to Mr Blackthorn's unusual occupation?'

'It's something we're looking into.'

'I see, and can you comment on the way that the body was laid out at the eastern end of the sanctuary? Have you uncovered any link to Satanic rituals?'

The question was a wild one, but Raven parried it with ease. 'We have no evidence to suggest anything of the sort.'

'Do you have any suspects yet?'

'We're pursuing a number of leads.' He smiled, careful not to overdo it. It was important to stay serious and give the appearance of being in control. In fact, as the interview progressed, he was gaining confidence. It was beginning to feel like he might pull this one off.

Liz smiled back, almost as if she knew something he didn't. 'Chief Inspector, it has been reported that Mr Blackthorn was killed in a manner reminiscent of a vampire attack, with a bite to his neck and his body drained of blood. Is there any truth to that, or can you quash that rumour?'

Raven certainly hadn't seen that one coming, but he had no time to speculate how the reporter had found out about the wound in Reynard's neck and his missing blood. He needed to give her an answer and squash this vampire rumour before it gained ground.

Tell the truth.

He hesitated. He couldn't possibly admit on live TV that Reynard had been medically exsanguinated. Gillian would go nuts. But how else could he explain that Reynard's killer had staged the murder to look like a vampire attack?

'Chief Inspector?'

Tell the truth.

Raven knew he was sweating. He could feel the perspiration on his forehead and the dampness on his shirt.

Look smart.

He brushed his hair aside, buying time to think.

Stay calm and stick to the facts.

The facts... what were they again? 'The murder...' He trailed off.

'Yes?' prompted Liz. He could see the amusement in her eyes and knew how much she was enjoying his discomfort.

Don't make it personal.

'There's no such thing as vampires!' he snapped.

The look on her face told him he'd blown it.

'I see,' said Liz. 'Then one final question. Should Whitby's goth weekend be cancelled?'

Raven's mind was spinning under her barrage of questions. It was all he could do to mutter, 'Well, I think that would be rather drastic, don't you?'

Liz swung back to face the camera. 'So there we have it. A dangerous individual on the loose, a possible link to Satanic rituals, yet the police maintain that there is no risk to the public. What do you think? Are vampires real? Have your say on social media. And now back to Adrian in the studio with the weather forecast.'

The cameras stopped rolling and Liz turned to him with a big smile. 'Thank you, Chief Inspector Raven, that was fantastic. The viewers will love it.'

Raven groaned. The interview had not achieved its purpose; rather, it had veered dangerously off course. Gillian would be furious.

He turned his back on the reporter and her camera crew and stomped away to rejoin Becca who was waiting for him at the edge of the car park. The look on her face was half sympathy, half dismay. 'Don't say it!' he told her. 'I lost control of the narrative.'

'Is that what you media people call it?'

'How would you describe it?'

A flicker of amusement crossed her face, but he knew that he was the joke. 'A king-size cock-up.'

CHAPTER 15

Becca maintained a diplomatic silence as Raven swung the car out of the car park, over-revved the engine and cursed as he narrowly missed the TV van. He was still a bag of nerves after his interview with Liz Larkin.

Becca had shared her boss's pain as she'd watched him struggle under the reporter's relentless grilling. Still, she was glad it had been Raven, not her, in front of the camera. Although he'd suggested she might be ready to take on a bigger role in the investigation, she didn't want that kind of responsibility. Not on a detective sergeant's salary, at any rate.

It hadn't escaped her notice how Liz had flirted with Raven before they were on air. That woman was shameless in her efforts to get what she wanted. As for her summing up at the end of the interview, it was clear she had twisted Raven's responses to fit her own agenda. And what had that agenda been? To stir up controversy and gain attention at any cost.

The cost here would be public disquiet and a loss of confidence in the police. Not to mention further speculation and unwanted commentary on social media. With so many people gathered together in Whitby for the goth festival, it couldn't have come at a worse time.

It wasn't until they were on the A171 speeding back towards Scarborough that Becca ventured to speak. 'I've been reading about the Order of the Dragon,' she said, taking out her phone.

Raven groaned. 'What about it?'

'It says here that the Order of the Dragon was a chivalric order, founded in 1408 by Sigismund of Luxembourg, who was King of Hungary and Croatia and later became the Holy Roman Emperor. There were twenty-one founding members, but perhaps the most famous was the Prince of Wallachia, Vlad Dracul, who took his title from its name.'

'Wait,' said Raven, 'you mean Dracula?'

'No, not exactly. Bram Stoker based his character on Vlad the Impaler, who was the son of Vlad Dracul. In Romanian, *Dracula* means *Son of the dragon*.'

Raven took a moment to digest the information. 'So why did Bram Stoker use Vlad the Impaler as the model for his vampire?'

Becca continued scrolling her way through the article. Not an easy task when Raven was driving at his usual hectic speed. 'It was partly his bloodthirsty reputation. By some estimates he killed nearly 80,000 people, mostly by impaling them on wooden stakes.'

Raven winced. 'Not a very pleasant chap.'

'No.' Becca continued reading. 'And partly because in Romanian, *dracul* also means *devil*, so his name could be taken to mean *Son of the devil*. But it was also because of what happened after he died. First he was decapitated, which was the traditional treatment reserved for anyone believed to be a vampire. And then his body was buried at Snagov Monastery in Romania, but when the tomb was later opened, it was found to be empty.'

'Creepy,' admitted Raven. 'So this secret society that Reynard and the others started was a kind of vampire appreciation society.'

'That's one way of putting it.'

'We definitely need to find out more about Nathan and Mia. I wonder how Tony's getting on?'

Becca checked the time. It was too late to expect even Tony to still be at his desk. 'I'm sure he'll let us know as soon as he's found anything interesting.'

'Sure.'

She lapsed into silence again, allowing Raven to return to his introspective brooding. It was what he did best, after all. She tilted her head to look at him once or twice during the journey, but his eyes were fixed on the road ahead, and his brow was furrowed in concentration.

As they approached the outskirts of Scarborough, Becca asked him, 'How is Hannah getting on? Has she found much to do in Scarborough?'

Raven grunted. 'She's off to a concert tonight. I'm hoping to catch her before she goes out.'

'Great. Who's she going to see?'

'No idea.'

Becca wondered what it must have been like growing up with Raven as a father. Had he taken the slightest interest in Hannah as a child? He'd probably missed more school plays and sports days than he'd attended.

Her own parents had been staunch attendees at every school event and parents' evening. She'd taken their constant involvement for granted, and had even found it annoying during her teenage years. But looking back, she realised how hard they must have juggled their commitments running the guest house to be there for her. Now that she'd finally moved out, she was really missing them. Not just her mum's cooking, but the way she'd always showed so much interest in whatever Becca was doing. It had sometimes felt intrusive and cloying, but now she was living with Ellie, she'd give a lot for a good old gossip with her mum after work. And as for her dad's quiet but reassuring presence, she was missing his hugs and steady words of advice. Perhaps she'd call round at the guest house this evening and say hello.

Maybe Hannah didn't miss Raven in the same way, because she'd never depended on him. Still, it was a bit rough on her, having come all this way to see him, only for him to spend all his time in Whitby.

An idea struck her. 'It's Saturday tomorrow, why don't I see if Ellie's free? She's always good fun, and I'm sure she'd be happy to hang out with Hannah and show her around.'

'That would be wonderful,' said Raven, and Becca could tell how grateful he was. 'Thank you.'

'You're welcome. All part of the service.'

★

After dropping Becca off at her flat, Raven drove on to Quay Street feeling calmer now that the interview with Liz Larkin was behind him. All right, he had completely botched it, and Gillian would be on him like a ton of bricks, but he would face that later. For the moment he intended to put the TV interview, the Order of the Dragon and the rest of the investigation out of his mind and focus his attention on Hannah. He might not get to see much of her this evening, but perhaps there would be a little time before she went out to the concert, or else he could stay up and catch her when she returned.

Letting himself into the house, he called out a greeting. He was met with silence. It was rare for the house to feel so empty. He had grown used to Barry's hammering and swearing, punctuated by occasional off-tune singing, but now the house was completely deserted. He checked the kitchen and went upstairs to the guest room, but there was no one around, neither his builder nor his daughter. Feeling frustrated, he called her on his mobile, knowing that once again he had no one to blame but himself if he'd missed her.

'Hi Dad.' There was a babble of voices in the background and it sounded as if she was outside.

'I've just got back to the house. Where are you?' He hoped he didn't sound like a nagging father, but knew he most likely did. It seemed there were only two modes to his parenting style – neglect and harassment.

'I'm in Whitby.'

It took him a moment to make sense of what she'd just said. 'Whitby? What on earth are you doing there?'

'I'm going to the concert, like I told you.'

'You said it was in Scarborough.'

'No, I didn't.'

'Yes, you did. At the spa.'

Hannah laughed. 'No, that's just where I saw it advertised. The concert is actually at the pavilion in Whitby.'

Raven let out a groan of frustration. 'Why didn't you say so?'

'You didn't ask.'

Shit. What was wrong with him? He was supposed to be a detective and a father yet he hadn't bothered to ask his daughter even the simplest of questions. His mind began to race through the implications. She must be going to the concert that was part of the goth weekend. He'd had no idea she was into that kind of music. Did he even know the first thing about her? 'What time does it finish?'

'Midnight.'

'And how are you planning to get back to Scarborough?' Now he really did sound like a nagging parent.

For the first time in the conversation, Hannah hesitated. 'Well, I'm not sure. I came here on the bus but–'

Raven's mind was made up in an instant. 'I'll come and fetch you.' His tone of voice admitted no refusal, or at least he hoped it didn't. 'I'll be parked at the top of the cliff next to the crescent.'

'Thanks, Dad.'

He was pleased to hear the relief in her voice and knew that he was doing something right at last. The kind of thing that normal fathers did all the time for their daughters. 'No worries, sweetheart.' He ended the call.

Midnight. That was still hours away.

If he'd known she was in Whitby he would have stayed there. Becca could have got a lift back with Jess. But of course he'd known nothing. He hadn't even thought to ask.

He made himself a couple of slices of cheese on toast and checked his emails. Nothing yet from Gillian regarding his performance on television, although he was sure a reprimand would be winging its way to him very shortly. He could probably find the interview online if he searched for it, but that was the last thing he intended to do.

He paced the empty house for a minute, angry with himself, angry with the world, then decided to go out. The concert hadn't even begun yet, but some protective instinct made him want to be in the same town as his daughter. He grabbed his keys and headed back to his car.

This time he drove at a more leisurely pace, allowing his mind to wander where it fancied. And soon enough, just as he'd known it would, it returned to Reynard Blackthorn and the perplexing circumstances surrounding his death.

The case was certainly a strange one, perhaps the strangest he'd worked on. Who would stage a murder to make it look like a vampire killing? Surely someone who knew that Reynard belonged to a secret society styling itself on no less a character than Vlad Dracula himself. And that pointed strongly to one of the other members of the Order of the Dragon. The accidental drowning of Nathan Rigby, followed by the suicide of his fiancée, Mia Munroe, were looking more than ever as if they might be tied to the case. And with three out of the original six members of the Order dead, that left only three suspects: Raj Sandhu, Aurora Highsmith and Lucille West.

Unless, of course, the artist, Eve Franklin, had decided to follow through on her death threats, in which case the deaths of Nathan and Mia were entirely unrelated.

Yet however many times he turned over the facts, each time a nagging doubt resurfaced: why had the killer gone to so much trouble and taken such a great risk to kill Reynard in that peculiar and elaborate fashion? What kind of message were they sending, and to whom was it directed?

On an impulse, Raven turned off the main road, following the sign to Whitby Abbey.

Like a moth returning to a flame, he felt a fool going back to the site of his recent humiliation, but there was something irresistible about the skeletal ruins of the abbey standing proud on the clifftop. Now that night had fallen and the news crew and hordes of visitors would have gone, perhaps he would glean some fresh insight from viewing the scene again.

He stopped some distance before reaching the car park and visitor centre, pulling up on the grassy verge of the road that ran along the back of the abbey. Once again the mist was creeping in from the sea, threading pale tendrils along the ground. The moon was rising over the sea like a metal disk, illuminating the ruins with a cold, unforgiving light. Icy air stung his face as he emerged from the car. There was no one around, and nothing separating him from the abbey grounds except a dry stone wall.

The wall was uneven, the weather-beaten surfaces of the stones showcasing an array of textures. Those at the base were smooth, making it hard to find purchase in the narrow cracks between them, while those at the top were jagged and rough. Moonlight traced lines of shadow, turning the stones a silvery grey and pale yellow, shining a spotlight on Raven as he struggled to gain a foothold on the unyielding surface. After a few attempts, his toes found a gap wide enough to hold his weight, and with a final heave he was over the top, wincing as the rugged capstones scraped against his thigh.

He landed with a thump on the other side and stumbled forwards, narrowly missing a strip of water that shone like a mirror in the cold light. A footpath ran along the edge of the pond, and he followed it, moving swiftly and with stealth. Soon the path ran out and he found himself trekking across the grass that surrounded the abbey. The uneven terrain lay blanketed in darkness, making the going precarious, and he slowed to avoid a fall.

He was approaching from the east, heading straight towards the great gothic arches that formed the eastern wall of the sanctuary. The moon was at his back, throwing his shadow before him.

The ruins held a stark beauty against the night sky. They had stood for almost a millennium facing the wrath of the North Sea winds, nothing between here and Denmark. Yet for all its glory, the abbey felt oddly insubstantial, as if it might vanish at any moment in a shimmer of light. This was a place where the veil between the rational and the supernatural felt precariously thin.

Raven cast his eyes upward, searching for a glimpse of heaven, but finding only the oppressive weight of centuries of history. The moon picked out the broken peaks of the abbey's walls, the dark archways of its empty windows, the dizzying heights of its teetering towers. Shadows clung to its crumbling masonry, even deeper than in the surrounding folds of land.

Just then, a smaller shape detached itself from the stone wall and moved towards the south side of the building. It was hard to make out, but Raven thought he saw a figure, creeping slowly amid the ruins. He was too far to see the stranger's face, or even to tell what kind of clothes they were wearing. But there shouldn't have been anyone here at all. The crime scene was still sealed to the public.

He set off after the intruder, starkly aware of the moon at his back, threatening to betray his presence at any moment. Crouching low, he picked a path across the rough ground.

The south side of the abbey was more ruined than the north – nothing but a series of arches and the stumps of foundation stones sticking up from the ground. He slowed to a crawl as he navigated a way through the darkness, taking care not to stumble headfirst into one of the open, shallow graves that lay dotted around.

By the time he reached the place he had glimpsed the mysterious figure, the intruder had vanished. The moon cast long shafts of light through the arches of the sanctuary, causing beads of water to glisten on the grass. The wind made a shrill cry as it whistled through the empty windows.

Raven peered between the ancient columns, but could see no one. Had he imagined the figure? It was easy to get spooked in a place like this.

He took a step into the darkness just as a great weight barrelled into his legs. The force knocked him off balance and he teetered for a moment, arms windmilling, before falling heavily and striking his shoulder against a stone jutting out of the ground.

He rolled and saw an animal turning round and charging back in his direction. A dog, huge and black, its eyes pools of orange in the darkness. It panted furiously as it came for him, opening its jaws wide to reveal sharp, canine teeth and a slavering tongue. The monstrous creature tore through the night, its powerful muscles rippling beneath its ebony coat.

Raven rolled away at the last moment, scraping the side of his face across the same rough stone that had jabbed so painfully into his shoulder. He curled into a ball and dragged his coat around him for protection.

The beast halted in its tracks, its head just inches from Raven's. Its jaws opened wide and it gave a series of barks, deafening up close. Raven slid away, propelling himself across the slippery ground as best he could. The dog came after him, its hackles raised, its teeth strong and white. Drool sprayed from its long tongue.

It barked once more and then it was off, turning and running away into the night. Raven watched it go, breathing hard in the chill air, the pounding of his heart loud in his ears now the animal had fled. It dashed between the stones and then was gone, as if it had never even been there.

Raven staggered to his feet and hobbled slowly back to the dry stone wall, every step an agony. The fall had set his leg on fire, and the pain in his shoulder wasn't helping one jot. He tasted salt and put his fingers to his cheek. They came away dark and slick. Blood.

Damn it all. How was he going to explain that to Hannah?

CHAPTER 16

'I love your hair,' said Hannah. 'It's amazing.'

The woman queuing before her at the pavilion box office had the most extravagant hair Hannah had ever seen. It fanned out around her head like a scented cloud before plunging down her back in a frothy cascade. In the evening gloom, the golden waterfall shimmered like bottled sunshine, contrasting vividly with the woman's dress of charcoal black.

She turned to Hannah, darkened eyes disdainful, blood-red lips dripping with contempt. Her face was shockingly white, stark against the black lace choker fastened around her long neck.

She was really working overtime to channel that vampire vibe.

Saying nothing in reply, she gave a haughty smile before turning back to converse with her two friends – a man in full steampunk gear complete with bronze goggles and meticulously groomed beard, and a woman in a leather jacket and ripped jeans, a cigarette drooping from her mouth.

Hannah shrugged. Most of the goths she'd encountered

so far had been much friendlier and willing to engage in conversation.

The queue shuffled forwards. Before long it was Hannah's turn to scan the ticket on her phone and receive a wristband granting her access to the concert venue. She entered the pavilion foyer where a diverse crowd, all in elaborate and outlandish costumes, created an atmosphere of friendly eccentricity.

Thanks to Vivienne, Hannah blended in effortlessly.

She was still shaken after her unsettling encounter with the dog at St Mary's Church, so she made her way to the bar and ordered half a pint of cider. She was pleasantly surprised by the price of the drink – so much less than she'd have paid in London – and took a sip to steady her nerves. She told herself repeatedly that Mr Swales's story of the barghest hound was nothing more than a myth, and that the dog she'd seen was no more a hell hound than the woman with the hair was a real vampire. But still, the incident had been more than a little unnerving. Perhaps it was partly because of the curious air of mystery that seemed to pervade the town of Whitby. With its wild coastline, clifftop graveyard and the ruins of a gothic abbey, it was no wonder that Bram Stoker had found so much inspiration for his novel here.

Armed with her drink, she made her way through to the auditorium where Velvet Nocturne was due to open the concert. The opening slot of a festival was often given to a new act, and Dante had described it as the band's big break. She hoped the performance would go well and it wouldn't be an embarrassing flop.

The band had already set up their instruments on stage, and the sound crew was going through some last-minute checks. After a few minutes, the band members came onto the stage, one by one, and were greeted by polite applause and a few cheers from the waiting crowd. Finally, Dante emerged from the wings.

He was dressed just as Hannah had seen him earlier in black leather jacket and shades. Easily the tallest member of the band, his long dark hair shone beneath the blaze of the spotlights. He sauntered languidly to the front of the stage and picked up the mic. 'Hello, Whitby!'

His greeting received a half-hearted response, the audience not yet warmed up, the auditorium still over half empty. But Dante took it in his stride, offering the crowd a cool smile in return. He really did have rockstar quality, and Hannah felt a flutter in her heart, a sensation she hadn't experienced in quite some time – excitement tinged with a hint of trepidation. She still had no idea what kind of music the band was about to play.

When it began, the first song was surprisingly good, opening with a fast drumbeat before bringing in keyboard and guitar. Hannah was already tapping her foot and feeling her body move to the rhythm when Dante's voice entered the mix. She had heard him speak earlier, but now that it was amplified over the sound system, his deep, sonorous voice seemed to resonate inside her, touching her in a way that was peculiarly intimate.

The band's blend of goth rock and synth music was novel to her – probably more to her dad's taste – but surprisingly catchy. She could get to like it.

The thought of her father triggered a stab of guilt about not telling him about her trip. She was glad he'd offered to come and pick her up, even though he'd sounded exasperated on the phone. The buses probably didn't run that late, and it would be a good chance for them to spend some time together, having missed each other so far.

Velvet Nocturne finished their first number to enthusiastic applause. They followed up with several more songs, varying in style and tempo, but each with the same characteristic drumbeat, heavy synths and guitar, and Dante's deep voice layered on top. Some of the lyrics were a bit dark and sinister for Hannah's taste, with words like "vampire", "cemetery" and "blood" cropping up rather too often. But by the end of the set she was swaying to the beat along with the other fans. When Dante took his final bow, the band left the stage amid enthusiastic clapping and cheers.

There was a break before the next act, so Hannah decided to pop outside for some air. A lot of people were still just arriving, no doubt coming to listen to the big-name act that would bring the concert to a close, not to Dante and his unknown band of musicians.

Outside the pavilion, small clusters of concert-goers gathered to smoke and vape. A heady mix of fragrances filled the night, but Hannah had never seen the appeal of the habit, and hurried past them into the cold, refreshing air beyond.

Security guards were stationed at the main exit, checking wristbands to ensure that only paid-up ticket holders could re-enter the venue. But a smaller exit led in the opposite direction, away from the pavilion and down towards the beach. Glancing at her own wristband, Hannah descended this smaller path, coming to a line of colourful beach huts separated from the sand by a railing. A thin mist lay along the shore, cloaking the beach in a ghostly layer of white.

There were no lights on the beach and it was dark in the lee of the cliffs, with only a hint of cool moonlight to light the way. The moon played across the surface of the sea, casting broken shards of silver across its swelling waters and turning the expanse into a shimmering mirror. Hannah stopped to watch it, enjoying the peace and calm of the waves washing steadily onto the shore after the deafening sound of the music.

Her visit to Yorkshire was turning out to be very different to how she'd imagined. She'd anticipated spending most of her time with her father, a thought that had filled her with apprehension, if she was honest. What would they have talked about? They'd never enjoyed a close relationship, at least not for many years. As a small child, he'd always been there for her, carrying her aloft on his broad shoulders, comforting her when she cried, making her laugh when she was grumpy. But as the years had rolled by, a distance had come between them.

Lisa had cautioned her about the visit, a bitterness in her voice. 'He'll let you down,' she'd warned. 'He always does.' If her mum found out about his current prolonged absence, Hannah could imagine her smugly saying, 'I told you so.' But Hannah didn't want to share her mother's resentment. She believed that her father could change. The note of concern in his voice and his quick willingness to come and pick her up from Whitby were reassurances of his affection.

Her few days in Yorkshire had already provided her with a fresh insight into his life that mere conversations wouldn't have achieved. To experience for herself the place where he'd grown up, to live in his childhood home and to walk in his footsteps were all new experiences for her. She was growing very fond of this far-off corner of the world, and warming to the gruff speech and frank openness of its residents. Her interactions with Barry and with Mr Swales in particular had reinforced her growing impression of friendly, albeit somewhat blunt, northerners. You were as likely to be treated to a scowl as much as a smile in these parts, but even that was a refreshing change from the sullen grimness of Londoners.

And she was perceiving something else for the first time. Her father's dedication to his work wasn't simply a character defect, as Lisa so often claimed. It was a calling to do good; a drive to make a difference and fashion a better world. It was a quality to be admired.

That was something Hannah wanted very much to do in her own life, even though she hadn't yet found her own calling. Perhaps she was more like her father than she'd realised.

Lost in her thoughts, she almost missed the sight of the woman with the stunning hair down on the beach. She must have left the pavilion before the end of Velvet Nocturne's gig and was alone on the sand looking out over the shore. Clad in black amid the darkness, she was almost invisible apart from the ghostly mantle of her hair.

She hadn't noticed Hannah, and Hannah felt a little

awkward approaching her in this deserted place. She didn't want to attempt another conversation with the snooty vampiress, only to be snubbed for a second time.

She watched as the woman began to walk across the sand, away from the pavilion. The mist swirled around her legs, making her seem to vanish into the night.

It was getting cold and Hannah wanted nothing more than to go back inside. Maybe she would find Dante in the bar having finished his act, or she could check out the other bands playing that night. Either way, she would be indoors, away from the damp and the cold. But something kept her where she was. She couldn't just leave the woman on her own.

Hannah caught a glimpse of a tiny light flickering. Was she lighting up? Hannah didn't see her as a smoker. It had been the other woman who'd had a cigarette in her mouth.

An ear-splitting scream rent the silence of the night. The cry had come from the sands.

Hannah started forward, then gasped as a ball of fire bloomed before her. 'Oh, my God!' She raised her hands to shield her eyes from the blinding light, but the initial firestorm was over as quickly as it had appeared. In its place was a horrifying spectacle.

The woman in the vampire costume was staggering across the sand, her hair ablaze. That magnificent hair that Hannah had admired and praised and that must have taken so long to prepare, was consumed in flames, doubtless made highly flammable by the mass of hairspray that had gone into supporting it. Had she accidentally set herself alight?

But no. Even as the terrified woman screamed for help, Hannah saw a figure dressed in black fleeing along the shoreline.

There was no time to worry about that now. Hannah ducked under the railing and jumped down onto the beach. The sand dragged at her feet as she ran, but she was at the woman's side in moments.

Up close she could feel the heat from the fire. The coils

of golden hair that fell to the woman's waist were already blackened and charred and now the blaze was spreading to her clothes. Flames danced eagerly along the chiffon sleeves that covered her thin arms, reaching around her torso like bright red tongues, engulfing her neck and face. She spun in a circle, her hands flapping uselessly at the fire. She would be scarred for life, her beautiful face unrecognisable, her gorgeous hair razed to an ugly stubble.

There was no time to think.

Hannah grabbed her hand and pulled her towards the sea. 'Run!' she shouted. 'Run to the water!'

The woman seemed incapable of understanding Hannah's words. She stumbled in her grasp, blinded by the flames, out of her mind with terror, screaming and wailing like a banshee.

But Hannah tugged at her relentlessly. The water's edge was just a few yards away. Heat scorched her own hand as the flames licked it hungrily. But she held on tight and dragged the burning woman with all her might towards the waves that rose to meet them.

A breaker surged against the shore, white foam frothing in the moonlight. Hannah flung herself forward, and together they stumbled and toppled into it, icy water closing over her head. The woman's hand slipped from hers.

Salt water filled her mouth as the wave broke over her, and the shock of the cold made her scream as she surfaced, fighting for air. The mist was rolling in like a thick blanket of cold, covering everything in a veil of white.

Hannah looked around for her companion.

She lay face-down in the surf, her dress reduced to rags, her skin burned raw. The sea had doused the flames, but the woman had borne the brutal brunt of the inferno.

Hannah seized her with both arms, lifting her clear of the water. With all her strength she hauled her onto the beach and turned her onto her back. Then she lay at her side, panting for breath.

She heard a shout and soon a man came running up to

her. It was one of the security guards, the yellow of his reflective jacket bright in the moonlight. 'Are you all right, love?'

'I'm fine,' gasped Hannah. 'My friend caught fire. I dragged her into the water.'

'She's not breathing.' The guard knelt at the woman's side, tilting her head back with one hand and lifting her chin with the other to open her airway. Then, pinching her nose closed, he blew air into her mouth. When she failed to respond, he began to press on her chest with the heel of his hand. He counted to thirty and started again. Still the woman lay motionless.

Another man came running over and wrapped a foil blanket around Hannah's shoulders. She was shivering uncontrollably, her teeth chattering like a woodpecker. 'Here, put this around you. Come away from the water.'

But Hannah couldn't take her eyes from the woman she had tried to save. Her body lay lifeless on the shore, unresponsive to all attempts at resuscitation. 'I tried to save her,' she told her rescuer.

'You did your best,' said the man. 'Now come inside to the warm. An ambulance is on its way.'

Still, Hannah stayed where she was. Her legs felt like lead, fixed to the spot. 'Did you see anyone?' she asked the guard. 'Someone running away from the beach? They were dressed in black.'

'Just you, love. No one else.' The man's eyes moved to the woman lying on the cold sand nearby. 'Just you and your friend.'

The beach fell silent, interrupted only by the relentless wash of the waves as they chased each other onto the shore. From the direction of the harbour, the twin flashes of the lighthouses broke through the velvet blackness.

And somewhere in the distance, a dog howled.

CHAPTER 17

Raven rose early the next morning, unable to sleep once the gulls had begun their morning chorus. He hoped that Hannah would have managed a lie in, but she too was up when he came downstairs, and was curled on the sofa cradling a mug of green tea. She gave him a wan smile and he bent over and kissed her forehead.

'How are you feeling?' he asked.

'Okay, I suppose.'

'Did you get any sleep?'

'A bit. You?'

'The same.'

The truth was he'd lain awake half the night, reliving the terrible events of the evening before.

After his foolhardy excursion to the abbey he'd returned to his car and driven to Whitby's west side, stopping on Crescent Terrace, a few doors down from Mrs Harker's guest house and just above the pavilion. There, after stepping out briefly to pick up a styrofoam cup of coffee from a late-night burger van, he'd settled back to wait for Hannah's appearance, congratulating himself that he had finally become the sort of father she'd needed when she was growing up.

Better late than never.

He winced as he tried to make himself comfortable in the leather seat of the car. Every move set off his leg or his shoulder. Shift one way and the ghost of the bullet in his thigh seemed to rise from its grave to haunt him. Twist the other direction and the fresh pain in his shoulder stabbed at him once again.

Better just to keep still and endure a dull throbbing from both. Not to mention the sharp pricking of the graze on his cheek.

That bloody dog, it had a lot to answer for.

His phone sprang to life with an incoming call, but the name on the screen gave him no comfort.

Detective Superintendent Gillian Ellis.

No prizes for guessing why she wanted to speak to him at such a late hour. That interview with Liz Larkin in the grounds of the abbey had been worse than a public relations catastrophe. So much for media awareness, Raven couldn't have been less aware of how to handle the situation if he'd been pitted against a chess grandmaster without knowing how any of the pieces moved.

He rejected her call and slid the phone into his jacket pocket. He'd deal with Gillian the following morning, with a good night's sleep and a handful of Nurofen to soften the impact.

He forced down the cooling brown liquid that the burger van had falsely advertised as coffee, each sip of the disgusting sludge a test of his resolve, and idly perused a flyer from the concert. There were various bands performing but he didn't recognise the name of a single one. He was out of touch. If anyone had quizzed him about his musical tastes, he'd have said gothic rock without thinking twice. But the truth was the scene had moved on, leaving him stuck high and dry in his own little world.

Story of his life.

The sudden arrival of emergency vehicles – two police cars and an ambulance – with their deafening sirens and blue flashing lights had roused him from his stupor. They sped past him and took a sharp left before the whalebone arch by the Captain Cook memorial. That could mean only one thing. They were heading to the pavilion.

Raven was on the move even before the ambulance had rounded the corner, his thumb against the start button, his foot to the floor. The M6 sped off with a screech of rubber, hot on the tail of the emergency vehicles and covering the short distance to the pavilion in the blink of an eye.

He pulled to a halt and clambered from the car. Crowds filled the area in front of the pavilion. They milled about while security guards did their best to herd everyone into some semblance of order.

Raven followed the police officers and paramedics as they pushed their way through the throng. It quickly became clear that some kind of incident had taken place down on the beach. He set off down the path that led past darkened beach huts and stumbled across the sands, hoping to God that Hannah wasn't involved.

Despite the best efforts of the police and security, crowds of goths were spilling onto the shore, drawn by the commotion. Hands held up mobile phones, taking photographs and videos of whatever had happened.

An area of sand close to the water's edge was cordoned off and uniformed officers were stationed at the perimeter, keeping interlopers firmly on one side of the barrier. Paramedics were attending to two people.

Sergeant Mike Fields was in charge of the operation. Raven ducked beneath the barrier and went straight to him. 'What happened?'

'Terrible tragedy.' Fields pointed to a prone figure on the beach. 'A woman died from burns after her hair caught fire. A second woman dragged her into the sea to try to save her. But she was too late.'

Raven approached the body of the dead woman with trepidation, afraid of seeing his daughter lying there. But although her hair was crisped to a cinder and her face charred and disfigured, the blackened remains of her outfit identified her as Aurora Highsmith.

He turned his attention to the other woman, expecting to find Lucille West, but to his surprise she ran towards him and threw herself into his arms, soaking wet and shivering.

'Dad!'

It was the voice he loved more than any other, and her cry split his heart in two. 'Hannah!'

She sobbed against his chest and he held her tighter than he'd done in a long time, not wanting to let her go. What was she doing here? And how could he have let her get so close to such a grisly scene of death? No father should ever have allowed it.

Once he'd established that she was unharmed, he insisted on taking her home immediately. Sergeant Fields wanted her to give a statement, but Raven said it could wait until morning.

'It's all right, Dad,' Hannah said. 'I'd rather do it now, while the memory's fresh. Besides, there's not a lot to tell.'

He waited impatiently while she told Fields how she had first noticed the woman in the company of two friends. No, she didn't know where the friends were now, she hadn't seen them again. She'd come outside for a walk and encountered the woman again on the beach.

Raven listened carefully as she described seeing the flame of a cigarette lighter, and particularly when she mentioned a dark figure fleeing the scene. His chest swelled with pride as she related how she'd acted on instinct, dragging the screaming woman into the sea to quench the flames.

'I didn't do the wrong thing, did I?' sobbed Hannah. 'By pulling her under the water?'

'No,' said Raven. 'You did a very brave thing. And now I'm taking you home.'

He had left the local police to deal with the body, knowing that he'd be back in Whitby once again in the morning.

He joined his daughter now on the sofa, reluctant to

leave her again. 'I want you to know that I'm very proud of what you did last night.'

'I didn't save her though,' said Hannah. 'Aurora, I mean.'

He had told her the victim's name the previous night. It was one of the first things she'd asked once she was in the safety of his car, on the way back to Scarborough. She'd also wanted to know who had killed Aurora and why, but he hadn't been able to give her answers to those questions.

Not yet, anyway.

'You can't save everyone,' he told her now. 'You can only do your best, and sometimes it just isn't enough.' It was a hard lesson, and one he'd had to learn himself early on in his police career. Even now, he found it hard to accept.

'Is that what it's like for you, Dad? As a police officer? You have to stay detached?'

'I could lie and say it gets easier, but the truth is that every failure hurts. Even when it's not your fault.'

She shot him a guilty look and he guessed what was coming. 'Mum would tell me to go home. She'd say it's not safe for me here.'

He'd been expecting this. Lisa would heap the blame on him for putting Hannah into danger and would want to get her away from Scarborough as quickly as possible. And he was really in no position to raise an objection. 'If you'd like me to drive you to the station and put you on a train, you only have to say. There's no shame in leaving. Especially since I haven't exactly been able to give you much of my time.'

'You haven't, have you?'

'I'm sorry.' He knew that her visit to Scarborough had been a disaster from start to finish, and that it was the same story as always. Work had come between them yet again, despite his best efforts to stop it. It would always be the same, no matter how hard he tried. He'd be a fool to deny it. 'So what do you want to do?'

Her face broke into a defiant smile. 'I don't want to run away, that's for sure.'

Raven put his arm around her. 'You're certain? Mum will be mad.'

She laughed. 'She's going to freak out, isn't she?' But the steel in her eyes told him of her resolve to stay. 'I don't want to leave just yet. I'm having a good time.'

'Really? Then stay as long as you want.' He regarded her tenderly. 'I'm going to have to go back to work again today, but I'll see if I can get away a little earlier this evening. In the meantime, will you promise me something?'

'What?'

'That you'll stay in Scarborough today? My sergeant said she'd hook you up with her flatmate, Ellie.'

'Sure,' said Hannah. 'Why not? I can't go back to Whitby anyway. My goth outfit is totally ruined.'

CHAPTER 18

By the time Raven arrived at the station, he had already decided on a plan. With four members of the Order of the Dragon now dead, the focus had to be on the survivors – Raj and Lucille. He also wanted to know more about the first two to die – Nathan and Mia. An accidental drowning and a suicide, supposedly. Well, that explanation looked less and less likely by the hour.

He was pleased to find that the rest of his team were already at their desks when he entered the incident room. Even Dinsdale had turned up and was looking ready for action.

Less welcome was the simmering presence of Detective Superintendent Gillian Ellis at the back of the room. If there was a hell catering specifically for police detectives, Gillian would be at its adamantine gate, ushering new arrivals into the fiery domain. Giving them a sharp stab up the arse with her trident for good measure. Raven waited to see what she would have to say, but she merely levelled him with a steely gaze, saying nothing.

Fine by him. He made his way to the front of the room, trying to regain his focus.

Six faces stared back at him from the whiteboard, their names neatly written beneath their photographs. Nathan Rigby, Mia Munroe, Reynard Blackthorn, Aurora Highsmith, Raj Sandhu and Lucille West. A photo of the red dragon tattoo found on Reynard's body had been fixed nearby, above the words "Order of the Dragon".

The dead now outnumbered the living, and Raven repositioned Aurora's photograph on the other side of the line that separated suspects from victims. He turned to face the room.

'One death is a tragedy, two a coincidence, three a pattern. Four of these people are now dead. It's time to bring in the other two for questioning.'

'You want to do that here?' queried Dinsdale.

'No, let's go to Whitby. Tony, can you call Sergeant Fields and ask him to make the arrangements? If they won't submit to voluntary questioning, tell him to arrest them.'

Tony's pencil was already jotting down the instructions. 'I'll do that, sir.'

'Do you want me to join you?' asked Dinsdale.

Raven considered his options. It would be good politics to invite Dinsdale to the interview. He was the most senior member of his team, and Gillian would approve of the move. But Raven's heart told him that Becca would make a better partner. The last thing he wanted was for Dinsdale to blunder in with the wrong questions and ruin everything. 'No need, Derek,' he said smoothly, 'I've got another task lined up for you. Could you take Jess with you to Whitby and dig up more background on Nathan and Mia? There has to be more to their deaths than the official version.'

Dinsdale's eyes narrowed dangerously at the snub. 'Background? What exactly did you have in mind?'

The question only bolstered Raven's certainty that he had made the right decision in keeping Dinsdale out of the main interviews. Did a detective inspector really need to be told how to do his job?

'Well, Derek, you could begin by speaking to the owner of the shop where Mia worked, and talking to Nathan's brother. Listen to their stories and find out if there's more to Nathan's and Mia's deaths than we already know.'

A muted grunt was the only acknowledgement forthcoming from the other detective. Jess looked anxious at her assignment and Raven gave her a reassuring smile, hoping he'd made the right call partnering her with Dinsdale once again. With such a small team available to him, it wasn't like he had many alternatives.

'Becca,' he continued, 'while we wait for Raj and Lucille to be brought in, I'd like to check out the hotel where Aurora was staying. Let's see if she left anything behind that might clue us into what happened last night.'

'Okay.' She lifted a file from her desk. 'I've printed copies of the witness statements that the Whitby police took from people on the beach last night.'

'Excellent work,' said Raven. 'Bring them with you. You can brief me as we drive.'

It was time for him to finally meet Gillian's stern gaze. 'Did you have anything to add, ma'am?'

Her hard eyes glinted back at him like polished diamonds. 'It sounds like you've got everything covered Tom. Just one thing. If any more media opportunities should present themselves...'

'Yes, ma'am?'

'Best to give them a wide berth.'

*

'What happened to your face?' asked Becca once they were in the car.

'My face?' Raven scratched at his cheek, wincing as his fingernail caught the plaster he'd stuck over the graze. He'd cleaned the wound after getting back to Scarborough the previous night, and bathed it in disinfectant, but it had been too painful to shave that morning, and his efforts to change the plaster had resulted in fresh bleeding. 'It's nothing.'

'Doesn't look like nothing.'

'Just a scrape.' He didn't feel like telling her he'd got into a tight spot with a big dog while skulking around the ruins of the abbey after dark. Acting stupid was one thing – admitting it, quite another. He'd already earned a reputation for rash behaviour and had no desire to tarnish himself further in her eyes.

At least the pain in his shoulder and thigh had eased off.

She could tell he was being evasive but had the good grace to drop the subject. 'All right, then. Do you want to run through the witness statements?'

'Let's do that.'

She thumbed through the sheaf of printed paper. 'The Whitby police will be taking more statements during the day, but these were done at the scene last night.' She sifted through the sheets and selected one. 'This is the statement Hannah gave. Is it okay if we start with this?'

The idea of his own daughter being an eyewitness in a murder investigation made the bile rise to his throat. But he swallowed it down and kept his eyes fixed on the road, determined not to show his misgivings. 'Of course.'

He listened as she read the report aloud, already knowing what it contained. He'd been at his daughter's side when she'd given it, and knew her words by heart.

Becca nodded in appreciation as she recounted Hannah's role in the drama. When she reached the part where Hannah had tried to save the burning woman, she reached across the steering wheel and gently placed her hand on his. 'Hannah's a very brave girl. You know that, don't you?'

'She is brave,' agreed Raven. 'Or foolhardy. Like her father.'

'You should be proud of her.'

'I am.'

Becca returned to the report, concluding with the arrival of the paramedics and police. 'Could Hannah have been mistaken about seeing someone on the beach? The first-aiders didn't notice anyone, and Hannah herself says that it was misty. None of the other statements I've read so far mention seeing a dark figure.'

'But someone else must have been there, or how could Aurora's hair have been set on fire?'

He recalled the mysterious figure he'd spotted creeping about the abbey. What had he seen, really? Nothing more than a shadowy form moving through the ruins. Insubstantial, more like a ghost than a person.

And yet the dog he'd encountered had been undeniably flesh and blood.

Flesh, blood and teeth. Mustn't forget about those teeth.

'What about sightings of a dog?' he asked Becca. 'Hannah said she heard a dog howl.'

Becca turned over the pages of the various reports. 'A couple of people reported seeing a large black dog in the vicinity. Do you think it's the same dog that Mrs Harker heard barking the night Reynard vanished?'

'The curious incident of the dog in the night. Could be.'

Becca continued to read through the reports, but there was nothing more that caught his attention. Only Hannah had seen the attack itself, and no one had seen the perpetrator leave the scene. He lapsed into a thoughtful silence.

'What's bothering you?' queried Becca. 'I can tell there's something on your mind.'

There were many aspects of this case that were bothering him, and not just how close Hannah had come to danger. The dark figure, the dog... it was almost as if they were one and the same. At the abbey, he'd seen the figure alone, and then the dog afterwards. Hannah had only heard the dog howling, after the stranger had vanished, and none of the other witnesses had seen anyone. It was almost as if the killer had turned themselves into a black dog.

But that was crazy thinking. He shook the idea from his head.

'What's bothering me,' he told Becca, 'is the way that Aurora was killed.'

'Sure, it was horrible.'

'That's not what I meant.' He sought for the right way to explain it. 'What I mean is, why set her on fire? Reynard's death was carefully staged to look like a vampire attack. Aurora dressed as a vampire, so it might have been logical to kill her by driving a stake through her heart.'

Becca looked sceptical at the suggestion. 'Perhaps that wasn't very practical.'

'And yet the murderer went to enormous trouble to exsanguinate Reynard.'

'Perhaps they had something else in mind this time.'

'A new theme?' He shot a sideways glance at her. 'That's what worries me.'

CHAPTER 19

'This a duff job,' complained Dinsdale. 'A detective of my experience shouldn't have to do something so routine.'

'Well, someone has to,' countered Jess. 'And really, I don't mind. It's nice to be out and about, don't you think?'

Dinsdale gave a snort. 'Just as long as this rust bucket doesn't conk out halfway there.'

They were back in the Land Rover, crossing the national park again, and Jess couldn't understand why he was being so grumpy. Unless that was just how Dinsdale was. The Land Rover may not have been the height of luxury, yet despite his obvious dislike of the rattling old vehicle, he hadn't offered to drive them himself in his Toyota. Jess didn't mind. She much preferred to be the one behind the wheel.

'At least we're not going to the arse-end of nowhere today,' he conceded. 'Maybe we can stop for fish and chips again by the harbour.'

Jess hadn't regarded Reynard's cottage as the arse-end of anywhere. Although the farmyard was a little run-down, its setting on the moors had been idyllic. But today they were heading for Whitby town centre. Raven had asked them to find out more about Mia Munroe and Nathan Rigby, the friends of Reynard and Aurora who had also died in recent years. And although Dinsdale had described the task as a duff job, Jess was looking forward to it. To her way of thinking, the two deaths certainly seemed worthy of further investigation.

She parked close to Skinner Street, and together they walked the short distance to the boutique on Flowergate where Mia had worked.

Dinsdale regarded the sign over the shop with disdain. 'Vivienne's Vamp & Victoriana. What sort of name is that?'

Jess thought it quite charming, but knew there was no point voicing her opinion to Dinsdale. What did it matter what the shop was called, in any case?

He peered in through the shop window, giving the clothes displayed on the mannequins a sullen look. 'Look at these! What normal person would want to buy this sort of rubbish?'

The display was eclectic, for sure. A purple floor-length frock trimmed with white lace jostled for attention with a daring outfit in shiny black leather. Sky-high stilettos studded with nails vied for space with witches' hats and jewelled masks.

Perhaps Dinsdale was right and no "normal" person would want to buy any of these items. Personally, Jess wouldn't buy any either, but she was intrigued to look inside the shop and meet Vivienne herself.

'Tell you what,' she said, 'why don't I do the interview with Vivienne, while you go and track down Nathan's brother?'

According to Tony's information, Nathan's brother, Alexander, owned a jet jewellery shop in the heart of the old town. The walk down Flowergate and across the swing bridge to Church Street would do Dinsdale good, and it would get him out of her hair for an hour or so. She could easily speak to Vivienne on her own. Dinsdale was right about that – it didn't need an experienced detective to conduct the interview.

'All right,' he said, as if it had been his idea all along. 'It'll be more efficient that way. You handle the weirdo, and I'll talk to the sensible person. We'll meet for lunch afterwards. Same place as yesterday.'

'Fine by me,' agreed Jess. She watched him go. Then, glad to be rid of him, pushed open the door to the shop. A bell tinkled as she entered and she found herself in a cornucopia of old-fashioned silk, lace, leather, and an array of fancy accessories to accompany the outfits – black parasols, wide-brimmed hats adorned with veils and feathers, fingerless lace gloves – in short, everything you could need for a goth weekend or a Victorian funeral with all the trimmings.

A few shoppers were examining the merchandise with interest, and a youthful assistant was hovering nearby, ready to help, but Jess made her way straight to the counter where a woman wearing a black dress and with long black hair and purple highlights greeted her warmly. 'How can I help you, love? We've a changing room just through here if you'd like to try anything on.' She indicated a dark corner of the shop where a velvet curtain was draped across a small cubbyhole. A plaster gargoyle perched above it, grinning wickedly down at the customers.

'I'm not here to buy,' said Jess. 'I'm DC Jess Barraclough from North Yorkshire Police. Are you Vivienne Nightingale?'

The woman pursed her scarlet lips. She eyed Jess thoughtfully, running pale fingers through the dark hair that framed her face. Her eyes were a piercing green, her earrings silver, fashioned into pentacles. She wore a choker of black and purple threads around her slim neck, and at her throat a moonstone radiated a soft glow.

Perhaps she had a book of spells tucked behind the counter, or a cauldron bubbling on a stove in the back room, eye of newt simmering away. She gave Jess a nod, setting her pentacles swaying. 'Yes, I'm Vivienne. Is this about the murders?'

It was inevitable that news of the latest death would have spread by now. Hundreds of people had been at the rock concert where it happened, and after Raven's disastrous TV interview, which Jess had watched with dismay, the two gruesome murders had become the number-one talking point of the town. She was aware that a hush had fallen over the shop as its customers strained to listen in to the conversation.

'Is there somewhere more private we could talk?' asked Jess. 'I'd like to ask you some questions about Mia Munroe.'

Vivienne's perfectly pencilled eyebrows shot up a notch. 'Mia? Let's go through to the back room.'

Leaving her assistant in charge of the shop, Vivienne took Jess to a room at the back of the shop. Disappointingly there was no bubbling cauldron. Instead, dresses in sumptuous fabrics hung from a rack along one wall. Several half-finished garments were draped over the backs of chairs. A complicated-looking sewing machine stood on a table piled high with swathes of purple, indigo and red velvet. Vivienne moved a mound of fabric aside so that Jess could sit down.

'Do you make all of the dresses you sell in the shop?' asked Jess, taking a seat amid the clutter.

'I make some of them,' said Vivienne, gathering her voluminous skirt to one side as she lowered herself into a chair. 'And I do alterations and repairs. Occasionally I get asked to create a bespoke dress for a client. Mia used to help me. We worked together to make her wedding dress.'

It was clear from the way Vivienne spoke that she had felt a great deal of affection for the dead woman. 'Tell me about her,' said Jess.

Vivienne's gaze drifted to the far wall as she gathered her thoughts. 'Mia was Scottish. She came from some remote island in the Outer Hebrides, I forget which one. All wind and rain, according to Mia – a bit like Whitby.' She gave Jess a half-smile. 'Anyway, she wanted to get away, and she had a real love of clothes and an eye for design – not to mention dextrous fingers – so she studied Fashion at Leeds. She had grand plans to go on to London, you know, to get into the fashion scene down there. But then she met Nathan at Leeds and the pair of them fell madly in love. They got engaged and she came to Whitby to live with him.'

'So, Nathan was originally from Whitby?'

'That's right. He studied Fine Art at uni and wanted to make a career of it. I can't say I liked him all that much. He could be quite arrogant and temperamental at times. Mia excused his behaviour, saying it was because he was an artist and his passion was just a manifestation of his creativity. But still, artists can be kind too, don't you think?'

'Did they live together?'

'Yes, in a tiny cottage on Silver Street. They were very poor, really. I couldn't afford to pay Mia a lot, and Nathan earned a pittance from his work, but young love can carry you through any hardship.' She smiled to herself, a flicker of warm memories in her eyes. 'Nathan could have joined his brother in the jet shop, but he sneered at that idea, saying he had a greater calling. He fancied himself as part of the avant-garde, pushing the boundaries of art. His style was – how can I best describe it? – challenging. But that won't get you far, not if you want to put food on the table. And especially if you have only half the talent you think you do. Most visitors to Whitby want pretty watercolours of the abbey, or perhaps some gothic prints of the ruins. Nathan hated doing that sort of thing, but Mia persuaded him to spend at least some of his time painting pictures people actually wanted to buy.'

'And they planned to marry?'

'Oh, yes. They were going to get married at St Mary's Church. As you might imagine, Mia wanted something really special to wear. She designed the dress herself, and I helped her make it. It was really quite unique. We made bridesmaids dresses too, for her two friends from university.'

'Would they be Aurora Highsmith and Lucille West?'

'That's right. The wedding was all arranged. But then tragedy struck. Nathan drowned.'

'Tell me about that,' said Jess.

Vivienne's shoulders sagged as she recalled the event. 'Nathan was always drawn to the sea. I suppose it was part of his artistic temperament. He liked to stand on the end of the pier, looking out to sea. One day he went out in a storm and never came back. His body was washed up on the rocks.' Vivienne demonstrated with a sweep of her purple-painted fingernails. 'Mia was inconsolable, as you might imagine.'

Vivienne's eyes sparkled with tears and Jess hesitated before asking, 'You miss her?'

'Terribly.' Vivienne withdrew a black-trimmed handkerchief from the bodice of her dress and dabbed at her eyes. 'She was a lovely girl. Gifted with a sewing machine and good with the customers. But more than that, she was a friend.' She bowed her head.

Jess knew what it was like to lose someone dear. She was still missing the man she had loved. Sometimes she would wake up in the middle of the night, unable to believe that he was gone, certain that it had all just been a nightmare. And each time, grief struck her all over again.

'Did Mia ever think about returning home? After Nathan drowned, I mean.'

Vivienne shook her head dismissively. 'What would she have done in the Outer Hebrides? There was nothing for her there. Here she had a job and her memories.' She hesitated. 'But maybe that wasn't such a good thing.'

'What do you mean?'

'The day after Nathan's death, she turned up at the shop all dressed in black. That wasn't so unusual for Mia, but there was something different about her. It wasn't simply grief, it was a kind of resolve. She spent a whole year wearing mourning dress, just the way the Victorians would have done. While she was working in the shop, she didn't look out of place. But around the town, she attracted a lot of unwanted attention. Except during the goth weekends, when she blended in perfectly.'

Jess knew what was coming. 'And after a year of mourning...?'

Vivienne gave a long sigh. 'After a year and a day, she put on her white wedding dress, walked up the steps to St Mary's, and threw herself onto the rocks below.'

It was a shocking story, and clearly painful for Vivienne to relate, but Jess couldn't simply accept it at face value. She probed deeper. 'Did Mia ever discuss suicide with you?'

'No. If she had, I would have insisted she went to counselling.' Her mouth turned down. 'Perhaps I should have done that, anyway. I hoped that the mourning was just her way of coming to terms with her grief. I never imagined...'

Jess knew she had to tread sensitively over the subject. 'In your opinion, was there anything to suggest that Mia may not have taken her own life?'

Vivienne looked shocked. 'Whatever makes you say that? The coroner ruled suicide and I've never questioned that.'

'Did she have any other kinds of problems in her life, apart from grief? Debts, drugs, disputes, anything of that kind?'

'No.'

'And did she leave any kind of note behind?'

Vivienne shook her head. 'No. She didn't tell anyone what she planned to do.'

'But you're sure she intended it?'

'Yes. She walked up to the church early that morning when there was hardly anyone else about. She must have walked right past the shop long before I opened up. I've thought about that so often. If only I'd seen her, I could have stopped her.'

Jess recognised survivor's guilt in the older woman. She had suffered from it herself, but her police training helped. Some people you just couldn't save.

'Even if you had seen Mia,' she said gently, 'you couldn't have known what she intended to do.'

'But I could have stopped her,' insisted Vivienne. 'No one else could have helped. Her family were miles away. Her friends hardly ever saw her. There was only me, and I let her down.'

Jess wasn't sure what else to say. She had explored every avenue she could think of. The case seemed open and shut. Mia had killed herself because of unresolved grief following the death of her fiancé. If Raven had hoped to find some link with the murders of Reynard and Aurora, Jess had been unable to find one.

She was about to get to her feet when Vivienne put out a hand to stop her.

'There's something else I ought to tell you. It seems silly, but since you're here asking all these questions...'

Jess returned to her seat. 'Yes?'

'In the weeks before she died, Mia said that someone was following her. I thought she was imagining it. But she insisted she was being stalked.'

'Who was it? A man? A woman? Was it anyone she recognised?'

Vivienne shrugged. 'She didn't know. She was never able to see their face. She just talked about a figure in black.'

CHAPTER 20

DI Derek Dinsdale didn't get it. Why couldn't people just dress normally? There were men his own age, for goodness' sake, dressed up like mad Victorian inventors or as Dracula or as sinister undertakers. The Whitby goth weekend didn't only attract youngsters. Middle-aged and even elderly goths were parading about town in large numbers, busy making a spectacle of themselves. You'd think people would grow out of wearing fancy dress.

He trudged his way across the swing bridge and into Church Street, giving a wide berth to anyone who looked particularly weird, but it was impossible to avoid them, there were that many. Sidestepping a man in a plague doctor's mask, he collided with the bustle of a large lady who was all made-up with her decolletage on display. She smiled at him as if he'd just made a pass at her. Good grief, she was well past retirement age. He scowled and moved on.

He found the place he was looking for halfway along the cobbled street. The shop's bay window was arrayed with necklaces, earrings and bracelets of black jet, mostly set in silver. His wife, God bless her, had passed away a few years ago, but she would never have liked this kind of jewellery. Like any sensible woman, Audrey had liked pretty things. Not lumps of black rock that looked like polished coal.

The jewellery shop was next to a café with a tempting display of scones and cream cakes in its window. Dinsdale stopped for a moment to have a look and to allow the tempting aroma of baking to percolate up his nostrils. He had a liking for scones. But you had to spread the jam first, then put cream on top. Some folk did it the wrong way round and ruined everything.

Idiots.

If he had time after speaking to Alexander Rigby, he'd treat himself to elevenses. Why not? There had to be some compensation for trekking all the way over to Whitby. He'd be late getting back to Scarborough as it was. And it wasn't as if inspectors got paid overtime like junior ranks.

He pushed open the door, and a bell tinkled overhead. The inside of the shop was quiet after the hustle of the street, and he took a moment to enjoy the peace. All he needed now was a chair to take the weight off his feet. A cup of tea wouldn't go amiss, either.

A man appeared from a back room and peered at Dinsdale over the glass counter. The proprietor, presumably. He looked to be in his early forties: slim, slightly balding and with a pair of reading glasses perched on the end of his nose. Dinsdale was relieved to see he was wearing an ordinary suit, not some ridiculous costume. He didn't think he could seriously interview anyone in a silly outfit.

'Alexander Rigby?'

'Aye. And who are you?' The man was your typical blunt northerner. Dinsdale started to feel more at home.

'Detective Inspector Dinsdale, Scarborough CID. I'd like to talk to you about your brother, Nathan.'

'Nathan? Why? He's dead.' Alexander Rigby crossed his arms in front of his chest.

'I know that.' Dinsdale stood his ground. 'But I still want to talk about him. Is there somewhere we can sit down?'

The man sighed in annoyance. 'I'll have to close up the shop.'

'You do that, then,' said Dinsdale. 'And why don't you put the kettle on while you're at it?'

*

The old stone walls and mullioned windows of Bagdale Hall made an imposing first impression. This, mused Becca, as she crossed the threshold of the Tudor manor house, was the kind of history she could relate to. Not obscure orders of medieval knights and battles against invading armies, but the indulgence and pampering afforded by a luxury hotel.

Inside the building, the impression of comfortable tradition was reinforced by the dark oak timbers supporting the ceiling, and the elaborately carved wooden fireplace that stood beside the reception desk.

For all her shortcomings, Aurora Highsmith's choice of residence in Whitby couldn't be faulted. Even vampires, it seemed, craved a little comfort when they weren't holed up in their coffins.

Becca crossed the tartan-patterned carpet of the entrance hall to the desk where a dark-suited young man was waiting. From the nearby dining room, the murmur of conversation and the clink of cutlery on crockery signalled that breakfast was still being served. The smell of bacon was in the air, but Becca had already fortified herself against its powers of seduction by eating a low-fat bowl of porridge for breakfast.

Oatmeal, one; crispy bacon, nil. A decisive victory of health over instant gratification.

But there would be plenty of opportunities for a re-match.

'How may I help you, sir, madam?' The young

receptionist beamed warmly at her and Raven, and barely faltered when Becca produced her warrant card.

'Do you have a Miss Aurora Highsmith staying here?' she asked.

'Yes, I believe that Miss Highsmith is still here.' The receptionist consulted his computer. 'She's due to check out this morning.'

'Is she?' That was news to Becca. Aurora had previously said she'd planned to leave Whitby on Sunday. In fact, she'd been told by Raven not to leave without letting the police know first. 'Well, I'm afraid that her plans have changed.'

The receptionist's smile had been replaced by a look of concern, especially now that Raven was leaning against the desk, thumbing idly through the brochures that had been placed there for the benefit of guests. Six foot two of stern-faced intimidation, clad in his usual black coat and wearing a carpet of dark stubble on his chin and neck. It didn't help that his cheekbone bore a nasty red graze, which was presumably the reason he hadn't shaved this morning.

How had he cut his face? Apart from his dodgy leg, he'd been injury-free when Becca had last seen him in Scarborough the day before. But as usual Raven had refused to talk about it. Another mystery.

'We'll need a key to her room,' she said to the receptionist.

'Is there a problem?'

Raven fixed him with a hard stare. 'There won't be, as long as you give us a key.'

The man hastily began to program a card key.

'Has Miss Highsmith had any visitors to the hotel during her stay?' asked Becca.

'Not to my knowledge. She's always been on her own whenever I've seen her.'

'You remember her, then?'

A flush of red came to the young man's neck. 'She's very, uh, memorable. With her hair and her clothes, I mean.' He handed over a key card. 'If you need anything else, just ask.'

'Don't worry,' Becca assured him. 'We will.'

They took the stairs to Aurora's room on the first floor, the limp in Raven's leg just a fraction more pronounced than usual. Donning nitrile gloves, Becca inserted the key and pushed open the door.

The room was grand, more like a suite, with a mahogany four-poster bed and a brown Chesterfield sofa in front of a stone fireplace decorated with antique tiles. Aurora certainly hadn't been afraid to treat herself to a little luxury.

As she entered the room, Becca bent down to pick up a postcard that had been pushed under the door. The picture on the card showed a painting of a young woman. Her exuberantly long red-gold hair cascaded over her shoulders and below the edge of the table at which she was seated. Becca turned it over. Printed text identified the painting as *The Bridesmaid* by John Everett Millais.

And beneath the text was a handwritten message.

In life she craved beauty; now she sleeps in beautiful death.

Becca showed it to Raven. 'It's the same handwriting as the postcard found in Reynard's cottage. The killer's sending us another message.'

CHAPTER 21

Dr Raj Sandhu wasn't looking his best. He sat slumped at the table, his head in his hands, his steampunk hat discarded beside him, his black hair sticking up at all angles. His clothes were crumpled, his wing-collar shirt hanging open at the neck. His beard, which had previously been tapered to a fine point was now rough with overnight growth. He raised his head as Raven and Becca entered the interview room, his face drawn and gaunt, his eyes puffy and bloodshot. He looked like someone who'd woken up on a friend's sofa the day after a fancy dress party and wondered what the hell he was still doing there.

Raven pulled a seat up, watching him wince as the chair legs scraped across the floor. 'Thank you for coming to see us this morning.'

'Did I have a choice?' asked Raj.

'Of course,' said Raven. 'You're not under arrest. This is a voluntary interview. You're free to leave at any time.'

Raj looked suspiciously from Raven to Becca. 'So I could just get up and walk out right now?'

'You could,' said Raven. 'But then I'd have to arrest

you. So I suggest you just stay in your seat and cooperate.'

Raj's head dipped, knowing he was beaten.

'Let's start by establishing some facts about last night. You went to the concert at the pavilion with Aurora and Lucille, is that right?'

'Yes,' said Raj.

'Did you all go together, or did you meet there?'

'We met for a drink at the Elsinore pub and walked to the pavilion together.'

'I see. And what time did you arrive there?'

'About seven thirty, I guess. I wasn't really looking at my watch.'

Raven already knew from Hannah's statement exactly what time Raj and his friends had arrived at the box office. So far everything the doctor had said appeared to be truthful and straightforward. Raven didn't get the impression that he was trying to hide anything.

'Tell me exactly what you did after entering the pavilion.'

Raj ran a hand through his matted hair. He really did look as if he'd been dragged straight from his bed. Perhaps he hadn't slept at all. 'We got there quite early. Most people hadn't yet arrived. I bought some drinks from the bar for everyone and then we went to listen to the first band, Velvet Nocturne. I'd never heard of them before. They weren't bad, I suppose.'

Raven wasn't interested in a review of the band's performance. 'And then what?'

Raj gave a mournful look. 'We kind of drifted apart. The girls wanted to get up close to the stage, but I prefer to stand further back so my eardrums don't get blasted. But it wasn't just that. Lucille and Aurora had started arguing as soon as we got to the pavilion and I guess I'd had enough of them. I went to use the bathroom and afterwards I decided I'd prefer to be alone.'

'So what did you do?' asked Becca.

'I went to stand by the bar. I didn't see either of the girls after that.' His head sank into his hands and he closed his eyes. 'And now I'll never see Aurora again.'

Raven gave him a moment to recover, then asked, 'Before you left them, did you notice Aurora speaking to anyone else?'

'I don't think so.'

'You don't seem sure.'

'Well, her hair always attracts' – he paused and shook his head – 'I mean attracted, a lot of attention. People would always stop to pay her compliments, to ask how she styled it that way.' He gave Raven a sideways look. 'That was why she did it, of course. She craved attention. But I didn't notice her having a proper conversation with anyone. Oh, wait a minute.' He clicked his fingers. 'When I got back from the bar, she and Lucille were chatting with that woman who runs the dress shop.'

'You mean Vivienne Nightingale,' said Becca.

Raj seemed surprised. 'You know Vivienne?'

'Vivienne's Vamp & Victoriana is where Mia Munroe used to work.'

'Yes,' said Raj. 'That's how we know her.'

'And what was this conversation about?'

'I don't know. Clothes? Music? Vivienne was just leaving when I returned with the drinks.'

'So,' said Raven, 'what did you do after the first band finished their set?'

'I went outside to clear my head. I think I'm getting too old for all this loud music.' His words trailed off. 'I know what you're going to ask. Did I see Aurora outside? Did I go down to the beach? But the truth is I didn't see anything. There were people smoking and vaping just outside the entrance to the pavilion, and I hate that, so I went and sat by myself on the wall. If you want to know what I was thinking, I was wondering what on earth I was doing in Whitby. One of my friends had just died, I wasn't enjoying the music or the dressing up, and I'd come to the realisation that I didn't really like Aurora or Lucille anymore. I was thinking about going home. And then the police arrived and it was all chaos.'

Raven recalled the scene first-hand. The police cars and ambulance with their flashing lights and sirens. The goths milling about. It was the ideal situation for the killer to vanish in the crowds.

A figure dressed in black? There must have been hundreds of them that night.

'Did you notice a dog?' he asked.

Raj seemed taken aback by the question. 'A dog? In the pavilion? During the concert?'

'Outside. Afterwards.'

'I don't know. I don't think so. What kind of dog?'

'Black. Large. Fierce.' Out of the corner of his eye, Raven caught Becca giving him a funny look. But he kept his gaze fixed on Raj.

'No. Nothing like that. But as I say, it was mayhem.'

Raven opened his file and withdrew a clear plastic envelope containing the postcard that had been left in Aurora's room at Bagdale Hall. The CSI team had checked it for prints but it was clean. He showed it to Raj. 'Does the picture mean anything to you?'

'Is this to do with Aurora's death?' Raj held the envelope by its edges as if afraid of being contaminated by the postcard it contained. 'I guess this is supposed to be Aurora? I mean, with the hair?'

'What about the message on the back?'

Raj turned it over and read aloud. '*In life she craved beauty; now she sleeps in beautiful death.* Well, it's no secret that Aurora was obsessed with how she looked.'

Becca cleared her throat. 'Would you mind showing us your tattoo?'

'My tattoo?' Raj appeared startled by the question. He looked ready to refuse, but then his shoulders sagged in acquiescence. 'All right.'

He removed his jacket and rolled up the ruffled sleeve of his left arm. And there it was. The fire-red dragon curled in a circle, its back arched, its tail looping around to meet its head. It was skilfully executed.

'Nathan designed these?' asked Raven.

'Yes. He produced the design and he inked the tattoos himself. I've thought about having mine removed, but it's not an easy process and there's no guarantee of success. You need laser treatment, which is painful and can leave scars. I guess I'm too much of a coward.' He rolled his sleeve back down.

'I get the impression,' said Raven, 'that you weren't the most enthusiastic member of the Order of the Dragon.'

'Well, no, I was never comfortable with it, to tell the truth. All that stuff about fighting against the Ottomans. It sounded too much like a crusade for my liking. I only went along with it because I wanted to fit in.'

Raven understood that feeling: doing something stupid to demonstrate your allegiance to a group of peers, or to impress a girl. He'd been guilty of it himself as a teenager. In his own case it had amounted to petty acts of crime, mostly shoplifting. He'd won the girl, even if he'd lost her later. But at least he hadn't made the mistake of having her name tattooed on his forearm.

'So this is where I have a problem.'

'Oh?' Raj looked wary.

'A tightknit group like that doesn't simply drift apart. Something must have happened.' Raven spoke from experience. In his own case, it was the sudden and tragic death of his mother that had stretched the already-fragile bonds of friendship beyond breaking point. He'd dumped the girl, turned his back on his friends and left Scarborough with the intention of never returning. It had taken three decades and the death of his father to make him return.

He leaned back in his chair and waited for Raj to speak.

The young man began to fiddle with his cuffs, not meeting Raven's eye. Raven let the silence drag out, knowing that it was one of the most effective weapons in a detective's toolkit. His patience was rewarded when eventually Raj looked up. 'Betrayal drove us apart,' he muttered.

'Would you care to explain?'

Raj's face drooped, his eyes turning dark as pits; his

cheeks shrinking to sunken hollows. 'When I first went to Leeds, I was very shy. I didn't know anyone and it was all so big and overwhelming. Everyone else seemed to be making friends and I was left on the side. And then I met Lucille.' He stared at Raven, a picture of hopelessness. 'She was special. I fell for her immediately, hook, line and sinker. It took her a little while to notice me, but after a while I became part of her circle. We were all outcasts of one kind or another, and that's what drew us together. Anyway, after our first year, Lucille and I became a couple. Mia and Nathan had already hooked up – they were made for each other. That just left Aurora and Reynard.'

Raven waited, knowing there was no need to intervene. Now that Raj had begun his story, he would tell it to the end.

'Reynard could never stand by and watch other people be happy. There was a darkness in his soul. If he couldn't have something, he wanted to destroy it. So one night, after we'd all had too much to drink, he managed to entice Lucille into his bed. Like I said, he had this dark attraction that women found hard to resist. She swore afterwards that it was just the once, and I believed her. She begged me to forgive her, and I tried my best, I really did. But… I guess that I'm not as forgiving as I would like to be.'

Raven nodded in sympathy, recalling the hurt he'd experienced on learning that Lisa had left him for another man. He'd tried to forgive her too, but in the end it had come to nothing.

Betrayal hurt.

'So you never truly forgave Lucille?'

Raj looked helpless. 'How could I?' he whispered. 'I loved her.'

'And you blamed Reynard for seducing her.'

'Reynard?' For the first time, a look of quiet ferocity entered Raj's eyes. 'He was supposed to be my friend. But he took the love that was most precious to me and deliberately destroyed it. I hated him with all my heart.'

CHAPTER 22

It was Barry who had recommended going to Peasholm Park, and to Hannah's surprise the place was proving to be well worth a visit.

It wasn't like any of London's parks. Much smaller than Hyde Park or even Kensington Gardens, Peasholm had none of the elaborate monuments and statues of its grander city cousins, but it was a whole lot more fun.

The park was ranged around a boating lake with a small but mountainous island at its centre. An oriental bridge guarded by stone lions joined the island to the bank, and a Japanese pagoda could be glimpsed peeping above the trees. A mini golfing green occupied one corner of the park, and boats in the form of dragons and swans could be hired by the hour. Hannah would have loved to take one of the boats out if she'd had someone to help her paddle. But her dad was at work and she wasn't due to meet Ellie until later, so she had to content herself with an ice cream and a leisurely stroll along the path that looped around the edge of the park.

A bandstand stood on a wooden platform in the widest part of the lake, but it wasn't in use this early in the season.

A nearby sign promised that during the summer months, an historic naval battle would be recreated in miniature on the water, complete with battleships and aircraft. Hannah found that very hard to picture. She'd have to see it for herself.

Yet even though the sun was doing its best to push through the grey cloud cover overhead, she found it difficult to keep her imagination from dragging up dark and terrifying images from the previous night. Sea mists and shadows seemed to close over her again as she relived the moments before the horrible attack.

The woman in the vampire costume, her amazing hair seeming to dazzle in the darkness; the sudden flash of light as her hair burst into flames; the frantic sprint across the sands and into the sea – there was nothing Hannah could do to stop it from replaying in her mind in a horrifying loop.

No matter how many times she revisited the event, there was nothing she could do to alter the outcome: Aurora dead in her arms as the waves washed over her, her scalp scorched to a cinder and her face and arms a mass of hideous burns.

And the smell, almost like brimstone. That acrid stink filled her nostrils even now.

'Are you all right there, miss?'

An elderly man had come up close beside her, an anxious look in his watery eyes. With a start, Hannah realised she had walked right up to the edge of the lake and was standing with one foot half over the water. She had almost fallen in.

She pulled herself together and took a step back. 'I'm fine. Thank you.'

He nodded and moved off, turning once to check she was okay.

Hannah took a deep breath, letting cool air fill her lungs. There was no smoke in the air now; no shadows; no fire.

She looked out across the lake at the artificial waterfall

that spilled from the top of the island. The sun was breaking through, leaving a soft sheen on the water. Ducks splashed about and swans glided serenely past, and nearby a squirrel dashed across the grass and up a tree.

Life going on as if nothing had happened.

She turned away from the lakeside and continued along the path.

The old man had reminded her of something and as she walked she realised what it was. Old Mr Swales up in the graveyard at St Mary's Church. He had recounted a similar event to Aurora's death, one that had occurred in the town bakery over a hundred years earlier. Poor Mary Clarke, the girl with the lovely hair which had caught fire at the bakery.

An eerie coincidence. The tale was the stuff of local legends, giving rise to whispers of a ghost that haunted the streets at night. Could that story have inspired whoever had set Aurora's hair alight? The idea gave Hannah the chills.

What else had Mr Swales said? He'd told her of the barghest hound, the black dog that appeared when someone was about to die. An even taller tale, to be sure. And yet Hannah had glimpsed exactly such a hound, running in and out of the gravestones just hours before Aurora had met her end. And she had heard a dog howl soon after Aurora was attacked.

That could have been any dog. Yet somehow she knew it was the same animal.

Her thoughts were cut short by the ringing of her phone. She reached for it and was alarmed to find it was her father. Why was he calling her now?

She answered it quickly. 'Hi, Dad. What's wrong?'

There was a pause before he replied. 'Nothing. Does there have to be something wrong?'

She breathed a sigh of relief. 'No, of course not. So, why are you calling?'

'I just wanted to make sure you're okay, sweetheart. How are you feeling?'

It was good of him to ask. 'You were worried about

me?'

'Not worried. Concerned.' He was trying hard to sound casual and completely failing to pull it off. Perhaps his concern was understandable under the circumstances. She was beginning to appreciate why he took his job so seriously.

'Well, there's no need to be concerned. I'm good. Really.'

'Where are you?' So that was the real reason for the call. He was checking she'd kept her promise to stay in Scarborough.

'Standing by the lake in Peasholm Park. I've just eaten an ice-cream and I'm watching the ducks and swans.'

'Good,' he said. 'Just be careful of the geese. They can be vicious. Especially when they get angry.'

Despite everything, she found herself laughing. If angry geese were the greatest danger in Peasholm Park, she knew she was safe there.

She knew what he was doing though. Trying to put her at ease.

She wondered briefly if she should tell him about Mr Swales' bakery story. Yet even as the thought occurred to her she dismissed it. If she started telling him the old man's salty tales, he really would worry about her state of mind.

'Don't worry, Dad. I'll be fine. I'll catch up with you later.'

She ended the call and set off around the lake once more. The sun had abandoned its earlier attempt to break through, and heavier clouds were mustering overhead. She shivered and drew her jacket closer to her. Mist and shadows swirled at the edges of her consciousness, and Aurora's face appeared once again.

I tried to save you, Hannah told the vision.

And what more could she have done? Everyone had said how brave she'd been, and that she'd done her very best.

It wasn't my fault.

And yet, despite her heroic efforts, she had failed to

save Aurora from the flames. Her actions felt like a futile gesture.

★

'He has no alibi for either murder,' said Becca. 'And he admitted to hating Reynard.'

'True.' Raven leaned against the doorframe of the interview room at Whitby, watching her face intently. Raj had been taken away, and they were considering what to do about him. 'So what do you think? Should we keep him in custody?'

Becca considered the matter carefully. She knew that Raven was giving her the chance to take the lead on the case. He was asking her to make a judgement call. Perhaps he was thinking of handing the investigation over to her while he went back to Scarborough to hang out with Hannah. Becca was keen to shoulder a little more responsibility, but she didn't think she was experienced enough to head up a double murder investigation.

Especially one as bizarre as this.

'I can't see what his motive for wanting to murder Aurora might be,' she pointed out.

'Neither can I, but perhaps that will become apparent under further questioning. Right now, he has a clear motive for one out of two murders, and as a doctor he must have had access to the medical equipment required to carry out an exsanguination.'

'Then let's hold him until after we've spoken to Lucille,' suggested Becca.

'And if he refuses?'

'We'll have to arrest him.' She shook her head. They didn't have sufficient evidence to make an arrest. 'Let's just ask Sergeant Fields to offer him tea and biscuits and ask him a load of tedious admin questions. That'll keep him here for an hour or so.'

Raven grinned in approval. 'Devious. Why don't you sort that out while I arrange for Lucille to be brought into the interview room.'

'Sure,' said Becca. 'I'd best check my supply of tissues too.' If Lucille was even half as emotional as last time, she'd need a whole box full.

Five minutes later, she and Raven were back in the interview room, with Lucille now occupying the seat that Raj had recently vacated. The crying had already begun.

Lucille accepted a tissue from Becca and wiped her eyes. It smudged her eyeliner and mascara, but this only added to her goth look. 'Thank you,' she murmured.

'I want to make it clear that this is a voluntary interview,' began Becca. 'You're free to leave at any time, but it would be in everyone's best interests if you stayed.'

'I understand,' said Lucille, her voice barely above a whisper.

'Let's start with the concert in the pavilion,' said Becca. 'Is it true that you and Aurora had an argument?'

A fresh wave of crying ensued. 'Did Raj tell you that?' Lucille asked. But without waiting for a response she went on, 'Well, it's true. We had a row, and Aurora stormed out.' She gave Becca an anguished look. 'If only she'd stayed inside, she'd still be alive!'

'We don't know that,' said Becca. 'Tell us what the argument was about.'

Lucille's expression turned even more miserable. 'It seems stupid now. Aurora had decided she wanted to leave the festival early. After what happened to Reynard, she said she'd had enough, and she wanted to go home. She'd already told the hotel she was checking out. I said she was letting everyone down and that she owed it to Reynard to stay. And she said I had no right to tell her what she owed anyone. She accused me of ruining everything back at university.'

'What did she mean by that?'

'I'd prefer not to say.'

'Was it connected with your relationship with Raj?'

Lucille stared glumly back. 'He told you about that?'

Becca nodded. 'He did. And he said that you and

Reynard had a one-night stand. Is that true?'

Lucille dissolved into tears again and Becca shot Raven a look of despair. She knew now why he had dumped this interview on her. She waited patiently while Lucille dabbed at her eyes and blew her nose.

When she had calmed down again, she continued. 'Raj and I were in a relationship. We were really happy together, but he was hardly ever around. He was always studying. I'm not saying that was an excuse, but it was a contributing factor. Anyway, Reynard and I were both lonely and one night after we'd had too much to drink, well, one thing led to another. Reynard could be really persuasive. It was hard to say no to him.'

'What was Raj's reaction?'

Lucille slumped in her chair, her voice dropping to a whisper. 'He never got over it. I tried it make it up to him. I told him it was just a one-off, and that I totally regretted it. I begged him to forgive me, but it was like he'd closed his heart to me. He was never the same again, and before long he told me it was over.'

For the first time in the interview, Raven asked a question. 'How did Raj find out about the affair?'

Lucille's face hardened a little. 'It was Aurora. She told him.'

Becca raised an eyebrow. This shed fresh light on the affair. If Lucille blamed Aurora for precipitating her break-up with Raj, might she still have held a grudge ten years on? Might Lucille, in fact, have blamed both Aurora and Reynard, and hated them because of that?

A knock on the door of the interview room interrupted her chain of thought. The door opened and Sergeant Fields poked his head inside. 'Could I have a quick word?'

'Of course.' Becca rose from her chair and went to see what was up.

The sergeant was carrying an object in a sealed evidence bag. 'We recovered this from the beach close to where the attack took place last night. Forensics have given it a once-over, but they couldn't recover any prints or

DNA.'

'What is it?' Becca took the bag from him and held it up to the light. One look was enough to tell her exactly what it contained. A cigarette lighter, its distinctive chrome casing inscribed with a pentagram.

'You can let Dr Sandhu go now,' she told Fields. 'We won't be needing him any longer.'

CHAPTER 23

It was too early to stop to eat, and Jess was in no hurry to catch up with Dinsdale. They'd arranged to meet by the fish and chip shop for lunch, but Jess figured she still had time to spare before she would be missed.

Instead of turning onto the harbourside, she carried on across the swing bridge into the eastern half of town. Alexander Rigby's jet shop was here on Church Street. As she walked past, she slowed down just enough to take a peek through the window. There was no one inside and the sign on the door said *Closed*.

She carried on past, turning off at the foot of the one hundred and-ninety-nine steps and onto Henrietta Street, a narrow road crammed with tiny terraced cottages. Black-clad goths were filing up and down the steps towards the church and abbey at the top of the East Cliff, and through a gap between the houses she caught a glimpse of the East Pier. The end of the pier was swathed in thin mist, but a flash from the lighthouse showed its location. A second flash from across the short mouth of the harbour revealed its twin. With a shiver she continued along the street until the cottages ran out. Now she was walking along the line of the coast, just a railing separating her from the beach. To her right, cliffs rose sharply, forming a steep and jagged barrier against the might of the North Sea winds.

She followed a path down to the pier and set off along it, gathering her parka around her against the chill.

The pier formed a divide between two waters. To her left, the slow-moving estuary met the salt of the sea within the tranquil confines of the harbour. To her right, the maritime realm was altogether wilder and untamed. Even today, with the wind calm and barely ruffling her long hair, fierce waves beat relentlessly against the wall of the pier. Spray flew into her face, and with every step she felt as if she was leaving the safety of land behind and setting out into a savage and violent territory. Rocks broke the surface in the lull between waves – sharp, black and treacherous.

What on earth had driven Nathan Rigby to venture out here during a storm?

With mounting trepidation she continued along the pier. The mist grew thicker the further she went from the shore, and she slowed her pace, terrified of stepping off the edge and plunging into those furious waters. The rhythmic blinking of the eastern lighthouse guided her, but it seemed an untrustworthy guide, more likely to lure her to her death like a will-o-wisp than lead her to safety.

Her fear crystallised as she reached the foot of the lighthouse and saw what lay beyond – a thin and rickety-looking bridge leading out across the waves to a walkway that seemed to stretch away to oblivion. She placed one foot onto the bridge and gripped the railings, her fingers white against the metal.

All around her, the sea churned and eddied as waves dashed themselves against the solid stone of the pier. Cold fingers of mist reached out to her, beckoning her on, as the waves crashed beneath her, throwing white foam against her cheeks.

Try as she might, she couldn't bring herself to go a single step further.

It was impossible to understand why a local like

Nathan, who must have been aware of the danger, would have ventured out here so recklessly during a violent storm. He must have known the peril he was placing himself in.

And yet for some reason he'd ignored it.

Jess turned away and retreated as quickly as she could, back past the lighthouse and along the pier. She didn't stop until the mist had cleared and the roar of waves against stone had diminished. Then she stopped and lifted her gaze, her fingers trembling.

Rising precipitously above the rocks stood the cliff, the grey of St Mary's Church perched on top. The drop from clifftop to shore must have been at least a hundred feet. She imagined Mia Munroe standing on the edge of that cliff in her white wedding dress before taking the fatal step that would plunge her to the rocks below.

Shocking though that was, Mia's impulse to hurl herself into oblivion was one that Jess could understand. In the black depths of her own recent bereavement, dark thoughts had been no strangers to her either. But Jess had friends and family to comfort her, and a job that gave her meaning. Without those props, might she too have made the same choice as Mia?

With a shudder, she set off briskly along the path to the town, glad to be back on dry land.

*

Becca placed the cigarette lighter on the table in the interview room. At her side, Raven stiffened, his attention fixed on this latest piece of evidence. Becca waited for Lucille's reaction.

'My lighter,' she exclaimed. 'Where did you find it?'

She reached for it, but Becca put out a restraining hand. 'I'm afraid that this is now evidence in a police investigation. It was recovered from the beach where Aurora was attacked last night.'

Lucille scowled in consternation. 'No, that can't be right. I still have mine.' She began searching through her jacket and trouser pockets, then with a deepening frown, inside her handbag. But no amount of rummaging could produce the lighter. 'I can't find it,' she muttered.

'That's because you left it on the beach,' remarked Becca.

Lucille set her lips in a flat line. 'I didn't,' she insisted. 'I used my lighter this morning.'

'Then how do you explain it being found at the scene of the crime?'

'It can't be mine. It just looks like it.'

Becca lifted the evidence bag off the table so that the polished surface of the lighter caught the light. The distinctive pentagram etching on the front was clearly visible. 'It's a very unusual design.'

Lucille shrugged. 'I bought it at the bazaar. Anyone here for the goth weekend could have done the same.'

'We can check that,' said Raven.

'Yeah,' said Lucille. 'Why don't you do that?' Her earlier vulnerability had vanished, to be replaced by a steady determination and quiet resolve. The sobbing and theatrics had been turned off like a light switch and Becca found herself wondering, not for the first time, if they had merely been an act.

'Let's return to the events of last night,' said Becca. 'You told us that you and Aurora had an argument. What happened afterwards?'

'Aurora stormed out of the pavilion.'

'Alone?'

'I certainly had no intention of following her.'

'So what did you do?'

'I looked for Raj. But he had disappeared.'

'So no one can verify that you stayed inside.'

Lucille gave a defiant pout. 'Probably about a hundred people could, if you asked them.'

'We'll be doing just that,' said Becca. 'If you can't come up with a better alibi.'

Lucille folded her arms across her chest. 'Is this still a voluntary interview?'

Becca looked to Raven, who gave a nod. 'It can be,' he told Lucille, 'just as long as you continue to cooperate.'

'I really don't know what else you want from me,' said Lucille. 'Raj vanished. Aurora and I had a row and she went outside. Then some lunatic set her hair alight. You ought to be treating me with more sensitivity. In case you haven't realised, she's the fourth friend of mine to die in the past few years.'

Becca narrowed her eyes. 'We're well aware of that. That's precisely why you're here. But in fact Aurora wasn't really a friend, was she? You've already said she was the person who told Raj about your infidelity. When we first met you at the White Horse & Griffin you described her as a mean bitch.'

'Well,' said Lucille. 'She could be a bitch. She was so self-centred.'

'And,' continued Becca, 'you blamed Reynard for seducing you. In your mind, he and Aurora were responsible for causing your break-up with Raj.'

Lucille presented an implacable expression. 'Well, they were.'

'That gives you a clear motive for both murders, and you don't have an alibi for either.'

'I do,' insisted Lucille. 'Like I said, I was in the pavilion when Aurora died.'

'That remains to be proved,' said Becca. She glanced across at Raven to see if he was going to contribute anything or if it was all down to her.

To her surprise he scraped back his chair and stood up. 'I think we're done for now. Thank you for coming to speak to us this morning, Miss West. You're free to go, but please don't leave Whitby without first clearing it with us.'

Lucille eyed him suspiciously. 'You're letting me go?'

Raven gave her a smile. For such a miserable bastard, he really did smile a lot. 'It sounds like we have our work cut out, checking up on that cigarette lighter, and speaking to everyone who was at the pavilion last night to see if they remember you.'

CHAPTER 24

The back room of the jewellers was small but tidy. Dinsdale had expected to find a messy workshop here, filled with all the paraphernalia and detritus of the jewellery trade, but the space was just a regular office with a desktop computer, a filing cabinet and a kettle for making tea. No doubt the work of polishing and setting the stones happened elsewhere.

He was pleased to find that Alexander Rigby knew how to make a proper cup of tea. Milk and two sugars, just the way it was supposed to be. No biscuits were on offer, but it was just as well to leave room for that scone later. He took a good slurp of tea and settled back into his chair.

Alexander took a seat behind the desk, knitting his fingers together. 'So,' he prompted, 'you've got some questions for me about Nathan?'

'Aye, I do.' But Dinsdale was in no hurry to ask them. He liked to get the measure of a man before delving into the nitty gritty, and it was always useful to gather some background information first. Get them talking about themselves, that was the way to find out if they were telling the truth. 'Lived here all your life, have you?'

'Aye. Whitby born-and-bred.'

Dinsdale nodded encouragingly. 'Tell me about your shop. Is it a family business?'

He could tell he'd found the right question by the way the man's chest puffed out in response. 'It was my great-grandfather who founded this place, and it's been handed down from one generation to the next.'

Every man had a flaw, and he'd found Alexander Rigby's without much bother. *Pride*. That would be his downfall.

'Does it all belong to you now, then?'

Puff that chest up. Let him boast.

'My parents are dead, so yes, it's all mine.'

And now comes the needle. Prick that chest and watch it deflate.

'What about your brother? Did he own a share?'

Alexander scowled in irritation at mention of his brother. 'Nathan owned half, but in name only. I would have paid him a salary if he'd pulled his weight, but I was the one who did all the work. The fact is, he was never interested in jet, even though it was in his blood. I thought he might change, given time, but he never did. He was just a big kid at heart.'

A big kid. So Alexander had looked down on his younger brother. Had thought him a waste of space.

'What happened to his share of the business after he died?'

'Nathan died without a will, so his half came to me.'

Dinsdale made a mental note of that, taking another swig of tea to collect his thoughts. When money changed hands, there was always motive. Perhaps Raven hadn't been barking up the wrong tree when he suspected foul play in the brother's death.

'So what did Nathan do for a living if he wasn't pulling his weight here?'

Alexander gave a dismissive wave of his hand. 'This and that. He tried his hand at being an artist.'

'And how did that work out?' asked Dinsdale, although

there was no need to ask. Alexander wasn't holding back on how little he'd thought of this brother.

'Not too well. Trouble was, Nathan had no head for business. He just painted whatever he fancied, hoping someone would buy it, but it was all too weird. Most people just want a nice picture they can hang above the fireplace, don't they?'

'That's very true.' Despite the man's boastfulness, Dinsdale was warming to the jeweller. He liked a man with his feet on the ground. Even though the black gemstones he sold were a little too dark for his own taste, there was clearly a market for that kind of thing, and Alexander's business seemed to be doing well enough. He decided to probe a little further. 'How close were you to your brother? There was quite an age gap between you, wasn't there?'

'Twelve years,' said Alexander. 'We didn't have much in common, to be honest. I went straight into the family business after leaving school, but Nathan wanted to go off to university. He was the first from the family to go, and I was proud to see him do well, but that's where he got a lot of his funny ideas from. Some of the people he met there!'

Dinsdale could easily imagine. 'You knew his student friends?'

'Oh, sure. They used to meet up in Whitby regularly. I tried to get along with them, especially Mia, since she was Nathan's girlfriend. She was a sweet girl. Too good for Nathan, if I'm being truthful. But the others he hung out with... I can't say I liked them.'

Having met some of Nathan's friends himself, Dinsdale quite concurred. He drained the dregs of his tea and set the empty mug on the desk. 'At university, Nathan and his friends formed a group calling themselves the Order of the Dragon. What was all that about, do you know?'

Alexander held up his hands. 'Typical Nathan. It was supposed to be a secret society dedicated to the dark side. That sort of nonsense appealed to him.'

'Apparently they all had dragon tattoos,' said Dinsdale. 'Was there any more to it than that?'

'Not to my knowledge.'

'I see.' Dinsdale leaned forwards, ready to get stuck into the meat of the interview. The rest had been warm-up. Building rapport. Encouraging Alexander to believe they were on the same team. This was where things got serious. 'Tell me about how he died.'

Alexander seemed to pick up on the change in tone. He sat up straighter in his chair. 'Don't you already know all about that from the police report?'

'I'd like to hear it from you.'

'Okay. It was January, two years ago. In the middle of a violent storm, Nathan went out onto the East Pier and was washed into the sea.'

'Now, why would he do a mad thing like that?'

Alexander shrugged. 'It was the kind of thing Nathan did. It probably appealed to his artistic temperament.'

'I expect so.' Dinsdale nodded his head in sympathy before putting the boot in. 'It suited you, though. Didn't it?'

Alexander blanched. 'What do you mean?'

'What I mean,' said Dinsdale, in his element now that the mask was off and the thumbscrews were being tightened, 'was that you benefitted directly from his death, since you inherited his half of the business. You've already told me you didn't get along with your brother and that he never helped out in the shop. He was just, if you'll pardon the expression, a deadweight.'

Alexander's eyes narrowed. *Fear? Anger? Both?* 'Are you suggesting I played some part in his death?'

'That's exactly what I'm suggesting. And what's your response?'

'My response is that the police investigated thoroughly and concluded that it was accidental drowning.'

'Hmm.' It was a good enough answer and Dinsdale couldn't find any holes to pick in it. Probably Raven was wrong after all, and there was nothing more to Nathan's death than a straightforward accident.

Folk drowned all the time. The sea was unforgiving.

That scone waiting in the café next door was starting to seem much more appealing than dragging this interview out much longer.

'I don't suppose you found any sort of note after his death?'

'If you mean a suicide note, then no. Suicide wasn't Nathan's style.'

'Hmm. And where were you at the time he died?'

'I was here, working in the shop, as usual. Mia called to say Nathan had gone out in the storm and hadn't returned home. She reported him missing, and later that night I had a phone call from the police. A body had been recovered from the rocks beyond the pier. They asked me to go and identify it.' He swallowed. 'It was Nathan.'

The scone was beckoning and Dinsdale rose to his feet, eager to be on his way. He was about to leave when he stopped and turned, one final nagging question demanding to be asked. It was best to get it off his chest, so he could enjoy his elevenses with a clear conscience.

'Was there anyone who might have wanted to harm Nathan?'

Alexander turned his face away. 'No. I don't think so.'

'No?' Dinsdale studied the man's profile intently. He had an instinct, honed from forty years of being on the receiving end of bare-faced lies, and that instinct was flapping a big red flag and blowing loudly on a trumpet. 'You told me Nathan didn't earn very much. Did he owe money to someone?'

'Money? I don't know what you mean.' Alexander shook his head as if that might make his problems go away.

But they were only just beginning. The jeweller might have been a good businessman, but he was a useless liar.

Dinsdale lowered his bum reluctantly to his seat. 'Yes,' he said. 'Money. How much did Nathan owe and who did he owe it to?'

That scone, it seemed, was going to have to wait.

CHAPTER 25

Thick grey mist was rolling off the sea again when Raven returned to the pavilion with Becca.

The crime scene looked completely different in the daytime. There were no emergency vehicles disturbing the peace with their shrill cries, and the only flashing lights were the steady blinking of the lighthouses that marked the end of the two piers. The crowds around the pavilion had long since dispersed, the beach itself was empty apart from a few dogwalkers, and even the police cordon had gone.

The tide had washed the sands clean.

Now the stark horror of the previous night had been replaced by a sense of quiet dignity as mourners made their solemn way down from the promenade bearing bouquets of flowers. One by one, or in pairs or small groups, they left their tributes next to the colourful beach huts to mark the place where Aurora Highsmith had met her death. The black-clad goths who had come to pay their respects may not have known the victim personally, but she was one of their own.

Two of the town's visitors, however, were noticeable by their absence.

'What if Lucille or Raj make a run for it?' asked Becca.

'Then we'll know we should have arrested them,' said Raven. 'But we had no option. There were no reasonable grounds to detain them. Even Sergeant Fields and his biscuits weren't going to keep them at the station forever. Besides, if Lucille's alibi turns out to be solid, we need to widen our net.'

They had already established, with the help of the local constabulary, that Lucille had been telling the truth about the cigarette lighters. Although she was unable to explain what had happened to hers, a couple of bobbies had paid a visit to the pavilion and verified that lighters of that same design were on sale at a stall in the bazaar. Interestingly, it was Eve Franklin, the stallholder who had shopped Reynard to the police over his illegal taxidermy, who sold the lighters and other accessories as a sideline to her artwork and candles. She had confirmed selling several of the lighters during the past few days, but claimed to have no idea who had bought them.

'Well,' countered Becca, 'I just hope you know what you're doing. This latest idea of yours is a crazy longshot.'

Raven was inclined to agree with her. 'Crazy longshots are one of my specialities.'

'True.'

Before leaving Whitby police station, he'd called Tony and asked him for a full list of everyone who had presented a ticket for the concert before the venue had been closed following Aurora's death. There had been hundreds of names on the list, but perhaps one of them might have recognised Lucille's photo and could confirm she had been inside at the time of the attack.

It was possible, too, that one of them might have noticed something that could help to identify the killer. It would be an enormous task. Every single one of the hundreds of concertgoers would need to be interviewed.

But perhaps there was a quicker way forward.

The media.

Despite his previous encounters with Liz Larkin, and

Gillian's warning not to go near the media again, Raven hoped that an appeal for witnesses to come forward might work. It would yield quicker results than waiting for the local police to work through all the witness interviews, and a full reconstruction of the crime would take too long to organise.

Swallowing his misgivings, he had called Liz Larkin.

She had readily agreed to broadcast a second interview to help jog people's memories. It had been her suggestion to do it outside the pavilion, explaining that an appeal from the scene of the murder would be most likely to generate a response.

'Although,' Becca pointed out, 'you might just generate a whole load of nuisance calls.'

'I'll take the risk,' said Raven. 'And look, I've come prepared.' He showed her a page of scrawled notes he'd made, just as his course instructor had told him to. This time he wouldn't allow Liz to conduct a free-ranging interview and ambush him with unexpected questions. It would be an appeal to the public to come forward with information. Nothing else.

Take control of the narrative.

'Just be careful,' warned Becca. 'She knows a lot more about how to do this than someone who's just come back from a three-day media awareness course. Look out, here she comes now.'

Liz Larkin was just as polished as always, her smile radiant despite the foggy weather, her blonde hair glinting even beneath stony skies. Today she was wearing an olive green trouser suit that matched her eyes.

'Remember,' hissed Becca. 'Just stick to the script.'

'Got it,' Raven assured her.

Liz trotted over to him in her heels. 'DCI Raven, we meet again.'

He acknowledged her with a polite incline of his chin. 'Liz.'

It seemed that she was unable to resist placing a manicured hand against his arm. 'The crew's ready to film.

Have you got your statement ready?'

Raven brandished his piece of paper like a charm to ward her off. He had already laid down the terms of his appearance when he called her to arrange the broadcast.

She withdrew her fingers and gave him a tight-lipped smile. 'If you'd like to expand your appeal into a full interview then we'll have time to air it on tonight's show.'

Raven almost felt sorry for her as he crushed her hope. 'There will be no interview,' he said. 'Just the appeal.'

The man with the headphones and clipboard appeared and began to boss them about. 'Okay, guys, let's get the camera rolling. I don't like the look of those storm clouds heading this way.'

Raven looked out across the sea and saw dark clouds gathering. A storm was brewing – one that would soon blow away the mist and fog. He took up position while the crew checked the light and sound levels.

'Okay, we're ready,' called the director eventually. 'Action!'

Raven referred one last time to his notes, then looked into the camera and spoke in a steady voice.

Stay calm and stick to the facts.

'Yesterday evening, a brutal and violent murder took place on the beach here at Whitby. Officers and paramedics were called to the scene, but despite their best efforts, a twenty-nine-year-old woman who had been at the concert in the pavilion was declared dead after having her hair set alight. This incident follows the recent murder of a man at the abbey. We are appealing for anyone in the vicinity of the pavilion on Friday night who feels they may have seen or heard anything suspicious to get in touch with North Yorkshire Police as soon as possible. We are particularly interested in sightings of a figure dressed in black seen leaving the scene. Meanwhile, our thoughts are with the family and friends of the two victims. Thank you.'

'Cut!' shouted the director.

Raven looked to Becca who gave him a big thumbs up. But it was Liz who was immediately at his side to congratulate him. 'Well done, DCI Raven. A very polished presentation. It's almost like you've been practising.'

If that was intended to be a dig at his previous disastrous performance, he chose to ignore it. 'Thank you.'

'I hope your appeal generates a good response.'

'I hope so too. Now if you don't mind, I have to get back to my inquiry.'

'Of course you do.' And yet she lingered, seeming unwilling to leave him.

'Was there something else?'

'Well...' Her eyes sparkled. 'You do realise that you're living inside a gothic mystery?'

'I'm sorry?'

'Yes, don't you see?' She laughed. 'I should explain that I studied English at university. That's what started me on my career in journalism. It strikes me that these murders have a lot in common with gothic literature.'

Raven could see Becca making her way towards him. He should be off already. He didn't have time for nonsense.

But Liz was on a roll. 'Let's go through the various elements.' She started counting on her fingers. 'Firstly, you've got not just one but two macabre deaths, one of them quite possibly linked to an occult ritual.'

'There was no occult ritual,' he insisted, 'just a staging of the murder scene.'

Liz carried on, undeterred by his objection. 'Then there's the mysterious dark stranger.' She lifted a third finger. 'And the weather effects – first mist, and now a storm on its way.'

Raven lifted his gaze to the far horizon. There was no denying that the weather was worsening.

'Then there are the monsters.'

Raven shook his head dismissively. 'We haven't got any of those.'

A smile flitted across Liz's red lips. 'Not literally, but look around you. There are people dressed as vampires, witches, hooded figures, skeletons, even someone in a demonic mask.'

'I suppose so,' said Raven, humouring her. Liz was right that some of the costumes worn by the festival goers were quite bizarre and scary.

Her hand brushed his arm once more. 'And let's not forget a brooding hero.'

Raven laughed. 'Now I think you're mocking me.'

'Not at all. Think of me as your secret admirer. The only trope you're missing is a black dog.'

Her comment caught him off-guard. 'A black dog?'

'Every good gothic tale needs one. The dog is a symbol of supernatural evil and an omen of death.'

Raven looked to Becca for help. She had been stopped in her tracks by the director, who was questioning her and taking notes on his clipboard.

'What happened to your face?' Liz raised her arm, brushing his cheek with her hand. 'That graze looks painful.'

The touch of her fingers against his skin was like electricity. Pain or pleasure, he couldn't tell which.

He caught her gently by the wrist and pulled her hand away. 'If you don't mind,' he told her, 'I really have to be going now.'

★

The restaurant was right in the heart of Scarborough and Hannah found it easily enough with the help of her phone. It was a classy kind of place with a relaxed ambience. The lighting was subdued, and guitar music played softly in the background.

It certainly didn't have the kind of bright and noisy student vibe that Hannah was used to. The diners looked to be mostly older couples, enjoying wine and conversation with their meals.

There was no one here who looked likely to be her dinner date.

Not that she had any clear idea what Ellie Earnshaw

might look like. All she knew was that Ellie shared a flat with her dad's sergeant, Becca Shawcross. And since Hannah had never met Becca either, that didn't give her much to go on.

However, none of the people sitting at the tables were women dining alone, and not one of them paid her any attention as she lingered awkwardly inside the doorway. She wondered if she'd got the wrong place or the wrong time. She checked her phone, re-reading the text that Ellie had sent her earlier, but there was no mistake. She was debating whether to send a message to find out if Ellie was on her way, when the manager came over to greet her.

'Hi, you must be Hannah. May I take your coat?'

The man was solidly built, with a pronounced forehead and steel-grey hair. His lips were thin, but his smile was broad and there was a twinkle in his eyes.

'Oh,' said Hannah, startled that he appeared to know who she was. 'Right, thanks.' She removed her jacket and handed it to him.

He hung it on a stand and ushered her to an empty table by the window, drawing out a chair for her to sit down. 'I'm sure that Ellie will be here any minute. Can I get you a drink while you wait?'

'Um...' Hannah wasn't sure what to say.

'It's on the house.'

'Really?'

The man seemed suddenly to realise she had no idea who he was. He slapped his big palm against his forehead. 'Ellie hasn't told you, has she?'

'Er, told me what?'

'I'm her father, Keith Earnshaw. This is my restaurant.'

'Oh, I see.' Hannah smiled as everything became clear. 'But how did you know who I was?'

He cocked his large head to one side. 'You're Tom Raven's daughter?'

'Yes.'

'I knew the Raven family growing up. You've got the look of them, all right.'

'Have I?' Hannah wondered what exactly "the look" was.

'Oh yes,' said Keith. 'You look like a young Joan Raven.'

'Do I? Actually I don't know who that is.'

'Joan would have been your grandmother.'

Hannah recalled the black-and-white photograph she had found in the house on Quay Street. The woman in the photo had looked kind and pretty. If that was "the look", Hannah was glad to have it. She was about to ask Keith what else he knew about the Raven family when the door flew open and a young woman burst in.

'Dad!'

'Ellie.'

The newcomer was in her mid-twenties with shoulder-length hair dyed a vivid red. She was dressed in a riot of colours and patterns with a paisley shirt over checked trousers. Knee-length boots, leather gloves and a pink beret completed the outfit. She seemed outrageously sophisticated and chic.

Ellie hugged her father and then came over to the table to greet Hannah with a kiss on each cheek. 'Sorry I'm late, has Dad been looking after you?'

'Very well, thanks,' said Hannah.

'Not too well,' said Ellie with a wink. 'I see you don't yet have a drink in your hands.'

'I was just offering one,' said Keith.

'What would you like?' asked Ellie. 'A glass of wine? Or a cocktail?'

'I don't mind,' said Hannah.

'Let's be wicked and have both. We'll kick off with a vodka espresso to get us going, then have a bottle of white with our food.'

'Coming up,' said Keith. 'I'll leave you ladies to peruse the menu.'

Ellie took a seat, then reached out and squeezed Hannah's hand. 'Fathers, eh? I hear that you've been abandoned by yours.'

It would have been easy to agree, but Hannah felt obliged to put up some defence of her dad. 'He hasn't abandoned me, exactly. He's just busy with work.'

Ellie nodded vigorously and dropped her voice. 'Becca told me about it. Two murders!'

Hannah hoped Ellie wouldn't want to ask about the murder she'd witnessed. It was one thing to give a formal statement to the police about what she'd seen, but she wasn't ready to talk to anyone else about it. It felt too personal, too private. She still hadn't fully processed the experience and come to terms with it.

Ellie seemed to pick up on her reticence. 'Don't worry, we're not going to be talking about any of that tonight. We are strictly here to have a good time!'

'Ladies.' As if on cue, Keith appeared with the cocktails and set them down on the table before retreating discreetly.

'Cheers!' said Ellie, clinking glasses with Hannah.

'Cheers!' The drink was potent, and Hannah took just a sip before setting it down. 'Your dad's great, isn't he?' she asked, keen to divert attention away from her own family and to find out a little more about Ellie's.

'Sure. We're very close. I never knew my mum, so Dad brought me up by himself.'

'I'm sorry.'

'Don't be,' said Ellie, running a hand through her scarlet hair. 'You can't miss what you never had, can you?'

'I guess not.' Hannah didn't dare ask what had happened to Ellie's mum. Instead, she tried to picture what it might be like to be so close to your father. So close, in fact, that he was everything a parent could be. She found herself liking the idea. 'So what do you do for a job?' she asked Ellie.

'Me? I run a brewery.'

Hannah lifted both eyebrows in surprise. 'You *run* a brewery? As in, you're the manager?'

Ellie laughed. 'I know, right? I'm far too young to be in charge of anything, let alone a brewery. To tell you the truth, sometimes I can hardly believe it myself. I'll tell you later how it came about. It's a bit of a long story.'

The evening was turning out to be full of surprises, and Ellie seemed to be quite a character. Hannah couldn't wait to hear more about her extraordinary life.

Keith arrived, bringing a bottle of white wine and some small plates of bread and olives. '*Bon appetit!*' Hannah didn't recall asking for anything, but perhaps this was how Keith treated all his diners.

'So,' said Ellie, tearing the bread apart and taking a bite. 'I hear you're a student?'

'I'm in my final year at Exeter.'

'Cool. And have you got a boyfriend? Or a girlfriend?'

'Nothing like that.' There had been a short-lived relationship during Hannah's first year but it wasn't something she liked to dwell on. 'How about you?'

Ellie glugged her cocktail and filled Hannah's wine glass. 'Far too busy. But I don't live alone. I share my apartment with your dad's sergeant, Becca.'

At mention of the mysterious Becca, Hannah's interest piqued. 'So what's she like?'

'Great. She's a couple of years older than me. She was engaged to my cousin Sam for ages, but... that all got very complicated.'

'So Becca's single now?'

'Yes.'

Hannah hoped she'd find out more about this young unattached woman her dad spent so much time with. Perhaps they'd even get to meet sometime. Her thoughts turned to Dante, and she began to formulate an idea. Although she'd promised to stay in Scarborough for the day, surely it would be safe to go to the gig Dante had mentioned the following day, especially if Ellie came with her. 'Are you doing anything tomorrow afternoon?'

'Nothing planned, why?'

'Do you want to come to see a band with me at the Abbey Brewery in Whitby?'

'Sure, why not?' Ellie downed the rest of her cocktail

and gave a grin. 'That sounds like fun.'

CHAPTER 26

The room at Whitby police station that Raven had commandeered wasn't half as big as the incident room in Scarborough but it would have to do. Sergeant Mike Fields had ferreted out a portable whiteboard from a storeroom and set it up at the front of the room. It was a bit dusty, but would serve. Raven stood before the board now, his team gathered together and ready to give an update. It had been a long day, and he was hoping to hear that real progress had been made.

They were all present – Becca, Jess and Dinsdale – and before starting, Raven dialled Tony's number in Scarborough and put him on speakerphone so he could listen to what was said and make his own contribution to the meeting. 'Can you hear me, Tony?'

'Loud and clear, sir.'

'Good,' said Raven. 'So, who wants to go first?'

'Why don't you start?' suggested Dinsdale. 'Since it seems that you've done most of the running today.'

'All right,' Raven agreed with reluctance. He was curious to find out what Dinsdale had been doing all day, although the chip fat stains on his tie told their own story.

But it was clear from the tone of his question that he believed he'd been sidelined, and there was no point antagonising him further. 'We started with a visit to the hotel where Aurora Highsmith was staying. It seemed that she'd changed her reservation and was planning to check out today.'

'A pity for her she didn't go sooner,' said Dinsdale.

'Quite. We searched her room and found this postcard.' Raven stuck a colour copy of the front and back of the card on the board and waited for Jess and Dinsdale to take their first look.

'*The Bridesmaid* by John Everett Millais,' said Jess. 'The woman with the long hair is obviously meant to be Aurora. She and Lucille were going to be bridesmaids at Mia's wedding. And what does the writing say? *In life she craved beauty; now she sleeps in beautiful death.*'

'The murderer has clearly departed from their vampire theme,' said Raven. 'It seems that in both murders the manner of death is related to some characteristic of the victim.'

'Reynard took the lives of animals in order to carry out his craft,' said Becca, 'and so the killer took his blood. Aurora was obsessed with her appearance and in particular her hair, so the killer used that as a weapon against her.'

'These killings sound like acts of vengeance to me, Raven,' remarked Dinsdale. 'Personal grudges. A vendetta.'

Raven was inclined to agree with the assessment. 'It's clear they're not random acts of violence. The postcards prove that the victims were known to the murderer, and the messages on the cards are clearly meant to explain the significance of the methods used to kill them. Though why the perpetrator felt the need to broadcast his purpose to the world isn't yet clear.'

'Some kind of self-justification?' suggested Jess.

'Self-aggrandisement, more like,' sneered Dinsdale. 'Someone trying to massage their own ego and demonstrate how clever they are.'

'The most obvious suspects appear to be Dr Raj Sandhu and Lucille West,' said Becca.

'Becca and I interviewed Raj and Lucille again today in the light of Aurora's death,' said Raven. 'We unearthed a rift in the group of four friends – a *ménage à trois* – you might call it, although all four were involved in some way. Becca, would you care to explain?'

'Sure.' Becca moved to join him at the front of the room and wrote the four names on the whiteboard: Reynard Blackthorn, Aurora Highsmith, Raj Sandhu, Lucille West. 'At university, Raj and Lucille were a couple. They seem to have been very close, but then Lucille had an affair with Reynard. Just a drunken one-night stand, according to her. The way she talks about it she seems to blame Reynard rather than accepting any responsibility herself. In any case, Aurora told Raj what had happened and the relationship came to an end. Lucille begged Raj to forgive her, but he never fully did.'

'So,' said Raven, picking up the thread, 'following the vengeance hypothesis that Derek suggested' – he waved his hand in Dinsdale's direction and was rewarded with a nod of appreciation – 'this gives both Lucille and Raj clear motives for the murders. Lucille held Reynard responsible for seducing her, and blamed Aurora for telling Raj what she'd done. Her inability to accept responsibility for her own actions fits the pattern of self-justification displayed by the messages on the postcards. Similarly, Raj hated Reynard for destroying his relationship with Lucille, and resented Aurora for bringing him the bad news. In this light, the messages on the postcards take on new meaning.'

Tony's voice came over the telephone line. '"*As he took the life from others, so it was drawn from him.*"'

'Thanks, Tony. Reynard didn't just take the lives of animals – he also stole the thing that was most important to Raj and Lucille. Similarly, the reference to Aurora's vanity indicates that her reason for telling Raj about Reynard and Lucille may have been selfish, perhaps related to jealousy.'

'But could it really be as simple as that?' interrupted Jess. 'Why go to such lengths to take revenge over a broken relationship?'

'These things run deep,' said Raven. An image of Lisa came to him, beautiful as always, yet treacherous. He had done his best to forgive her adultery, but in the end it had proven impossible. Divorce had been the solution, but under different circumstances, might he have nurtured a loathing so black it could have driven him to commit murder?

Knowing the pockets of darkness that lurked in every human soul, he couldn't easily dismiss the notion.

'And remember,' said Becca, 'how close this group was. They even had matching dragon tattoos as a sign of their allegiance to one another.' She continued her summary of the latest interviews. 'Neither Raj nor Lucille have alibis for the time of Aurora's death. We know they were in the pavilion shortly before the murder, but after Aurora left, the other two became separated. Moreover, a cigarette lighter recovered from the scene of the crime is identical to one that Lucille used.'

'So Lucille is our prime suspect?' asked Jess. 'How does she explain the lighter?'

'She claims to have lost hers, and in fact the same lighters are being sold by Eve Franklin at the goth bazaar, so we can't say for sure that the lighter used to set Aurora's hair on fire belonged to Lucille.'

'Moreover,' added Raven, 'the method used to kill Reynard – exsanguination – points the finger firmly in Raj's direction. So we have to regard both Raj and Lucille as our key suspects.

Tony's voice came over the phone again. 'What about this Eve Franklin? She reported Reynard to the police for illegal taxidermy and was responsible for a hate campaign on social media. She must be a suspect in Reynard's murder, and if she sold the lighters, we can't rule out the possibility that she killed Aurora.'

'But why would she have done that?' asked Raven.

'Perhaps she had some personal reason,' suggested Becca. 'Eve seems like the kind of person who would harbour a grudge.'

'True,' conceded Raven, writing her name on the board. 'And we mustn't forget the two other members of the Order of the Dragon, Mia Munroe and Nathan Rigby. Their deaths are suspicious and may be related.' He turned to Dinsdale and Jess. 'Now let's hear how you two got on.'

'I'll start, if you like,' said Jess, full of her usual enthusiasm. 'This morning I went to the clothing shop where Mia worked and spoke to the shop owner, Vivienne.'

'That would be Vivienne's Vamp & Victoriana?' asked Raven.

'Yes. Vivienne confirmed what we already knew, that after Nathan drowned, Mia spent a year in mourning and then threw herself off the East Cliff wearing her wedding dress. But Vivienne did say that Mia had reported being followed by a mysterious stranger dressed in black during the weeks leading up to her death.'

'A mysterious stranger?' The mysterious figure Raven had seen lurking at the abbey ruins came to mind, as well as Hannah's report of a dark figure leaving the beach immediately after Aurora's death. It was becoming harder to shrug off Liz Larkin's remark about gothic mysteries always involving the presence of a dark, mysterious stranger. 'Couldn't Vivienne have been more specific?' he grumbled. 'Half the people in Whitby right now are dressed in black.'

'No, sorry,' said Jess. 'But afterwards I walked over to the East Pier and out as far as the lighthouse. I wanted to check out the place where Nathan drowned.'

'And?'

Jess shuddered. 'I can't understand why someone who'd lived in Whitby all their life would have gone onto the pier during a storm. It's pretty wild out there. If a big wave came, there'd be nothing to stop you from being washed over the edge. It's almost as if... I don't know... he did it on purpose.'

'You mean he wanted to die?' asked Raven.

Jess gave a shrug of her shoulders. 'I don't know. It just seems very strange, that's all.'

'All right,' said Raven. 'What about you, Derek?'

Dinsdale stirred himself back to life, brushing what looked like cake crumbs from the lapels of his suit. 'I paid a visit to Alexander Rigby, Nathan's brother, at his jet shop. Just like you asked me to.'

Raven sensed that Dinsdale was still nursing a grudge about being asked to undertake such a mundane interview. 'And did you turn up anything useful?'

'As a matter of fact, I did.' Dinsdale was looking rather pleased with himself. 'I must say, Raven, it's just as well you asked a senior detective to conduct that interview.' He directed a look in Jess's direction. 'A less experienced one might have missed the crucial signs.'

Jess flushed pink and looked away.

Raven gave a sigh. The DI had clearly uncovered something, but there was little hope he would simply get on and say it. Instead, Raven resigned himself to Dinsdale dragging out his moment of glory.

'Oh yes,' continued Dinsdale. 'I dug out two interesting pieces of information. First of all, following Nathan's death, Alexander inherited his half of the jewellery business, so that gives him a clear motive for his brother's murder.'

Raven narrowed his eyes. 'You're suggesting that Nathan didn't drown accidentally?'

'That would tie in with what young Jess had to say, wouldn't it?' said Dinsdale. 'But it's only a hypothesis. I don't have any evidence yet.'

'Okay,' said Raven. 'What was the other piece of information?'

At this, Dinsdale really did look like the cat that had swallowed the cream. 'It seems that at the time of his death, Nathan Rigby was up to his eyeballs in debt.'

'And do we know who to?'

'A loan shark by the name of Donovan Cross.'

Raven pondered the new information. 'And you think that Nathan's death might be related to this debt?'

'It's worth following up, don't you agree? Never mind all this goth nonsense – dragons and mysterious strangers and what-not. Let's go after a good old-fashioned villain instead.'

'All right.' There might well be something in Dinsdale's lead, and if not, it would be a good way to push him to the sidelines of the investigation without ruffling his feathers. 'Why don't you and Tony look into this Donovan Cross. Tony, you dig out any background material you can find on him, and Derek, you track him down and see what he has to say for himself.'

'Very good, sir,' said Tony, and Dinsdale nodded his consent.

'What about the dog?' asked Becca.

'Ah yes, the black dog.' The symbol of supernatural evil and an omen of death, if you could believe a word that Liz Larkin had to say. The dog that had barked outside Mrs Harker's guest house at the time of Reynard's abduction. The dog that had almost savaged Raven at the abbey. The very same dog that witnesses had reported fleeing from the beach.

Or perhaps there were a lot of black dogs in Whitby.

'Any news from forensics on that hair that was found on Reynard's body, Tony?'

'Actually, sir, there is. I was going to mention it. It's been confirmed as a dog hair. Now they're trying to identify the breed.'

The news confirmed Raven's misgivings. The black dog was part of the story whether he liked it or not. Wherever the murderer went, the dog went too.

'Is the dog a suspect, then?' queried Dinsdale, his voice thick with sarcasm.

Raven chose to ignore the remark. He had to concede though, that there was something unnatural about the animal's appearances. Although the dog and the mysterious stranger seemed inseparable, they had never once been sighted together. It was almost as if they were one and the same; that human could become beast at will, much like a certain fictional vampire had done on landing at Whitby.

He shook the notion from his head. He was tired, that was all, and Liz Larkin had a lot to answer for, planting the seed of supernatural mystery in his imagination. As if he didn't have enough to worry about already.

'There's a matter that concerns me,' he told the others. 'Raj and Lucille are strong suspects but if we're right about this being a personal vendetta, then they're also potential victims. I think an officer should be assigned to watch over them for the remainder of their time in Whitby. Becca, can you ask Sergeant Fields to arrange it? And one last thing – Tony, has there been any response to my public appeal for information?'

He really hoped there had. If he'd endured an encounter with Liz Larkin for nothing, he'd be more than a little annoyed.

'Sir, we've been inundated. The phone lines haven't stopped ringing since the broadcast went out. Most of them are crank calls about headless horsemen and that sort of thing. But there is a photographer who has come forward with information. You should probably speak to him in person. I can send you his details.'

'You do that, Tony,' said Raven. A photographer he could handle; headless horsemen were another thing entirely.

CHAPTER 27

The Board Inn was a cosy pub at the end of Church Street right opposite the Whitby Jet Heritage Centre. Raven was glad to get into the warm interior and away from the brisk wind that had begun to blow. That storm he'd spotted rolling in earlier was poised to break at any moment. Already the air felt heavy with moisture.

The photographer was easy to spot among the goths in their assorted costumes and headgear. He was sitting at a window table with a professional camera equipped with a formidable lens.

Raven approached. 'Mr Thewlis?' Tony had sent the photographer's details, and a quick phone call had secured this hasty meeting.

'Call me George,' said the photographer, rising from his seat and extending a hand. 'And you must be DCI Raven.'

'Guilty as charged.'

The man gave a weak smile. He'd clearly encountered police humour before. 'Can I get you a drink?' His own pint glass was nearly empty.

'I should buy you one,' said Raven.

'I won't say no.'

Raven made his way over to the bar and returned with a pint of beer and a glass of mineral water.

George accepted the drink gladly and took a hearty mouthful, wiping his mouth with the back of his hand. 'I needed that! It's thirsty work being on your feet all day, but I never miss the goth weekend. I've been coming here for years and always get loads of great photos. When people have gone to that much effort to dress up, they're happy to have their pictures taken.'

'You're a professional?'

'Freelance. I sell what I can to various rags.' He shrugged, as if he found the idea distasteful. 'A man's got to make a living somehow.'

Raven didn't care how George Thewlis earned a living. But he was interested in why he'd contacted the police following Raven's televised appeal. 'You told my colleague you had something that may be relevant to the murder inquiry?'

'Sure,' said George. 'I was enjoying a bite to eat in another pub' – the photographer's day seemed to consist of little more than a succession of visits to pubs, punctuated with a smattering of photography – 'when you popped up on the telly asking if anyone had seen anything suspicious near the pavilion yesterday evening. Just so happens I did.'

'Yes?' said Raven.

The man reached for his camera and switched it on. 'I started going through my photos from last night and I found something interesting. Take a look.' He selected a photo, zoomed into it, and handed the camera to Raven.

The image on the screen was dark and grainy and Raven strained to make it out. The photographer had captured an image of the beach immediately after Aurora's hair had been set alight. The sky was as dark as the sand and sea, and a thin layer of mist muddied the detail. But there, in the centre of the image was a bright torch of orange where the victim's hair had caught fire.

'Can I zoom in any closer?' asked Raven.

'It's already at max,' said George. 'I wasn't intending to take a picture of the beach at all, it's just in the background of another shot. That's why the focus isn't sharp.'

But there was enough here for Raven to work with. There, lit by the halo of Aurora's hair, was Hannah. And off to one side, moving quickly away, was a dark blur.

Raven studied the image, trying to make out details. A fleeing figure in a black hooded cloak, their face covered by a mask. 'What is that costume they're wearing?' he wondered aloud.

'I think it's a plague doctor's outfit.'

Raven's breath quickened. He stared hard, seeking clarity in the infernal darkness. The outline of the plague doctor's mask gleamed reddish brown, made diabolical by the glow of the fire. It was the first proper sighting of the mysterious stranger. And not just an eyewitness account – an actual photograph. 'How can I get a copy of this?'

'No problem,' said George. 'Just give me your phone number and I'll send it to you now. The file contains all the metadata, so you'll be able to see the precise location and time.'

Raven gave him his number and George deftly tapped it into his phone. 'Should be with you any second.'

Raven felt his phone buzz and saw that the image had arrived as promised. 'Thanks very much, George.'

'Glad to be of help. Hope you nail the bastard.'

With a sudden start, George jerked his head and stared out of the window, his eyes growing wide with surprise.

Raven followed his gaze and saw an extraordinary sight.

A parade of goths was filing slowly past, dressed in their usual sombre attire, soundless apart from the tread of many boots on the pavement. Each one held aloft a flickering candle.

'Excuse me, Inspector,' said George, downing the remainder of his pint and grabbing his camera, 'but I have to get this.'

Raven followed him outside, finding himself in a flowing river of black, purple and scarlet. He fell into step alongside a middle-aged couple dressed in steampunk costumes. The man's leather coat matched his top hat, which was furnished with brass gears and cogs. The woman's hair was gathered into an elaborate bun, her voluminous dress so long it brushed the cobbles.

'What's happening?' Raven asked them.

The woman turned a doleful face towards him. 'It's a tribute to the dead. We're paying our respects to the fallen. The taxidermist and the girl with the hair. You must have heard about them.'

'I have,' said Raven. The candlelit procession was a sight to behold. Scores, perhaps hundreds of goths marching as one along Church Street, the flames of their candles guttering in the rising wind.

George was in his element, turning his lens and snapping away as if he'd hit the jackpot. Perhaps he had. His photos would probably be appearing in some newspaper the following morning.

Raven walked alongside him. At the foot of the one hundred and ninety-nine steps the group paused for a moment of silent reflection before beginning the ascent to St Mary's Church. Raven cast his gaze over the sea of faces, searching for anyone in a plague doctor's mask, but there were none to be seen.

'Coming up the steps?' asked George.

Raven eyed the long climb up to the church with annoyance. 'I think I'll stay down here.' Why did everywhere in this town have to be up a hill or at the top of a flight of steps? The place was even worse than Scarborough.

He watched as the parade passed by and ascended into the night, climbing back and forth up the long flight of steps and out of view. He stopped just long enough to send the photo of the hooded figure to Tony, then wandered in the opposite direction, down Tate Hill Pier, needing a moment of quiet reflection to himself.

The strong bonds of fellowship he'd observed in the goth community drew a stark contrast with the brutal and macabre killings of Reynard Blackthorn and Aurora Highsmith. The procession he had just witnessed seemed to be largely spontaneous, a gesture of sympathy from mourners who hadn't even known the victims personally. Could one of these people really be responsible for such barbaric murders? Might the killer even be a close friend of the victims?

His experience told him that it was often the ones we loved best we had to fear the most.

At the end of the short and stubby pier he stopped and looked out across the oil-black water of the estuary, its surface made choppy by the gusting wind. The goth weekend had touched him in a way he hadn't anticipated. After spending time closely observing and speaking with the festival-goers, he had been forced to confront his own identity. He'd always thought of himself as a bit of a goth, but he saw now that he was just a pale reflection of the real thing. The life he lived was so much more conventional than the folk who came to Whitby twice each year to make their wildest fantasies a reality.

Had the passing of the decades guided him inevitably down this straight and narrow road? Many of the people at the festival were his own age, or older, so that was no reason. Then was it the ties of family that had bound him so firmly to conventionality? A different set of choices might have led him down a different path. One where he broke free of those ties, casting his wings wide and living beyond the constraints of the mainstream.

Yet if the price of that freedom was a life without Hannah, he knew he had made the right choices, and would choose them again, a thousand times over, no matter how appealing the alternatives on offer.

As long as he had his daughter, he would have no regrets.

In the distance, the twin lighthouses at the ends of the

East and West Piers flashed their warnings every fifteen seconds: the eastern lighthouse short and stubby; the western one tall with a square platform at the top. He was reminded of the lighthouse at Flamborough Head, further down the coast, where another murder investigation had reached its appalling conclusion. A lighthouse was a beacon of safety, but it was paradoxically a place of danger too, marking concealed rocks and treacherous currents.

A heavy raindrop fell against his face as the storm finally broke. The wind gained strength and soon sheets of water were streaming from the obsidian sky. He ought to get indoors before his coat got soaked. Already cold water was running down his face, plastering his hair to his skin.

But before he could leave, he spotted movement on the other side of the harbour.

There, as the light on the West Pier blinked, a pair of figures appeared at the top of the lighthouse, moving quickly. He squinted into the rain, trying to make sense of the shifting shapes. Two people flitted across the square balcony, high up, where no visitor should be. Their shadowy forms moved silently in the darkness, drawing apart then coming together in a desperate struggle.

Lightning forked overhead, shocking in its suddenness, burning the scene into Raven's vision and making it as clear as day.

A dark and crooked mask concealed the face of one of the figures. The other's eyes were hidden behind amber lenses that blazed as the light caught them.

Framed by the brightness, the figures wrestled together, locked in a deadly dance. They struggled for supremacy, grappling with each other, right to the very edge of the balcony. Then, as if in terrifying slow motion, one of them plummeted over the safety railings, falling to the ground, then lying still. The other watched from the top of the lighthouse, then seemed to vanish.

★

For a moment Raven stood paralysed. Had he really just witnessed someone being thrown to their death? He didn't want to believe it, but he knew what he had seen.

He reached for his phone and called for backup. Then, cursing the body of water that lay between him and the lighthouse, he set off back to Church Street, stumbling as fast as he could and pushing against the crowds of goths still pouring across the bridge into the old town in silent tribute. He slipped on wet cobbles, his right leg burning in protest at each jolt. Minutes passed.

Over the bridge he staggered and onto the harbourside, earning himself scathing looks from people who thought he was drunk, and down to the West Pier as fast as he could force his legs to move.

By the time he got there, two police cars were already on the scene and an ambulance was on its way, its siren rising above the roar of the storm. The blue lights of the police cars flickered eerily in the night.

Sergeant Mike Fields was waiting for him. 'One victim; no sign of the perpetrator. We've begun a search of the area.'

'Let me see the body,' said Raven.

'I'll warn you, it's not a pretty sight.'

He made his way to the foot of the lighthouse, his breath coming in ragged gulps, his thigh a ball of fire.

A dark form lay on the pier, jacket and trousers a tangled mess, arms twisted in impossible positions. The victim's skull had broken wide open, disgorging a spray of blood and brains across the wet stone. Already the rain was washing it clean, making dark rivulets in its wake.

Raven knelt at the victim's shoulder and carefully drew aside the crumpled felt hat and bronze-coloured goggles that covered the victim's face. Blank eyes gazed back at him; the eyes of Dr Raj Sandhu.

CHAPTER 28

When her father came downstairs on Sunday morning, Hannah was shocked to see him looking so worn. His skin was as pale as death, and dark circles shadowed his eyes. He looked like he'd barely slept.

'Coffee?' she suggested. She'd finally worked out how to operate the fancy machine with its steel knobs and levers and its hissing steam dispenser. It seemed like an extraordinarily cumbersome way to produce a hot beverage, but she knew how much he adored it.

'That would be wonderful.' He sounded inordinately grateful.

'Shall I make scrambled eggs? It's my speciality.' She didn't usually go to so much bother in the morning, contenting herself with a bowl of muesli, but since coming to Scarborough she'd developed a real appetite. It must be that famous sea air. 'To be fair, it's the only cooked breakfast I know how to make.'

'You're an angel.' He sat down at the table.

He'd messaged her the previous evening to say he'd be back late and not to wait up for him. Something had come up in Whitby, but she wasn't to worry.

So naturally she'd gone straight to her phone to find out what was happening. There had been photos and videos on social media showing a candlelit procession and vigil in memory of Reynard Blackthorn and Aurora Highsmith. It was a moving sight to see so many people gathered together in memory of two who had been lost. The line of goths snaking through Church Street and up the steps to St Mary's, all of them holding candles aloft, had made for a haunting and magical sight.

Hannah felt a keen personal bond with Aurora, the woman she'd met so briefly and had tried in vain to save. Although it was true that Aurora hadn't been very kind to her during their fleeting encounter at the pavilion, that no longer mattered. It seemed that being dead excused a lot of bad behaviour. And even though she knew she was being irrational, she felt a twinge of guilt that she'd failed to save the burning woman. Hannah was sorry not to have taken part in the vigil and to get a chance to pay her respects.

There were reports, too, of an incident at the lighthouse on the West Pier. No one seemed to know exactly what was going on but police cars and an ambulance were mentioned. She guessed this was what had delayed her dad. There was speculation about someone falling from the top of the lighthouse – or had they been pushed?

She had stayed up till nearly one, scrolling through the news and rumours, waiting for him to come home. But in the end she had fallen into a fitful sleep, waking early to the sound of seagulls.

'So, what happened last night?' she asked him as she cracked eggs into a glass jug and heated butter in the frying pan.

'A man fell from the top of the lighthouse. We think he was pushed.'

'Oh God, that's awful. Was he killed?'

'I'm afraid so.'

'Who was it?'

He hesitated briefly before replying. 'It'll come out

sooner or later, so I might as well tell you now. It was another of Aurora's friends. His name was Raj Sandhu.'

'So all three victims knew each other?'

'That's right.'

'That's horrible.' The butter started to sizzle and Hannah quickly beat the eggs and poured the mixture into the pan. 'So what will happen now?'

Her father rubbed his forehead with his thumbs. 'The fourth friend, Lucille West, will be arrested.'

'You think she killed the others?'

'That's the working theory.'

It seemed shocking that someone could murder their closest friends, especially in such a horrifying manner. But in a way the news came as a relief. Hannah was glad now that she'd said nothing to her father about Mr Swales's tale of Mary Clarke and her burning hair. There was obviously no connection between the death of the poor girl in the story and the three murders that had taken place.

She stirred the eggs until they were light and fluffy, then shared the food between two plates. 'Here you go.'

'Thanks, love.'

'So you'll be going back to Whitby this morning?'

'I'm sorry, but I don't have any choice,' he said.

'Don't worry, I understand. You have a job to do. An important one.' She was only just beginning to realise how important it was. Her mother had never spoken about his work. It had always been simply a reason to blame him for not being around.

'This is delicious, by the way,' he told her through a mouthful of eggs.

'Thanks.'

'So tell me about your night out with Ellie.'

She knew he was changing the subject, and she knew the reason why: he wanted to protect her, the way he always had. She loved him for that, and didn't mind. She knew that he wasn't allowed to discuss the details of the case with her. He had never talked about his job, so it was no surprise that she'd never fully appreciated it. 'We had a great time,' she told him. 'Ellie's dad owns a restaurant in town and he served us free food and drinks all night.'

'Wow. Sounds great.'

She recognised the tinge of concern in his eyes when she mentioned the free drinks. She had never once seen him touch alcohol and had never thought to ask why. Suddenly she wanted more than anything to know the reason, to find out all about him and ask the questions she had never thought to ask. But she recognised this wasn't the right moment. She would make time later, when all of this was over. For now she just said, 'Don't worry, we didn't go mad, just shared a bottle of wine.'

'Okay. I'm sure you were very sensible.'

He had finished his food and she could tell he was ready to leave. 'Don't worry about the washing-up,' she told him. 'You need to be on your way. I'll clear up afterwards.'

'You're a star.' He rose and kissed her quickly on the forehead. 'Catch you later. I'll try to be home at a normal time tonight.'

She wondered if she ought to tell him about her plans to go and watch Velvet Nocturne at the Abbey Brewery, but decided against it. There was no need to add to his worries. It was only an afternoon event and Ellie was coming too.

In any case, they knew who the murderer was now. They would be safely behind bars very soon.

★

The door at the foot of the lighthouse had clearly been forced open. Raven stooped to inspect it, noting the broken brass padlock, now marked with a police evidence marker. The entire West Pier had been cordoned off and closed to visitors. Raj's body had been removed to the mortuary and the area where he had fallen tented off. Local police had conducted a thorough search of the area the previous evening, under the direction of Mike Fields, but the killer had long since vanished into the night.

At least the storm had abated and the mist that had swathed the town and harbour in recent days had cleared. Water lapped gently against the stone wall of the pier, making soft gurgling sounds, and a glimmer of sunshine threatened to break through the thin grey covering of cloud. Raven's coat cast a pale grey shadow against the square wall at the base of the lighthouse.

He stepped through the doorway, ducking low to avoid the lintel and gritted his teeth as he began his laborious ascent to the top. The steps that spiralled around in an elongated corkscrew might not have numbered one hundred and ninety-nine, but there were damn well more than enough of them, and they were steep buggers at that. His old war wound was making its unwelcome presence felt after the previous night's athletics, and he knew that this fresh exertion would only aggravate it further. Why did he always find himself investigating murders at the top of long climbs?

As he trudged up the steps he lamented the fact that this was to be Hannah's last full day in Scarborough and he'd been forced to desert her yet again. Her visit to the town had been an unmitigated disaster from start to finish and he wouldn't blame her if she never wanted to return to Yorkshire. He promised himself that in the summer he'd make time for her, even if that meant switching off his phone and making himself impossible to reach. Perhaps they could go somewhere together. Somewhere as far away from Scarborough as possible.

Becca and Holly were already waiting for him at the top of the lighthouse.

The CSI boss greeted him when he finally emerged, completely breathless, into the space that housed the light. 'Who needs to join the gym when you get to work in a place like this, eh?'

Raven had no breath to answer her, and merely grunted an acknowledgement while he waited for his breathing to return to normal. 'Found anything?' he asked when he could speak again.

'Yes, this.' Holly passed him a sealed evidence bag.

He already knew what to expect and wasn't surprised to find a third postcard inside the clear plastic bag. The front of the card showed a photograph of the two lighthouses taken from the seaward side. In the image, the sky was a clear blue and the water was calm. He turned it over. On the back was a message penned in the now familiar handwriting of the killer. He read aloud, *'Even the faithful may stumble and fall.'*

'Clearly a reference to Raj and Lucille's relationship,' remarked Becca.

Raven grunted his agreement. There could be absolutely no doubt now. The three murders had been carried out by Lucille West in an act of vengeance for the way she believed she had been mistreated.

Even though it was Lucille who had been unfaithful to Raj, somehow she had convinced herself that she had been wronged. It was necessary, Raven supposed, for a murderer to justify their actions with a certain amount of self-delusion. How else could they live with the consequences of their bloody acts?

'Where is Lucille West now?' he asked. 'Has she been arrested?'

He could tell from the expression on Becca's face that the news wasn't good. 'Lucille's gone missing. Officers went to her room at the Black Horse last night but she wasn't there. She hasn't returned. Her phone is switched off and nobody knows where she's gone.'

'Has she checked out?'

'No, all her belongings are still in her room at the Black Horse.'

'Shit,' swore Raven. This investigation had gone so disastrously wrong, it could spell the end of his career. 'We need to find her before she gets away.'

'There are officers stationed at the railway station and the bus depot. Local taxi firms have been warned not to pick up anyone matching her description.'

Raven smiled. 'I can see that I've left the operation in

good hands. What we need to do now is circulate Lucille's name and photo on social media. Let's put out a description of the plague doctor's outfit too, in case she's in disguise. Surely she can't hide for long in a town this small.'

'I'll get onto it right away,' said Becca.

CHAPTER 29

The half-timbered room at the Black Horse was cosy and comfortable, but quite extraordinarily messy. Its ensuite bathroom was stuffed full of toiletries. Black eyeliner, black mascara, kohl and black lipstick littered the sink area. Lucille's suitcase stood on a stand at the foot of the bed, its zip half-open. Black clothes tumbled out of it, spilling onto the carpet.

Raven couldn't possibly have lived in a place where everything seemed to have been cast aside so haphazardly. He needed things in the right place, and in the proper order. Was Lucille always so untidy, or had she fled the room in a hurry?

Becca snapped on a pair of gloves and started rummaging through the suitcase. 'No plague doctor's outfit in here. Do you think she took it with her?'

'Possibly.' Raj's killer had certainly been wearing a mask of some description. But Raven had been too far away across the harbour to make out any details of their costume.

He let his gaze wander around the compact room. Was this really the den of a serial killer? It was full to bursting with Lucille's clothes and personal effects. Where could she have stored the plastic container, syringe and tubing used to drain the blood from Reynard Blackthorn? Where had she kept the bolt cutter used to break into the lighthouse? And where, for that matter, was the black dog that had been spotted so often whenever the killer struck?

'I don't suppose this place allows pets?' he asked.

Becca gave him a funny look. 'I can ask the manager if you like.'

'No need. I wasn't being serious.'

'Then what are you thinking?'

'I'm beginning to doubt that Lucille is the murderer.'

'But if she isn't, then–'

Raven finished the sentence for her. 'She might be the next victim. And if that's the case it's even more important that we find her quickly.'

Becca moved to the bedside locker and picked out a couple of receipts from the pile of junk deposited there. 'Look at these. She must have gone shopping yesterday.'

There was a receipt for £95 for items of clothing from Vivienne's Vamp & Victoriana. There was also one for £120 from Rigby's Specialist Jet Jeweller's. Lucille had been splashing out on herself.

'These two names keep cropping up,' said Raven. 'Vivienne Nightingale and Alexander Rigby.'

'You think they might be involved?'

'They clearly are involved,' said Raven. 'But is there more to their involvement than meets the eye?'

'What are you thinking?'

An idea was forming in Raven's imagination. Just a germ of a conjecture, but it was quickly putting down roots and taking shape. 'Vivienne and Mia must have been very close. Jess told us they worked on Mia's wedding dress together. What if Vivienne secretly blamed Mia's friends for deserting her when she most needed them?'

Becca picked up the theory and ran with it. 'The postcard we found after Aurora's death drew attention to the fact that she was going to be a bridesmaid at Mia's wedding.'

'That's right. Raj said he saw Vivienne talking to Aurora and Lucille at the pavilion just before Aurora was killed. And now Lucille has gone missing and the last person to see her might well have been Vivienne.'

'Come on then,' said Becca. 'What are we still doing here?'

*

'Oh, yes,' said Vivienne, returning the receipt to Becca. 'Lucille came here yesterday. She bought a few items from me. A pair of knee-length boots, a leather choker and some lace gloves. They looked fabulous on her.'

After leaving the Black Horse, Becca and Raven had crossed the swing bridge to Whitby's west side and walked from the river up the sharply-sloping street of Flowergate. The hill had set Raven cursing and he'd resorted to hauling himself up the steepest stretch using the handrail provided.

Becca, tactfully, had refrained from comment. She knew how hard her boss was finding it to navigate the hilly town. The investigation seemed to be pitting the geography of Whitby itself against him, forever sending him up and down hills and steps. He stopped to catch his breath after the climb, commenting, 'Perhaps I should have stayed in London.'

'Not every investigation in Yorkshire involves hill-climbing,' she'd told him. 'Anyway, I bet the fish and chips are rubbish down south.'

He'd cracked a smile at that. 'Well, that's true enough.'

Becca now found herself in the most outlandish clothes shop she had ever visited. Vivienne's Vamp & Victoriana housed a treasure trove of the unique and bizarre. Here, jet-black corsets with intricate lace trimmings hung alongside bustle skirts in deep purple, their layered ruffles cascading to the floor. Leather jackets, studded with industrial rivets and buckles, vied for attention beside high-collared Victorian blouses. Green and black-striped tights dangled next to fishnet stockings, while blood-red lace-up boots stood prominently on a shelf. A centrepiece mannequin showcased a gown of midnight blue, its full skirt adorned with embroidered silver spiders.

It was like a dressing-up box for some very wicked little girl.

But as Becca continued to peruse the clothing on display, she realised how accustomed she had grown to this extravagant style. The initial shock had worn off, and the attire that had once seemed bizarre appeared more and more normal. By comparison, ordinary clothes looked bland and boring. Moreover, her perspective on the goth community had shifted. She no longer perceived them as outsiders, excluded – or excluding themselves – from mainstream society. Instead, it occurred to her that maybe the goths were on the inside, looking out.

She regarded the owner of the shop with curiosity, trying to work out what Vivienne's outfit was supposed to be. A black dress flowing with sensual curves in the bodice. A skirt so long it brushed the floor and hid her feet. Hair as wild as a galloping horse. Pentacle earrings, heavy with dark stones.

She was a bit witchy. All she was missing was a pointed hat.

'You know Lucille well, then?' Becca asked her.

'Yes,' said Vivienne. 'She comes here every time she's in Whitby to buy something. She was a close friend of Mia's. I measured her and Aurora for bridesmaids' dresses, but didn't get round to making them before the wedding was called off. Please don't tell me something has happened to her. I'm already in shock after what happened to Aurora. Not to mention Mia and Nathan. I don't think I can take any more bad news.' She looked pleadingly from Becca to Raven.

'We don't know if anything has happened to her,' said Becca. 'At the moment we're trying to trace her steps from yesterday. Do you remember what time she came to the shop?'

Vivienne brushed a strand of ebony hair away from her eyes. 'It was mid-afternoon. About three o'clock.'

'Was she on her own?' asked Raven.

'Yes.'

'And how did she seem?'

'Well, upset, obviously. We talked about Aurora and Reynard. Lucille had drifted apart from them over the years, but it's still devastating when someone you've known that long dies, especially in such awful circumstances. Lucille said she wished she could have done more for Mia, and that she held herself partly responsible for Mia taking her own life.'

As Raj had hinted, the jealousies and betrayals that had driven a wedge between the group of friends had turned to feelings of guilt and shame at their failure to help Mia during her time of crisis.

'And what did you say to that?' asked Becca.

'Well, obviously, I told her it wasn't her fault.'

Becca tilted her head to one side, picking up on an undercurrent of doubt in Vivienne's words. 'But privately, do you think it was?'

Vivienne pursed her lips, unwilling to reveal more. But eventually she said, 'I think that Mia could have used more support from her friends after she lost Nathan. Apart from me, she had no one to turn to. She must have felt abandoned, so far from home with no one to console her. If Lucille and the others had been more attentive, perhaps it would all have turned out differently.'

It was much as Raven had suggested. Vivienne blamed Mia's friends for not being around to support her.

'You were close to Mia,' said Becca, 'almost like a mother. Did you feel responsible for her?'

Vivienne shifted uneasily, dark hair swishing across her face. 'Responsible? I did my best for her.'

'But her friends didn't.'

'What are you saying?'

'You were at the pavilion the night of the concert, weren't you?'

'Yes.'

'The night Aurora was murdered. Where were you last night?'

Vivienne's green eyes hardened. 'You suspect me of killing Aurora and Raj?'

'I'm asking if you can account for your movements.'

Vivienne considered the matter. 'It must be exhausting being so suspicious of people all the time, but I suppose you're only doing your job. Let me put your mind at rest. After I closed the shop, I took my new assistant out for a meal. I like to treat people whenever I can. We went to a nearby restaurant and bar. Call them. They'll tell you we were there until late.'

Becca turned to Raven, whose face was grim. 'We'll check your alibi,' he said. But it was obvious from his expression that his theory had been punctured.

Becca did her best to recover gracefully from the setback. 'So, what else did Lucille say to you when she called in yesterday?'

'Nothing much. I told her to look after herself, and she hugged me and thanked me for everything.' A look of anxiety creased Vivienne's forehead. 'There was something... final... about the way she talked, as if she wouldn't be coming back. You don't think...' her words trailed off, the anxious expression turning to one of alarm.

'We don't know what Lucille intended to do,' Raven told her. 'That's why we're here. When she left, did she give any indication of where she was going?'

'Well, yes. She mentioned that she was going to call in and say hello to Alexander.'

'That would be Alexander Rigby, who runs the jet shop?'

'That's right.'

Raven exchanged a glance with Becca. The jet shop was to be their next port of call, and there might have been nothing more to Lucille's visit than a desire to buy some jet while in Whitby. And yet the name of Nathan's older brother kept cropping up again and again. 'How well do you know Alexander?' asked Becca.

'How well?' Vivienne gave a nervous laugh. 'I know him rather well, in fact. He's my husband.'

★

It was a Sunday, and Dinsdale breathed a sigh of relief that he didn't have to trek all the way to Whitby again. Especially in that rickety excuse for a car that Jess Barraclough drove. He had pictured the old Land Rover conking out in the middle of the moors, and having to wait half the day for a breakdown van to pick them up.

Instead he hauled himself into his own car – a Toyota Avensis estate, manufactured in Derbyshire, not too many miles on the clock, a five-star safety rating and a comprehensive breakdown policy included with his insurance – and took it to the address on Newborough that Tony had given him.

The slightly rundown offices of Cross Payday Loans were closed for the day, but they confirmed Dinsdale's initial impression of seediness. He hadn't previously encountered this Donovan Cross, but he knew the type well enough. In his opinion, any man going by the name of Cross could be up to no good, especially if his business was lending money to folk who didn't have any.

And if Cross had anything to do with the death of Nathan Rigby then all the better because it would prove his instincts were spot on. He'd show Raven he knew how to do his job. And more to the point, he'd prove it to Gillian. It would be nice to climb one more rung up the ladder before his retirement and finally get the recognition he deserved. He pictured an office of his own and a shiny nameplate on the door: *DCI Derek Dinsdale*. It had a nice ring about it, he couldn't pretend otherwise.

He carried on driving, and soon found himself in the rather more affluent surroundings of Queen Margaret's Road in the shadow of Oliver's Mount. The Porsche 911 standing in front of the double garage of the detached house only reinforced his belief that Cross was not to be trusted. How could you earn that kind of money lending to ne'er-do-wells like Nathan Rigby? Only by robbing the poor buggers blind. Cross Payday Loans might be the legitimate façade that Cross hid behind, but underneath he was nothing but a good old-fashioned loan shark.

He parked his Toyota next to the Porsche, noting the splashes of mud all over the alloy wheels of the sports car, rang the doorbell of the mock-Tudor house and waited.

The door was opened by a rather stunning blonde with a tan so orange and a pair of boobs so vast that they, just like the black-and-white timbers of the house, had to be fake.

He eyed her up and down, admiring the shortness of her skirt and the low cut of her top. She was a tart all right, the kind who sniffed out money like a pig with its nose in a feeding trough. 'Mrs Cross?'

She folded her bronzed arms across her substantial chest. 'Yes, who are you?'

'DI Derek Dinsdale from Scarborough CID.' He fumbled in his pocket for his warrant card. 'Is your husband in? I'd like a word.'

'Donny?' She gave him a scowl and retreated into the hallway. 'Sure, he's right through here.'

Donny, mused Dinsdale as he trudged after her into the house. *Makes him sound cute and cuddly.*

Donovan Cross was certainly not cute and cuddly. The man browsing a motoring magazine in the huge front lounge was a big ugly brute and no denying it. He didn't look best pleased to see Dinsdale and didn't bother to stand up. 'Who's this?' Cross addressed the question to his wife. 'It's Sunday. You know I don't do business on a Sunday.'

'It's the police,' said Mrs Cross. 'DI somebody-or-other. He asked to see you.'

'Oh, he did, did he?' Cross rubbed thick stubby fingers over his smoothly shaven head. 'Well he can bloody well take his shoes off before he leaves a mess all over the carpet.'

Dinsdale wondered if the entire interview was going to be conducted in the third person, with Cross's wife as the go-between. That would make things very tedious indeed. He contemplated ignoring the demand to remove his shoes, but decided it would be easier to comply. Slipping them off his feet, he took a seat on a massive leather sofa that almost swallowed him whole.

'I'll leave you boys to it,' said Mrs Cross, withdrawing from the room and closing the door behind her. No offer to bring tea or biscuits. Dinsdale sighed.

'You got some ID?' said Cross.

Dinsdale flashed him the warrant card. 'DI Derek Dinsdale.' It would be *so* good if that could be DCI.

'And what do you want to talk to me about, DI Derek Dinsdale?' Cross made a show of indifference, flicking through his glossy magazine, pretending not to care. But at least he had the brains to remember a name. Unlike his wife.

'Nathan Rigby.' Dinsdale tossed the name into the room, watching to see how it landed.

The wrinkling of the bald head told him it had hit home. 'What makes you think I know that name?'

'You strike me as the kind of man who knows his business and remembers the name of a punter.'

Dinsdale knew exactly how to play a sleazeball like Cross. Big greedy fish in a tiny little pond, that was Cross's problem. He probably got enough respect from his seedy loan-shark henchmen, but respectable people shunned him like cholera.

Flattery. That was the way to breach Donovan Cross's defences.

Cross looked up, a glint in his eye that showed he was lapping it up. Oh Yes, Dinsdale knew how to play a scumbag like this, all right. He'd been doing it all his working days.

'Might be that I know who you're referring to. What of it?'

'Tell me about him.'

Cross closed his magazine, shutting away the pictures of fast cars. 'He was a punter, as you say. Or rather, a customer, as I prefer to call them. I run a respectable business. All above board and properly regulated.'

'How much did you lend him?'

'You know I can't tell you that. I have a duty to keep my customers' personal data confidential.'

No denial there, at any rate. So Cross *had* lent money to Nathan. 'And did he pay you back?'

'Like I already said, that's not something I can tell you. Unless you have a search warrant?'

'In my experience,' said Dinsdale, 'people who demand to see warrants or won't answer a straight question usually have something to hide.'

'Not me,' said Cross, trying to look like he meant it and failing dismally.

'So what interest rate did you charge him on his loan? Fifty percent? A hundred?'

Cross didn't rise to the bait. 'Fair and responsible lending, that's the way I play, Inspector, not like some of those other sharks out there.'

But Dinsdale wasn't interested in those *other* sharks, only the one sitting right in front of him.

He tried a different tack. 'Why did Nathan come to you for a loan in the first place?'

Cross shrugged. 'People come to me all the time, and always for the same reason: they have nowhere else to go. Nathan didn't know how to handle money, and he didn't have a proper job. People like that can't just go to a regular bank. They'd be laughed out of the manager's office.'

'Whereas at your place, they're always welcome. As long as the rate of return is high enough to keep you supplied with fast cars and Mrs Cross with fake tits.'

It was all part of the game. First the flattery, then the insults. And Dinsdale could do insults all day long, given the chance.

Cross's heavy brow furrowed in consternation. 'I don't

know what you want from me.'

Dinsdale went for the kill, asking the question all this preamble had been leading up to. 'I want to know why Nathan Rigby walked onto a pier in the middle of a storm when he must have known the danger.'

But to his surprise, Cross's face cleared and he almost smiled. 'About time.'

'What do you mean?' asked Dinsdale. This wasn't the response he'd been expecting.

'What I mean,' said Cross, 'is why would Nathan have done such a stupid thing? More to the point, who benefited from his death? Because it certainly wasn't me. He died owing me an arm and a leg, and there was no way for me to get it back.'

'Why not?' demanded Dinsdale. 'If your loans were legitimate?'

Cross winced. 'Let's just say that I wasn't in possession of all the paperwork I needed to prove the amount he owed me.'

Dinsdale nodded slowly. It was like he'd suspected all along – the payday loans company was just a front for an illegal lending operation behind the scenes. Money lent off the books to those in need of cash at any price. Sky-high interest rates and bully-boy tactics in dark alleyways. But that was no longer his main concern. 'So who did benefit?'

'It's obvious, isn't it?' said Cross. 'Before Nathan came to me, he'd been borrowing heavily from his brother. But Alexander couldn't keep shelling out cash at that rate, especially when Nathan made no effort to repay the money. Alexander had a business to run. Wouldn't it have been so much more convenient if Nathan *accidentally*' – he drew air quotes around the adverb – 'fell off the pier during a storm?'

CHAPTER 30

The call from Dinsdale came just as Raven and Becca were leaving Vivienne's shop.

'Derek,' said Raven. 'What have you got for me?'

'A significant breakthrough, I'm pleased to say.' The smugness in Dinsdale's voice implied he'd all but cracked the case.

'Tell me,' said Raven.

He listened as Dinsdale described his encounter with Donovan Cross and expounded his theory that Nathan Rigby had been pushed into the sea so that Alexander could free himself from the burden of his brother's debts and at the same time inherit the whole of the jewellery business. 'You've got to admit it's a compelling motive,' concluded Dinsdale.

'It certainly needs following up,' said Raven.

'I'm glad you agree. I could come over to Whitby now, if you like. We'll interview Alexander together, you and me.'

'That's okay, Derek,' said Raven quickly. 'Becca and I are just on our way to speak to him now. We'll take it from here.'

He ended the call and thought about what he'd just heard. Could Dinsdale be right? Had Alexander Rigby killed his own brother, thereby indirectly precipitating Mia's suicide? It was a plausible scenario, but did it have any bearing on the present murders?

He explained Dinsdale's thinking to Becca.

'He could be right,' she conceded. 'What if the other friends discovered what Alexander had done? They might have tried to blackmail him, and he decided to kill them all, one by one, making it look like a personal vendetta between members of the group.'

'We need more information about Nathan's body after it washed up,' said Raven. 'What state was it in? Did the pathologist have any concerns about the cause of death?'

'Would you like me to give Felicity a call?'

'Please,' said Raven, relieved that Becca had volunteered and he wouldn't have to brave the pathologist's brusque manner.

He listened in to the one-sided conversation.

'Hi, Felicity. Becca here... Yeah, good thanks, thanks for asking... And you?'

How was it, wondered Raven, that Becca had such a good relationship with the pathologist when his was so strained? Was it something he'd said? Or something he hadn't said? Or was it just the way he looked?

'Yes,' said Becca, with a sidelong glance in Raven's direction. 'He's with me now. Yes. No. No, really. No.'

Raven wondered what Felicity could possibly be asking. Nothing good, was his guess. It was best if he didn't ask.

'Listen,' said Becca, 'I was calling to ask you about Nathan Rigby. That's right, he fell off the pier at Whitby and drowned. Did you have any concerns or doubts when you carried out the post-mortem?' She listened as Felicity spoke, Raven itching to know what was being said, wishing Becca would put the call on speakerphone. 'Oh, you did? Oh, did he? Mm, that's really interesting. Thanks... Yeah, speak soon.'

'What did she say?' asked Raven impatiently when she ended the call.

'She said the body showed signs of head wounds, but it was impossible to tell if they were the result of a physical assault or a result of being washed up on the rocks.'

'Which throws some doubt on the verdict of accidental death,' said Raven. Much as he hated to admit it, DI Dinsdale might be onto something for once.

*

Alexander Rigby was busy dealing with a customer when Raven and Becca turned up in his shop. While they waited, Raven browsed the jewellery on display. There were pendant necklaces of highly polished jet set in sterling silver, matching earrings, delicate bracelets and dozens of different rings to choose from. None of it was cheap, but he toyed with the idea of buying Hannah a pair of earrings as a gift. Her birthday was coming up and an expensive present would go some way to make up for the way he'd been obliged to abandon her for much of her visit. Then again, maybe she wouldn't appreciate a memento of her time in Whitby after her experience with Aurora. And he gave up the idea entirely upon realising with dismay that he wasn't familiar enough with her tastes to tell what kind of jewellery she might like. Did she even have pierced ears?

'Can I help you?' Alexander Rigby had finished serving his customer and was looking from Raven to Becca, quite possibly in the hope that Raven was there to buy something special for his decidedly younger girlfriend.

Raven soon disabused him of that idea. 'DCI Raven and DS Shawcross from Scarborough CID. We'd like to ask you a few questions.'

The smile slid from Alexander's face, to be replaced by a frosty expression. 'I've already spoken to one of your lot. Dinsdale, I think his name was. He was here yesterday, asking all sorts of questions.'

'Well, we have more questions for you.'

Did Alexander turn a shade paler at that prospect, or was it just the shifting light? Outside, clouds were gathering once again, snuffing out the sun's weak efforts to break through the gloom. 'Very well,' he said with a sigh. 'But this is costing me good money in lost business. I hope it won't take long.' He turned the sign on the door to *Closed,* locked up, and invited them into a room at the back of the shop.

'We're investigating a series of murders that have taken place in the town during the past few days,' said Raven once they were seated. 'No doubt you're aware of them.'

'Yes, of course.' The suspect's face gave nothing away, but Raven had the sense of a man who was trying very hard to keep himself together.

'We've just come from speaking to your wife.'

'Vivienne?' Alexander looked anxiously from Raven to Becca. 'What does she have to do with anything?'

'Mr Rigby,' continued Raven, 'where were you on Wednesday night? After, say, eleven o'clock?' Wednesday night or the early hours of Thursday morning was when it had all begun, when Reynard Blackthorn had been lured to the abbey and his blood drained from his body.

'Wednesday?' The question seemed to throw him off balance. 'I was at home in bed.'

'Can anyone corroborate that? Your wife, perhaps?'

His face fell. 'Vivienne was away that night at her mother's in Runswick Bay.'

'I see,' said Raven. 'And what about Friday night? Earlier – around seven to eight in the evening.' That was the evening Hannah had gone to the concert at the pavilion and watched as Aurora Highsmith's hair was set on fire.

Alexander brightened. 'I can account for Friday night. I was at the concert at the pavilion. Vivienne and I went together.'

'Mr Rigby,' said Becca, 'forgive me for saying, but you don't strike me as a goth.'

He laughed nervously. 'No, I don't go in for all the

costumes, not like Vivienne. I just pull on a pair of black jeans and a jacket. But I do enjoy the music. There was a band I hadn't heard before – Velvet Nocturne – they were quite good.'

'Did you spend the whole evening with your wife?' asked Becca.

Alexander touched a hand to his temple. 'Well, I... uh, no, actually. I did lose sight of her for a while. It was all a bit chaotic after the, uh, attack took place.'

'I see. And what about Saturday night?' Raven cast his mind back to the moment he'd stood on Tate Hill Pier and watched Dr Raj Sandhu topple to his death from the balcony of the lighthouse. He tried to picture Alexander as the mysterious figure in the plague doctor's mask. It was by no means necessary to stretch his imagination. The husband of Vivienne Nightingale, it seemed, was quite adept at dressing to fit any situation.

'I, er, stayed late in the shop on Saturday. Stock checking.'

'So again, you have no alibi?'

'No.' Alexander was beginning to sound like a man defeated.

Raven drove home his advantage. 'Does the name Lucille West mean anything to you?'

'Yes, she was one of my brother's friends.'

'Did she come to your shop yesterday?'

'Yes, she did. She bought a jet brooch. Quite old-fashioned, really. It was late afternoon, perhaps about four o'clock.'

'A jet brooch?' queried Becca. 'Like a piece of mourning jewellery?'

'Yes,' said Alexander. 'She told me she was buying it in memory of her dead friends.'

'Her dead friends,' repeated Raven icily. 'That would be your brother, Nathan, his fiancée, Mia, and her other friends from university: Reynard, Aurora and Raj. Five in total.'

'That's a lot of mourning, Mr Rigby,' added Becca. 'A

very unfortunate state of affairs.'

At the litany of names, Alexander seemed finally to crumble. He bent forward, dropping his head into his hands and began to sob.

But for once, Becca's supply of tissues remained firmly in her pocket.

When Alexander finally looked up, he looked like a broken man. 'About Nathan... There's something you need to know.'

'What?' Raven looked at him sharply.

'Nathan didn't drown.'

CHAPTER 31

It was fun to be heading back to Whitby with Ellie for company. Before setting off, Ellie had insisted on lending Hannah a black biker jacket and doing her makeup for her, giving her the most dramatic goth eyes she'd ever seen. Ellie herself had gelled her crimson hair so that it stood up in a goth-punk style. Together they set off in Ellie's convertible sports car, turning more than a few heads as they went.

Being with Ellie was like having the big sister Hannah had never had. Growing up as an only child she'd always envied her friends who had siblings, even though they seemed to spend most of their time bickering. Ellie, by contrast, was easy-going and generous to a fault.

They left the car in a car park next to the railway station, crossed the swing bridge to the east side of town, and meandered down Church Street, admiring the beautiful jet jewellery on display in the many shop windows. They treated themselves to ice-creams and then embarked on the climb up the one hundred and ninety-nine steps to St Mary's Church. It was the final day of the goth weekend and the graveyard was full of vampires and goths posing for photos.

'I met a strange old man here the other day,' said Hannah. 'He told me a story about a woman whose hair caught fire in the town bakery. It turned out to be rather prophetic given what happened later.'

They stepped off the path and began wandering through the gravestones.

'Whitby is full of ghost stories,' said Ellie. She laughed. 'Perhaps your old man was an apparition himself.'

'No, I can assure you he was very real. I talked to him and shook his hand.' She looked across to the bench where she had sat with Mr Swales. Sure enough, leaning on his stick and looking out to sea, sat the old man. He seemed as much a part of the landscape as the gravestones. 'There he is now. Come on, I'll introduce you to him.'

They crossed the graveyard to where Mr Swales was sitting as still as a statue. Hannah had the uncanny sensation that he'd been waiting for her to return, but dismissed the notion as quickly as it occurred to her. He obviously came to this spot regularly, and had probably been coming for years.

'Good afternoon, Mr Swales. How are you today?'

The old man's weathered face broke into a grin, revealing more than one missing tooth. 'Well, if it isn't Miss Hannah Raven.' He held out his bony hand.

Hannah was impressed that he'd remembered her name. The old man's face may have looked about a hundred years old, but his mind was as quick as a whip. 'This is my friend, Ellie Earnshaw.'

'Very pleased to meet yeh, Miss Earnshaw,' said Mr Swales. 'Are you two young ladies in a hurry, or can yeh spare five minutes to keep an old man company?'

Hannah checked her watch. There was plenty of time before the gig at the brewery was due to start. 'We'd love to.'

Mr Swales shuffled along the bench to make room for them. It was peaceful to sit there, gazing at the sea which today was shimmering a silvery grey. The sea, Hannah realised, was different every time she saw it. It changed continuously from one moment to the next, in constant motion. No wonder Mr Swales was content to sit here and watch it for hours on end.

It was moments like this that she wanted to cherish and remember from her visit to Yorkshire, not the terrifying ordeal on the beach the other night. In fact, as she sat there, in the company of her two new friends, the pale sunshine warming her face, the night terror receded, almost as if it had never happened.

It was Mr Swales who broke the silence.

'Terrible thing what happened t'other night,' he said, shaking his head. 'Down at the beach, I mean. Especially coming so close after that body was found at the abbey.'

Hannah had no desire to tell the old man that she had witnessed the attack on Aurora at first hand. The last thing she wanted was to relive that horrible event, especially now that she was beginning to find peace and put it behind her. 'Horrible,' she agreed. 'My father is the detective leading the police investigation.'

'Is he now?' Mr Swales looked suitably impressed and more than a little interested. He leaned closer. 'Strange coincidence, me telling you the story of Mary Clarke, just before that poor woman had 'er hair set afire.'

'Yes, it was.'

He nodded and Hannah thought he'd said all he was going to say on the subject. But then he leaned closer still. 'And now there's this business at the lighthouse.'

'The man who was pushed off the balcony,' said Hannah. 'My dad says the three murders are connected.'

'Aye, well, I daresay he could be right about that,' said Mr Swales.

There seemed to be something troubling him.

'What is it?' asked Hannah. 'Do you know anything?'

'Well, it might just be an old man's fancy.'

'Go on,' encouraged Ellie. 'Tell us what you think.'

Mr Swales settled back in his seat. 'You sure you want to know?'

'Of course.'

'It's just that the way those people met their deaths seem, to my way of thinking, to be very much like local tales. I've already told yeh the story of Mary Clarke whose hair was set afire, and you don't need me to tell you that Dracula came to Whitby for you to spot the similarity with the man whose blood was drained.'

'No, everyone knows that story,' said Ellie.

'Well, did yeh ever hear the story of the West Pier lighthouse ghost?'

'No,' said Hannah. 'Tell us.'

Mr Swales didn't need any encouragement. 'It's said that the West Pier lighthouse is haunted by the ghost of an old lighthouse keeper. One night, when a terrible storm was raging, the keeper looked out and noticed that the light in the lighthouse had gone out. Now, this could have been catastrophic for those mariners out at sea and heading for the safety of harbour. As yeh might have heard, the rocks along the coast here are cruel, and many a poor soul has lost their lives on these shores.'

The old man looked out to sea, almost as if he could see that storm raging, the waves crashing against the rocks at the base of the cliff, and hear the cries of the sailors.

'So,' he continued, 'this lighthouse keeper hauled on his boots and his coat, braved the winds and rain, and set off to rekindle the light. He could have been washed into the swirling waters himself, the wind was howling that strong and the waves were breaking over the pier. Rain was falling in torrents and by the time he reached the lighthouse, he was completely soaked through. As he climbed the winding staircase to the top, he dripped a trail of water behind him. Anyway, he managed to relight the lamp, so that those at sea would be safe.'

Mr Swales cast a haunted look in Hannah and Ellie's direction. 'But as he made his way back down the steps, which were now all wet from the water that had dripped off him, he slipped and plunged to his death. And ever since that night, when storms come to Whitby, there are folk what claim t'ave seen that heroic lighthouse keeper making his fatal journey towards the lighthouse. And some even say they've seen the ghostly image of a man lying at the bottom of the steps.'

'What a tragic story,' said Ellie.

'It just goes to show,' said Mr Swales, 'that bad things can happen to good people.'

Hannah's mind was leaping ahead. 'And so all three murders have parallels with local legends?'

'Reckon they do,' said Mr Swales. 'Though what that means, I couldn't rightly say.'

*

'So you're telling me that Nathan isn't dead?' Raven had to resist the urge to grab Alexander Rigby by the lapels and shake every last drop of truth out of him. The man's admission of a moment earlier had turned everything on its head.

'No,' said Alexander, looking like a man who had just offloaded the biggest secret of his life.

'You'd better tell us everything, Mr Rigby.'

'Of course.' Alexander looked down at his hands, then up at Becca, and finally at Raven. Finding no sympathy in either detective, he took a deep breath and launched himself into his confession. 'Nathan was hopelessly in debt. He was always useless with money. All through university I had to subsidise him. I hoped that when he settled down with Mia, things would get better, but they just got worse. Nathan wanted to be an artist. He had talent, for sure, but he didn't know how to direct it. None of the stuff he painted sold. I don't think he even wanted to sell it. He talked about putting on an exhibition, about moving down to London, about becoming the next David Hockney, but it was all a pipe dream. Mia did her best, working for Vivienne and trying to persuade Nathan to turn his hand to something that would sell, but it was a hopeless task.'

Raven listened in silence. When a suspect had begun to talk this freely, it was better to let them continue uninterrupted.

'I urged him to talk to Mia, but he refused. He was too ashamed. He kept coming back to me for money, but I didn't have limitless pockets. Things got out of control. Then he got involved with a loan shark called Donovan Cross. That only made matters worse.'

Raven could easily imagine it. He had seen similar scenarios play out time and time again, a spiral of debt sucking people under and pushing them into desperate straits.

'And then one night, a man was washed off the pier during a storm. Nathan was there – he often went down to look at the sea during bad weather – and saw it happen. He tried to help the drowning man, but it was too late. His body washed up on the rocks.'

'Who was it?' asked Raven.

Alexander shrugged. 'I honestly don't know. But it gave Nathan an idea. A stupid idea. I tried to talk him out of it, but he pleaded for me to help. He said there was no other way out.'

'You identified the drowned man, saying it was your brother.'

Alexander grimaced at the accusation but couldn't refute it. 'I didn't want to. I knew it was wrong. I told Nathan it would crush Mia. But you have to understand, he was at his wits' end. He couldn't see beyond his debts. This way, he could escape his troubles and start a new life. All he needed was someone to identify the unknown man and tell the police it was him.'

'And that person was you,' said Raven.

Alexander nodded. 'I was his next of kin. And I have to admit, part of me was relieved. If he'd carried on, he'd have bled me dry, and the business too. I had to think about Vivienne.'

'Does she know?' asked Raven. 'Was she in on it too?'

He shook his head. 'No, Vivienne had nothing to do

with this. She's completely innocent.'

'And what about Mia? Is she really dead? Or was that all some elaborate deception too?'

Alexander's face crumpled. 'Ah, Mia. That was the real tragedy. I told Nathan he should tell her what he intended to do. I said she'd understand, she'd forgive him. But he was too ashamed. He kept saying she'd be better off without him, and I persuaded myself that it was for the best, that she'd get over him, she'd move on. How was I supposed to know she would kill herself?'

Raven leaned back in his chair, dismayed by the sorry story he had just heard, but satisfied that the man before him had finally told the truth. 'And where is Nathan now?'

Alexander shook his head, burying his face in his hands again. 'I'm sorry. I'd tell you if I knew. But I haven't seen or heard from him since the night he faked his death.'

*

Raven was still reeling from the shock of Alexander's confession when his phone rang. He gave it a cursory glance, ready to reject the call, but when he saw Hannah's name on the screen he forced himself to change gears quickly.

'Hi, sweetheart. Everything good? I'm a little busy right now.'

Hannah was excited, her words tumbling out at breakneck speed, just like they used to when she was little. 'Dad, listen. I've just been talking to a man called Mr Swales and he told me an incredible story that explains exactly why the murders were carried out the way they were.'

'Mr Swales?' Raven dragged his fingers through his hair, struggling to make sense of what he was hearing. 'Sorry, who is Mr Swales?'

'He's this nice old man I've got to know. He sits on a bench at St Mary's churchyard and he's full of interesting stories. I think he might be an old sailor or something.

Anyway, the other day he told me the story of Mary Clarke who died after her hair caught fire, just like the way Aurora's hair was set alight. And now he's told me about a lighthouse keeper who fell to his death from the lighthouse in the middle of a storm. Don't you see? It's exactly like the latest murder!'

She paused for breath and Raven began to catch up. As he parsed her somewhat garbled message, he homed in quickly on the key point. 'Wait, you've been up at St Mary's Church? In Whitby? Today? You promised me you'd stay in Scarborough.'

'Dad!' cried Hannah in exasperation. 'That's not the important thing! What matters is that all three of the murders are based on local legends from the town. Whoever's carrying them out is working from a script.'

Raven gazed at the phone, his temper rising. 'Never mind that,' he told her. 'What were you thinking of, coming to Whitby when I specifically asked you not to? You knew the danger – you witnessed one of the murders yourself!'

'Dad! I'm not in the slightest danger. I'm here with Ellie. And Mr Swales is here too.'

The frustration in her voice told him he had disappointed her yet again. He tried to calm himself down and focus on the substance of what she'd said. Fanciful as these stories sounded, and whoever this Mr Swales might be, if Hannah was right and the bizarre nature of the murders had a rational explanation rooted in local legends, then... then what?

What did that mean?

CHAPTER 32

Becca was staring at him, mouthing a question, her brows raised high in curiosity. She was clearly desperate to know what was going on. And Raven could hear Hannah breathing on the other end of the phone in anticipation of his response. 'Dad? Are you still there? Can you hear me?'

'I'm here, darling. I'm just thinking about what you said.'

'You don't believe me.' Her accusation was filled with anger.

'No, I do believe you. It's just that... I don't know what to do with the information.'

'Well,' said Hannah in exasperation, 'neither do I. I just thought you should know.'

He still felt hurt by her disobedience. The fear that had seized him on learning she was back in Whitby refused to go, making his heart throb loudly and squeezing his chest like a metal band. But he could hear the pain in his daughter's voice, even louder than the thumping of his own heart.

He struggled to master his emotions and think things

through.

What did her theory prove, other than that the murderer possessed a good working knowledge of Whitby town legends and a meticulous eye for detail? It showed that not only had each murder been carried out in a manner that drew attention to the victim's character defects or traits, but had a basis in local lore too.

The person who fitted the bill perfectly was Nathan Rigby.

Born in Whitby, he had lived in the town most of his life and knew each victim intimately.

'Listen,' he told Hannah. 'I'm glad you called me. Are you with Mr Swales now?'

Her voice still carried resentment. 'Yes.'

'Then stay at the churchyard and make sure he does too. I'm going to send someone to interview him.'

'You are? So you're taking my idea seriously?' The bitterness was gone, replaced by longing. All she needed, it seemed, was his approval. Just what every daughter wanted from her father.

He swallowed his anger and gave her the approval she craved. 'I am. Absolutely. And Hannah?'

'What is it?'

'Stay safe.'

He had only just ended the call when his phone rang again. 'Sorry,' he said to Becca, 'I'll tell you what Hannah said in a minute.' He answered the latest call, which was from Sergeant Mike Fields.

'Raven, it's Fields here. We've just received a report of someone sleeping rough in the vicinity of Mulgrave Castle. There have been sightings of a black dog in the area too. I'm about to send an officer to check it out. Do you want to get involved?'

Raven had the sense that events were moving faster than he could keep up with. 'What and where is Mulgrave Castle?'

'It's a ruined castle just to the west of Whitby. No more than five miles as the crow flies.'

'Five miles.' Nathan Rigby was young and – now that he was no longer dead – presumably fit. Five miles on foot would be nothing to a man used to sleeping rough and living off the grid. Could this be where the undead man was hiding out? The report of the black dog was compelling. It had to be worth a shot.

'Let's do it,' said Raven, in the mood for action after his altercation with Hannah. 'And send an officer to the churchyard at St Mary's. My daughter is waiting there with an old man who has important evidence to give. Make sure she's safe and listen carefully to everything she says.'

If Fields was surprised at this request, his voice betrayed nothing. 'Very good, sir.'

'And send another officer to Rigby's Specialist Jet Jeweller's on Church Street. The proprietor, Alexander Rigby, is going to be helping us with our inquiries.'

'Are you going to tell me what's going on?' moaned Becca after he hung up.

'I'll fill you in on the way,' said Raven. 'Come on, let's get moving.'

*

'Where the bloody hell is this castle?' Raven could be a grumpy bastard at the best of times, but after his phone call from Hannah he was in a right state. Never mind media awareness, he needed to be sent on a basic communication course. Becca sat in the passenger seat of the M6, securely strapped in, enduring his foul mood and reckless driving until her own patience ran out.

'Slow down, or you'll get us both killed,' she snapped. 'And then tell me what's wrong.'

'Everything's wrong. And it sounds as if your friend, Ellie, is partly to blame.'

The BMW accelerated around a corner on a narrow country road that was little more than a track and Becca's head jerked back against the headrest. She was used to Raven's appalling driving, but this was too much. 'How can Ellie possibly be to blame for anything?'

Raven's knuckles tightened white around the steering wheel. 'She's here in Whitby with Hannah. And I made Hannah promise she'd stay in Scarborough.'

'So that's Ellie's fault?'

'Well, who would you blame?'

'Blame?' Becca and Raven had crossed swords several times before, though never this seriously. She'd thought they were a team. But if he was determined to make it personal by dragging Ellie into the argument and holding her responsible for his own failings as a father, she had no intention of backing down. 'Hannah's a grown woman. She can do whatever she wants, not what you tell her. If your parenting skills are anything like your team management skills then it's no surprise she didn't confide in you. So I'd say that if anyone's to blame, it's you.'

The BMW rounded the crest of a low rise, tyres straining to hold the road. 'Don't you dare lecture me about my own daughter. Did you know that Ellie and Hannah were coming to Whitby today?'

Becca pursed her lips. 'Ellie did mention a gig at the Abbey Brewery this afternoon. They were going together. I thought it would be good for Hannah to get out with someone her own age.'

'Oh, you did, did you?' Raven turned to face her, his eyes blazing with fury. The car veered dangerously to the left. He righted it just before it clipped the hedgerow that flanked the road.

'Yes,' said Becca, 'if it hadn't been for Ellie to keep her company, Hannah would have spent her whole time by herself. It was because you neglected her that she ended up alone at the pavilion when Aurora was attacked.' The accusation was harsh, and Becca regretted it as soon as the words were out of her mouth. But there was truth in them, and perhaps Raven needed to hear that truth.

He hit the brake and the car screeched to a halt, throwing her forwards as the seatbelt tightened around her. He switched off the engine and slid the gearstick into park.

She feared his temper was about to reach some new crescendo, and shrank back in her seat, scared for the first time that his rage might turn physical. But instead he leaned his forehead against the steering wheel and began to sob.

Becca sat still, stunned by the sudden change in his demeanour. For a long while she couldn't say anything, just watched this man, who had always seemed so strong and unyielding, break down in front of her like a tree felled by a gale.

His anguish was as violent as his fury and he seemed to lose all restraint as he gave himself over to crying. His voice came through ragged breaths as he struggled to speak. 'I'm sorry,' he choked, his voice barely audible over the sobs. 'I'm so sorry.' He twisted his face to look at her, his eyes red-rimmed, his voice cracking. 'You didn't deserve any of that. None of this is your fault, it's all mine. I'm a complete failure of a father.'

'No, you're not,' Becca said gently, reaching out to touch his arm. 'Hannah loves you.'

Raven shook his head, his face strained with guilt. 'I am. There's no point pretending I'm not. But instead of facing the truth, I let my anger get the better of me.'

Becca hardly knew what to say. She had never seen Raven like this before. 'Here,' she said, handing him some tissues. 'Take these. Crying doesn't suit you.'

His snivelling subsided and he accepted them meekly. 'Thank you,' he croaked.

'You're welcome. They're just tissues. I hand them out like sweets.'

He blew his nose and accepted another handful. 'I don't deserve it.'

'Don't be silly.'

'Your kindness, I mean. You're a real friend, Becca.'

'Glad to be, Raven,' she said quietly. 'Now stop being such a cry-baby. We've got a criminal to catch.'

*

The country road became a lane and then a track wandering along the edge of a farmer's field. Raven grimaced as the M6 lurched across the bumpy surface and metal scraped against stone. Soon even the dirt track petered out beneath a canopy of trees. A patrol car was already there with Sergeant Fields and a second uniformed officer waiting patiently for his arrival. Raven killed the engine and got out of the car.

'Raven,' said Fields in greeting. 'It's about a quarter of a mile on foot from here. Follow me.'

He set off at a brisk pace, with Becca and the other officer at his side. Raven plodded along behind as best he could through thick grass and undergrowth. This was all he needed – a cross-country trek leading to some godforsaken place in the middle of a forest. What had seemed like a good idea over the phone was fast losing its appeal and he wondered why he hadn't just left the job to his fitter, more capable colleagues.

Fields was explaining something of the history of the castle to Becca, and Raven caught fragments as he stumbled across the rough ground. '...three castles built over the centuries. The first was in Viking days, the second was destroyed during the Civil War. You can still see the ruins of the walls and the keep. You all right back there, Raven?'

Raven grunted. He was barely listening to Fields's patter. He was still filled with remorse for the way he'd snapped at Hannah and argued with Becca. He'd been so worried about his daughter, he'd lost sight of what really mattered in any relationship – trust. Hannah wasn't a child any longer, but a grown woman and he had no right to boss her about.

He'd been thinking of her as a little girl, clinging to the past as a way of making up for all the time he had lost. The occasions he hadn't been there for her. The hugs and kisses she'd needed but had never received. The love he'd felt but had been unable to express.

He had to let that go. He couldn't change the past. And he mustn't allow the present to blight the future.

'The third castle is still in use. It's part of the Mulgrave Estate, over on the other side of the woods, near Lythe.'

They were trekking now through a dense patch of woodland and Raven was struggling to keep up. The ground underfoot was uneven; the winding path between the trees poorly defined. Woody roots protruded from the loose soil, snaking out before him as if deliberately trying to trip him up. He snagged his coat on a bramble and had to stop to extricate himself. Predictably, his right leg was burning with the exertion.

The last straw was when he had to splash across a shallow beck. Another good pair of shoes ruined. Mud oozed into his socks as he squelched across the boggy ground on the other side. His misery was complete.

As he emerged from the woods, the outer wall of the castle suddenly rose in front of him like something out of a fairytale. This building was certainly well hidden. A handy place to stay if you were pretending to be dead but needed to pop over to Whitby for a spot of killing.

The question was whether Nathan was still here.

Fields lowered his voice. 'There's an entrance this way.'

Raven followed the others around the outer edge of the wall and in through what must once have been the main gate but was now just a gaping hole. A small ruined keep stood in the middle of the large green bailey. They approached with caution, but the place appeared deserted, home to neither man nor dog.

The keep was open to the sky. An earthy tang assaulted Raven's nostrils as he entered, along with the unmistakeable smell of mildew. Water glistened on the tower walls, green with moss and algae. It was a dreary and inhospitable place to live.

Yet there were signs that someone was camping out. A rolled-up sleeping bag. Blackened stones from a fire. Discarded cans and bottles. Raven picked his way through the belongings. He poked at the sleeping bag with his toe and saw the long black nose of a plague doctor's mask sticking out from underneath.

'Raven, look. I just found this.' Becca handed him a postcard.

The card showed an old sepia image of a woman wearing a nun's habit, her eyes gazing piously towards Heaven. He turned it over. On the back was a cryptic message.

She forgot her vow and must relearn it through suffering.

There was no time to wonder what it meant because the enclosed space of the keep was suddenly filled with the barking of a large dog.

CHAPTER 33

Raven knew that bark. He'd heard it at close quarters in the ruins of the abbey. Now here it was again, in the ruined tower of the castle.

There was something about that dog and wild, lonely ruins. A dramatic streak. A taste for the gothic. A penchant for appearing all of a sudden where it wasn't wanted.

Raven and the dog had a lot in common.

The animal stood at the entrance to the keep, filling the doorway with its presence and the stone chamber with its metallic bark. The sound reverberated off the tower's walls, louder than ever in the confined space.

Raven didn't know dog breeds, but he knew a big bastard when he saw one. And this was one hell of a beast. Huge, black and ferocious. Its eyes seemed to glow in the half-shadows, its thick coat as dark and glossy as polished jet.

The dog came closer, pushing its massive head inside the keep. Its jaws hung open, saliva drooling from teeth as sharp as knives and white as moonlight.

'Down, lad,' said Sergeant Fields, one arm outstretched as if to seize the dog by the scruff of the neck.

But his voice warbled weakly. His act was convincing no one, least of all the dog.

The beast took another step into the tower, barking again.

'Easy, boy,' said Becca. It turned its head towards her, eyes fixed on hers. 'Take it easy now. There's no need to be scared.'

Easy for her to say, thought Raven. But the tactic seemed to be working. The dog ceased its barking and trotted forwards, paws clattering on the stone floor of the castle. It sidled right up to her and dipped its snout.

Becca rubbed it gently, running her hands over the bridge of its nose and across the back of its neck. Raven wondered if the beast would take her arm off, but the dog seemed to like it.

From the entrance, a man's voice called out, 'Quincey?'

Quincey? Suddenly the dog seemed to lose all its menace. How could you be afraid of a dog called Quincey?

Raven started towards the entrance, emerging into daylight. In front of him crouched a thin man, dressed in a black jacket and combat trousers over hiking boots. His hair was a shock of dark thatch, unwashed and uncombed. He looked like he'd been on the road for a long time, sleeping under hedges or in derelict buildings.

Like a ruined castle, for instance.

'Nathan Rigby?'

The man stood up straight, turned and fled.

Raven lurched after him, his right thigh on fire even before he had started. He risked a quick glance behind him, but Becca was still busy with the dog and Sergeant Fields and his assistant were nowhere to be seen.

Bloody hell. Why did there always have to be a chase?

Nathan Rigby was lean and fit. A result, no doubt, of fending for himself in the wild. He sprinted across the green space of the castle courtyard and dashed out through the gap in the outer wall.

Raven lumbered after him, his legs as heavy as lead, as much a drag on his progress as a means of propulsion. His hands slid on wet stone as he pushed himself through the gateway and stumbled down an earth embankment.

Nathan had vanished.

Cursing the gloomy forest and the world in general, Raven set off through the trees, dodging between tall trunks and ducking beneath low-hanging branches. Twigs snapped underfoot and wet leaves slapped his face, but he kept on running.

God knew what had happened to Fields and his deputy, but ahead Raven caught a glimpse of a black figure, pushing through the undergrowth. The thought of that man setting Aurora's hair alight as Hannah watched in horror was enough to spur Raven on. This was the man who had shoved Raj to his death and drained the lifeblood from Reynard. He was a killer and had to be caught.

Raven forced himself onward.

He crashed through brambles, stamped on ferns and stumbled over hidden roots, feeling his chest tighten and his breath come in ragged gasps. His leg was one great ball of flame.

There would be hell to pay for this tomorrow. But he pressed on regardless.

Up ahead he heard a splash and then a cry. Pushing his way heedlessly through a clump of bracken he emerged at the bank of the beck he had crossed earlier on his way to the castle. Nathan had fallen into the water and was thrashing about, struggling to regain his footing.

Raven threw himself into the stream, wrapping his arms around the young man's waist and grappling him into submission. Yet as he dragged him down, his own head dipped beneath the surface. He gulped down a mouthful of icy water before recovering his balance and staggering back to his feet.

Nathan lashed out and pulled away, hauling himself up the opposite bank. But Raven tackled him again, dragging him down the muddy slope and back into the beck before forcing him into submission.

He was a scrawny thing to look at, although his arms

and legs were tight with muscle. His skin wore a light tan, testament to long days spent outdoors. And there, on the back of his neck, was the blood-red mark of a dragon tattoo.

'You've got a lot of life in you for a dead man,' gasped Raven.

He snapped cuffs over the man's wrists and stretched out beside the fugitive, his chest heaving. As they lay there, side by side on the boggy banks of the stream, the woods fell silent at last, save for their heavy panting and the distant cawing of a crow.

*

Never mind shoes, now Raven's whole suit was ruined. He returned to the castle, dripping, sodden, and caked in mud. But at least Nathan Rigby had been arrested, and his black dog pacified.

Quincey, it seemed, had been quick to switch sides under Becca's calm reassurance, recognising a change in fortune and setting petting and belly rubs ahead of loyalty to his former master. A doggy treat had sealed the deal. Who knew what else the resourceful sergeant kept in her pockets along with wads of tissues?

Nathan, meanwhile, was showing no desire to help the police with their inquiries. Bedraggled, defeated, yet still defiant, he refused to answer Raven's questions.

Raven shoved him roughly into the hands of Sergeant Fields. 'Show him the postcard.'

Fields nodded to his deputy, who produced the card, now safely sealed within the protective confines of an evidence bag and showed it to the suspect.

Nathan eyed it briefly, but his expression gave nothing away. Satisfaction? Regret? There was no trace of emotion in those cold, blank eyes.

'What does this mean?' demanded Raven. '*She forgot her vow and must relearn it through suffering.*' He pushed the image of the pious nun into Nathan's face, making him turn away.

It was the first time in Raven's career he had interviewed a suspect who was officially dead. He regarded the man before him with a sense of repulsion. With his haggard appearance, Nathan Rigby did indeed look like a creature lately risen from the grave. And given the havoc he'd wrought, it was hard not to think it would have been better if he really had been washed off the pier in that storm.

'We know who you are and what you've done,' said Raven. 'There's nothing to be gained from silence.'

Yet it seemed that silence was all Nathan was going to give.

Raven persisted with his goading. 'Your name is Nathan Rigby. You faked your own death to escape your debts and begin a new life. How well is that going for you?'

His only response was a sneer.

Raven tried a different tack. 'Your brother is Alexander Rigby. He's already admitted to falsely identifying your body. Your fiancée was Mia Munroe. How did you feel when you heard she'd killed herself?'

At last, Nathan turned his hollowed-out eyes to look at Raven. 'My beautiful Mia.' His voice was hoarse, his words slow and stumbling. The inevitable consequence of a life lived in the shadows with only a stray dog for companionship.

'She's dead, Nathan. Because of what you did.'

'No.' Nathan shook his head in flat denial. 'She's dead because of *them*.' The accusation was a bitter one, infused with bile and black hate.

'Who, Reynard? Aurora, Raj? They were Mia's friends, Nathan. They were *your* friends.'

'They should have looked after her when I was gone. But they were too busy with their own selfish lives. That's why Mia threw herself from that clifftop.'

'No,' said Raven, 'Mia killed herself because she thought you were dead.'

'She was better off without me.'

'So that's what you told yourself. That you weren't to blame. That it was all someone else's fault.'

'I could never forgive them.'

Every murderer crafted a warped version of reality in which they were the victim. Or the hero. In the story they fabricated, they were never the villain.

Raven had no time or appetite for Nathan Rigby's self-pity. He proceeded to the most pressing question of all. 'And what about Lucille?'

A sly smile tugged at the corners of Nathan's thin lips. 'You'll never find her in time.'

His words offered Raven a slender hope. 'Is she still alive?'

But Nathan ignored the question. 'She should have been faithful to Raj. She was a cheater and a liar.'

'So that was her fatal flaw,' said Raven. 'But how is she going to relearn her vow through suffering?'

Nathan continued as if he hadn't heard. 'It's not my fault. She earned her punishment.'

Raven raised his voice to a shout, brandishing the postcard before him. 'Where is she? What does this message mean?'

But all he got was that flat, dead-eyed stare of indifference. Nathan Rigby would go – or return – to his grave before revealing what he'd done with his final victim.

Raven turned to Becca instead, his anger igniting a sudden spark of inspiration. 'I know how we can find out what's happened to Lucille.'

CHAPTER 34

'**H**annah, are you still in the churchyard?'

'No, but don't worry, Dad. I'm perfectly safe. Mr Swales finished speaking to the policeman you sent, and now Ellie and I are having a cup of tea with him in a café.'

The phone signal in the middle of the woods wasn't the best, but it was good to hear Hannah's voice once more. And a relief to know she was no longer in danger, now that Nathan Rigby had been arrested.

'Good,' said Raven. 'Stay right where you are. I need to talk to Mr Swales myself. Can you tell me the name of the café?'

He took the name and hung up. Then he told Becca his plan.

'It's another crazy longshot,' she said, her eyes as narrow as the odds.

'But better than nothing. Which is what we currently have.'

She shrugged. 'You talked me into it. Let's go.'

They left Nathan Rigby in the capable hands of Sergeant Fields, and the dog in the rather less confident charge of his constable, then made their way back to the BMW, splashing once more across the icy beck. Raven's suit was a mess, but there was no chance of changing clothes anytime soon.

He took the journey back to Whitby at a slightly more measured pace and left the car as close to the café on Church Street as he could manage, considering the crowds of goths still flocking about the town centre. There would be a parking ticket waiting for him on his return, but that was of little concern now.

He burst into the café and found Hannah dressed in a black leather jacket, her eyes made up with heavy shadows. Sitting next to her was a woman with ruby-coloured hair. It took him a moment to place her as Becca's flatmate, Ellie Earnshaw. The last time he'd met her, during the course of an investigation, she'd sported a pixie-style haircut with purple highlights. He had half a mind to be cross with her for bringing Hannah to Whitby, but brushed that quickly aside. Instead, he turned his attention to the old man sitting opposite the two women.

He was truly ancient in appearance, his wrinkled face as weathered as one of the crumbling headstones in the graveyard where Hannah had met him. His hair was thin and snowy white, and yet his face was ruddy and he was holding forth with animation, apparently in the middle of relating some story. Hannah and Ellie were laughing at whatever he was telling them.

He stopped mid-flow and turned to Raven. 'Ah, you must be Hannah's father.'

'Dad,' said Hannah. 'This is Mr Swales.'

'Very pleased to meet you,' said Raven, shaking the old man's firm but bony hand.

'You should be right proud of yer daughter,' said Mr Swales. 'And 'er delightful friend, Ellie.'

'I am,' said Raven. 'Very.'

He couldn't stop himself from giving Hannah a quick hug. Then he took a seat at the table.

'So you're the detective investigating these murders,

are yeh?' said Mr Swales.

'Yes,' said Raven. 'And I need your help. A woman is missing and the only clue we have to her whereabouts is this postcard.'

Becca handed him the card and he passed it to Mr Swales.

The old man peered at the image of the nun through rheumy eyes, then turned it over. '*She forgot her vow and must relearn it through suffering.*'

'Do you know what it means?' asked Raven. 'Hannah told me you found a connection between each of the other murders and a local legend.'

'Aye,' said Mr Swales pensively. 'And I think I know which legend this refers to.' He turned the card over once more and pointed to the picture of the nun. 'This poor lady must be intended to be Constance de Beverley. Back in the days when the abbey was a working convent, Constance, who was one of the nuns, fell in love with a handsome knight. Knights in them tales are almost always handsome, you'll find. The ugly ones never seemed to find their way into stories. Anyway, Constance was unable to stop 'erself from breaking 'er vow of chastity. The other nuns were most un-Christian in their response. In order to punish 'er, they bricked 'er up inside the walls of the abbey. It's said 'er screams went on for many days until she finally fell silent. And now the ghost of poor Constance haunts the ruins at night.'

Hannah's face was a mask of horror. 'Do you think this poor woman has been bricked up inside the abbey?'

CHAPTER 35

Raven had done everything within his power to avoid climbing those damn steps, but it seemed there was no way he could get out of it now. He had to get to the abbey without delay, and that meant putting one foot in front of another until he was at the top.

How hard could it be, really?

Bloody hard. Especially since he had just completed a cross-country run through tangled woodland and muddy beck, tripping over every tree root in sight. And quite a few that had remained hidden.

He lifted his eyes to take in the full measure of the challenge, but the incline was too long for him to see beyond the first fifty steps. Beyond that the twisting stairs may as well have climbed all the way to the sky for all the difference it made.

Becca had already called Sergeant Fields and instructed him to organise a search of the abbey, but it was Raven and Becca who were on the scene, and they would have the first opportunity to start looking for Lucille.

If only he could manage to get himself up there.

'Why don't you go ahead without me?' he suggested. 'I

can go back and fetch the car.'

'No way,' said Becca. 'It's miles by road. You're not getting off the hook that easily. Come on. We'll do it together.' She offered her hand and he gave it a scowl.

But what choice did he have? None at all.

If Lucille was entombed within the abbey grounds, then every second counted.

He took Becca's hand and groaned as he lifted his right thigh to mount the first step.

She hauled him up. 'Good. Only one hundred and ninety-eight left to go.' She was already dragging him towards the next step.

'It would help a lot,' he muttered through gritted teeth, 'if you didn't count every single one of them as we went.'

It took a lot of groaning and a lot of cursing, and a fair bit of resting on the benches that partitioned the ascent into a series of separate flights, but eventually they reached the end.

The top of the steps was marked by a tall engraved cross. The grey of St Mary's Church rose before them, surrounded by its crumbling headstones and beyond it lay the sea. A fine sight to behold, if Raven could have spared any energy for it. But it was all he could do to keep going.

From the church, it was a relatively short and level walk to the abbey itself. It was late afternoon now and shadows lay long across the abbey grounds. The weather had turned fairer, helping to keep the chill from Raven's bones. He cast his gaze across the grey ruins, despairing at the prospect of finding Lucille here. If her burial place had been anywhere obvious, surely it would already have been discovered by a visitor or one of the English Heritage staff. She must have been drugged or gagged, or else her cries would have alerted someone to her presence.

'Where do we start?' asked Becca, clearly sharing his misgivings.

'At the nearest point,' said Raven. 'Then work outwards. Keep together. Look for any loose stone or sign of disturbance.'

By the time they had completed a search of the nave, reinforcements were arriving. Jess was first on the scene, followed closely by a team of Whitby constables. 'Spread out!' ordered Raven. 'There are tombstones and other remains beyond the main building.'

He was scouring the nooks and crannies of the north transept by the time Tony and Dinsdale showed up. Dinsdale was his usual grumpy self, presumably because his theory that Alexander Rigby had murdered his own brother had proved to be wide of the mark. But to his credit, his discovery of Nathan's debts had been a key point in unravelling the mystery. Regardless of his feelings, Dinsdale joined the search.

Not long afterwards, Fields himself appeared with more officers. 'Any sign of her?' asked the sergeant.

'Nothing,' cried Raven. 'We keep searching. Give special attention to the lake on the far side of the grounds.' The lake was close to the place Raven had climbed over the wall during his somewhat foolhardy night-time explorations. 'Look for any signs that the earth has been disturbed.'

He resumed his own search in the choir of the ruined abbey. But there was simply nowhere to hide a person. The stones that remained were massive and well-nigh immovable. He was close to the place where Reynard Blackthorn's body had been positioned in the former sanctuary. But Reynard's corpse had lain in full view.

Raven circled the outside of the abbey, but again there was nothing. He walked towards the lake, retracing his steps of the other night. Becca, Jess, Tony, and Dinsdale were traipsing over the ground, heads down, looking for anything out of the ordinary. Fields and his fellow officers were approaching from the opposite direction, poles in hand, probing for soft soil. The only sound was the occasional cawing of the crows circling overhead.

After nearly an hour of fruitless searching, they gathered beneath the large east window of the abbey, faces downcast.

'What did you expect?' grumbled Dinsdale. 'There's nowhere here to hide a body. This nun story sounds like a red herring.'

Raven made no attempt to reply. He didn't need to bring down team morale any lower than the level it had already sunk to. But it was hard to refute Dinsdale's logic. How could Nathan have possibly hidden Lucille here?

'If I was going to bury someone,' mused Sergeant Fields, 'I might choose somewhere that was easier to dig, like the beach.'

That was a fair point.

'But high tide was an hour ago,' said Tony. 'If Lucille was buried in the sands...' he left his conjecture unfinished.

'Any other ideas?' For all Raven knew, Lucille was already dead. But he wasn't giving up until he'd combed every likely location. 'This is still a rescue mission until I say otherwise.'

Becca looked thoughtful. 'There is something we could try. But it's another longshot.'

Raven gave her a smile of encouragement. 'You know what I think about longshots.'

★

'Quincey,' said Becca. 'Nathan took the dog everywhere. Mrs Harker heard it barking the night Reynard was abducted, and a dog hair was found on his body. The dog was spotted again the night Aurora's hair was set on fire. Chances are, Quincey was with Nathan when he buried Lucille. Could we use the dog to help us find her?'

'Shouldn't we bring in a police dog?' muttered Dinsdale. 'They know what they're doing.'

'It will take time to organise a dog handler from Scarborough,' said Raven. 'We should at least start with Nathan's dog. What have we got to lose?' He turned to Sergeant Fields. 'Where is the animal now?'

'It's down at the station. I'll give the guys a call and get them to bring it straight here.'

'Do it,' said Raven. 'And we'll need an item of Lucille's clothing. She was staying at the Black Horse on Church Street.'

The idea of going down all those steps and back up again filled him with nausea. 'Jess, could you run down to the Black Horse and fetch some clothing?'

'No problem.' She set off at a brisk jog.

They left the abbey grounds and made their way to the nearby churchyard. If Lucille wasn't at the abbey, then the church seemed like the most promising location. There was no particular reason to suspect that Lucille was there, but they wouldn't know if they didn't look. 'Get this place cleared,' Raven told Fields, 'and start your officers searching the grounds.'

Before long, the churchyard was sealed off to the public, and officers had begun a search of the church itself.

By the time Jess returned from the Black Horse, a police car was arriving. Raven heard a bark and turned to see the black dog being brought over on a leash. In daylight the animal wasn't half as frightening as it had seemed to Raven in the middle of the night in the grounds of the ruined abbey. It appeared to be in good health despite its adventures and seemed positively eager to get involved. Now that it was in responsible hands and free of Nathan's influence, it was docile enough.

It was big though. It may not have been a hound from hell, but it was one hell of a hound.

Jess sprinted over with an item of clothing wrapped in a plastic evidence bag. 'I've brought Lucille's nightshirt,' she said breathlessly.

'Then let's give it to the dog,' said Raven.

Jess kneeled and the dog trotted over to her. It cocked its head and regarded the assembled group with curiosity.

'Here, Quincey,' said Jess, removing the nightshirt from its bag and offering it to the dog.

The animal needed no further encouragement. It buried its long nose in the black cotton and immediately started barking.

'He recognises the smell,' said Becca. 'See how excited he's getting.'

'That's all very well,' muttered Dinsdale, 'but does he know what to do about it?'

'We just have to let him off the lead,' said Jess. 'And trust that he'll understand what we want from him.'

Raven nodded to the dog's handler.

The constable unclipped the lead and the animal bounded off across the churchyard, darting around gravestones. It hurtled towards the edge of the graveyard and the treacherous cliffs where Mia Munroe had fallen onto the rocks below. Raven grimaced, dreading the thought of being responsible for the death of the dog in addition to Lucille.

But there was no need for him to worry.

The dog stopped by a grave at the furthest corner of the churchyard. It sniffed and pawed at the ground. It let out a whine, almost a howl, that sent shivers down Raven's spine.

'Come on,' he ordered, setting off across the long grass.

By the time he reached the grave, the others were already there. 'It's an empty tomb,' said Sergeant Fields.

Raven frowned. 'How do you work that out?'

'The inscription on the headstone, see? *O hear us when we cry to Thee, For those in peril on the sea.* It's from the seafarers' hymn *Eternal Father, strong to save.* Sailors who were lost at sea were given mock burials.'

Raven crouched down and examined the grave. The soil around the flat stone had clearly been disturbed, as if someone had recently dug around it. That was all the proof he needed.

'Open it up,' he ordered. 'Get that stone lifted.'

He knew he was at risk of getting into all kinds of trouble. If Fields was wrong and the grave turned out to be occupied, he would be facing not only Gillian's wrath, but a disciplinary inquiry. You couldn't carry out an exhumation without permission from the Home Office.

But it wasn't the first time he'd put his career on the line and it wouldn't be the last.

And if there was the slightest chance that Lucille West was under that stone, it was coming up, come what may.

The local police had equipment in one of the cars and before long the heavy stone was being levered up. Within moments, it was clear of the ground.

'Careful,' cautioned Fields. 'Don't let it slip.'

Raven held his breath as younger and fitter officers manoeuvred the stone, raising it inch by inch. A wrong move now could prove fatal if Lucille was inside the tomb and still alive. Very slowly, daylight reached its bright fingers into the hollow of the grave.

Raven peered over the shoulders of the men, straining for a glimpse of clothing or anything that might reveal the presence of a living person, but as darkness receded and the space beneath the gravestone grew wider, there was still nothing to see. 'She must be here,' he murmured.

Quincey was lying nearby, watching the work unfold, his huge head resting on his paws. Had the dog been wrong? Was there nothing there but an empty void? Raven swallowed, his throat dry, a feeling of sickness in his stomach.

A shout cut through the silence. One of the constables scrabbled to his knees. 'Hold it!'

'What is it?' asked Fields. 'What can you see?'

'It's her!'

Raven leaned in and caught a glimmer of pale skin. He watched as two more officers stepped forward to assist in lifting the stone. This was perhaps the most delicate and critical moment in the operation. If the heavy stone slipped and fell now... Raven closed his eyes, unable to watch.

But before long it had been shifted safely aside and the grave stood open.

The body of Lucille West lay in the shallow space, pale as death, her mouth taped closed, her wrists and ankles bound tight by rope. Her eyes were closed and her body unmoving. Was she already dead?

It was Becca who reacted first. Crouching down, she pressed two fingers against Lucille's neck, feeling for a pulse. For a moment no one dared move. The only sound was the distant crashing of the waves on the rocks below. Then Becca looked up directly into Raven's eyes. 'She's alive!'

CHAPTER 36

The concert at the Abbey Brewery had kicked off later than planned, due to the police activity at the nearby abbey and later at St Mary's. But the rescue operation had concluded successfully and Hannah had been relieved to get a call from her father telling her that Lucille West had been found alive.

'It was all thanks to your quick thinking,' he'd told her.

'And Mr Swales,' she'd pointed out. But her heart had swollen at the pride evident in his voice.

'You did something amazing today,' Ellie had told her. 'You saved a woman's life.'

It was difficult to grasp the reality of that. All she had done was listen to an old man's story and draw a connection between a gruesome legend and the case her father was investigating.

It was hard to comprehend how this man, Nathan Rigby, could have found inspiration in such a horrible tale to wreak revenge on his former friends. Hannah didn't know how her father could spend his time dealing with such terrible people. But she was glad that somebody had the guts to do it.

After picturing the horror of a woman being left to die inside a tomb, she wasn't sure she wanted to go and hear Velvet Nocturne play. The band's dark songs with their sinister lyrics weren't exactly what she needed to hear right now. It might be better just to go back to Scarborough and wait for her dad to get home.

But it was Ellie who persuaded her to go. 'Come on, you told me the lead singer's hot, right?'

'Dante.'

'You have a crush on him?'

Hannah felt her cheeks grow warm. 'A bit.'

'Then we have to go. It's as simple as that.'

In the end she enjoyed hearing the band play and watching Dante perform. He was his usual cool and enigmatic self – tight black trousers and T-shirt, mirrored sunglasses, dark stubble – and she felt a thrill every time he looked her way.

Which was quite often, it seemed.

He caught Hannah's eye and smiled. She smiled back, her heart doing a little flip-flop. There was something irresistibly charismatic about him.

'He likes you,' said Ellie, giving her a nudge. 'He likes you a lot.'

'Maybe.'

The band played the same set they'd performed at the pavilion, and the last song finished to thunderous applause and cheers. The crowd were enjoying themselves, the combination of music and beer having the usual harmonious effect. Dante bowed and looked out across the audience.

He was so good-looking. So glamorous. So out of reach.

Yet he was there on the stage in front of her. He looked her way again and her insides turned to jelly.

Was he going to come over and say hello?

She imagined what it might be like to be the girlfriend of a famous rock star, to appear on his arm, to be photographed and attend events.

And then a dark-haired woman standing at Hannah's side ran up onto the stage and threw her arms around him. From the way she and Dante embraced, they were clearly a couple. He hadn't been looking at Hannah at all.

She felt a tear smart her eye and wiped it away.

Ellie took her by the arm. 'Come on, your mascara's running. It's time to go.'

'Yes,' said Hannah. 'Take me back to Scarborough.'

★

'So is Lucille going to be all right?' asked Ellie. 'Was she injured?'

'Not physically,' said Becca. 'She's recovering in hospital. She ought to be ready to leave in a day or two. But psychologically it's going to take much longer to come to terms with what happened.'

They were back in their shared apartment overlooking Scarborough's North Bay and Becca felt good to be home. Although Whitby was just a short drive along the coast, the town had a different feel to Scarbrough. The smell of the sea, the shape of the waves rolling across the bay, the calls of the gulls – they were all subtly different. And as for the fish and chips, they just didn't compare in Becca's opinion, although she acknowledged that this was a matter of debate.

Ellie shuddered. 'Buried alive! She must have thought she was going to die. I don't like tight spaces even at the best of times. I'd have gone bat-crazy in that grave.'

Becca also found herself recoiling at the idea of being sealed inside a tomb. Lucille had lain in the darkness for hours, unable to scream or shout for help. But was that any worse than the other means of execution Nathan had devised for his former friends? Reynard, drained of his blood until his heart stopped beating. Aurora, set alight. Raj thrown to his death from the lighthouse.

By any measure this had been a bizarre case. Normally, the details of a murder would have been kept confidential, but here the crimes had played out like a public performance, with news spreading like wildfire among the festival goers and broadcast by that TV reporter, Liz Larkin. Becca hoped she had seen the last of her. And more to the point, that Raven had seen the last of her.

'Did he really do it because he blamed his friends for not looking after his girlfriend?' asked Ellie. 'That's just sick.'

'Yes.' Becca had just returned from an interview with Nathan in which he'd eventually opened up and set out his twisted logic. 'He couldn't accept his own responsibility for what happened to Mia. He walked away from his debts by faking his death and assumed that his friends would step in to look after her. But they were busy with their own lives. Revenge was a way for him to try to shift the blame onto them. That's why he left those messages on postcards. He wanted to draw attention to the weaknesses in their character.'

Becca had divulged a few of the details of the case to Ellie. Normally she would have kept them to herself, but with so much in the public domain already, there seemed little harm in sharing a little more with a close friend.

'And how did he manage to sneak around without being caught?'

Becca pictured the plague doctor's costume with its hideous mask, first caught on the photographer's camera and then discovered in Nathan's hideaway at Mulgrave Castle. 'He wore a disguise to conceal his identity. That's why he waited for the goth festival before putting his plan into action. He knew that with everyone dressed up, he'd be able to go wherever he wanted without anyone knowing who he was. But of course his friends recognised him as soon as he removed his mask. He knew they would all be in town and he knew where they would be staying. He visited them one by one and they went with him willingly. Remember, they thought he was dead, so imagine their astonishment when he turned up alive. They must have been happy to see him. At first.'

'There's one thing I don't understand,' said Ellie. 'If Nathan faked his death, who was the drowned man?'

It was a good question. When asked, Nathan had been unable to offer much insight. He'd confirmed what Alexander had previously said – that Nathan had been down near the pier and had seen a man washed into the sea by a huge wave. As to the identity of that man, he had nothing further to add. Tony had begun to make enquiries and had found a missing persons report relating to an Estonian man who had not returned to the guest house where he'd been staying.

'The body will have to be exhumed,' Becca explained, 'so that DNA and other tests can be carried out.'

Ellie shook her head. 'How horrible.'

'By the way,' said Becca, eager to change the subject, 'thanks for looking after Hannah.'

Ellie smiled. 'No problem. I'm glad you introduced me to her. We had a great time together. I'd like to see her again, if her visit hasn't put her off Scarborough forever.'

'It hasn't been easy for her, has it? Nor for Raven.'

Mention of Raven made Becca reflect on the new side she'd seen of her boss during the investigation. The worried father, desperately anxious about his daughter's safety. She understood his concern, but as with all things, Raven had taken it too far.

He'd apologised for his bad behaviour during the drive to Mulgrave Castle and she'd forgiven him and put his outburst behind her. He'd even asked for her advice about a birthday present for Hannah and she'd been happy to help.

The more she saw of Raven, the more complex he seemed to become. Police officer, colleague, husband – now ex-husband – and father. Each facet cast him in a new light, yet she fancied she was beginning to perceive the whole picture. The incident on the way to the castle had brought them closer together than ever, and she wondered if she might now add "friend" to the list of roles.

'Come on,' said Ellie, 'let's go out for a drink. You

deserve it after all you've done.'

Becca yawned. She simply didn't have Ellie's limitless capacity for late nights and alcohol. She needed to start setting boundaries. And seeing Raven and Hannah together had made her think of her own parents. 'Actually,' she said, 'I'm going to call in at the guest house this evening to see Mum and Dad. And then I'm going to have an early night.'

CHAPTER 37

It had been a week since Nathan Rigby had been arrested and charged with three counts of murder and one of attempted murder. Six days since Raven had driven Hannah to Scarborough train station and watched as the 10:54 to York had pulled out with her on board. Five days since she'd returned to university for the summer term.

It would be two months before she completed her final exams and three months before she returned to stay with him again. He had already booked the final week in July as leave, making it clear to Gillian that these dates were non-negotiable.

In the meantime, he and Hannah had made a promise to keep in touch more regularly and to make time for a weekly Skype call.

This was the first of those calls.

'Hi, Dad, how's it going?' Hannah waved at him from the screen of his laptop. A juddery, pixellated image that scarcely did her justice, but was enough to make him catch his breath at the feelings it stirred in him.

'Great, thanks. Did you get back all right?'

'Yeah, no problem. I spent a night in London and then came down to Exeter the next day.'

'And how is your mum?'

'She's good. She's glad I had a nice time in Scarborough, even though you were busy some of the time.'

They shared a conspiratorial smile.

Before Hannah had left, they'd agreed not to tell Lisa what part Hannah had played in the events in Whitby which had been making frontpage headlines for the past week. The spate of bizarre killings had shocked the nation. Lisa didn't need to know how close Hannah had come to danger. There were some things that were best kept between father and daughter.

'So is the case all wrapped up now?' she asked.

'Yes. Nathan Rigby admitted everything. He'll get life. And my boss congratulated me on being a media pro.'

Hannah laughed. 'You? A media pro?'

'Well, I'm getting there.'

In their debriefing session after the investigation, Gillian had congratulated Raven on his use of the media to generate the lead that resulted in the photograph of the plague doctor, but had been furious about the series of leaks to the press that had dogged the investigation right from the start. She had blamed Raven.

Raven had vehemently denied being behind any such leak. He strongly suspected Sergeant Mike Fields of having a hand in that. Fields hadn't liked having his town overrun by goths. When challenged, Liz Larkin had refused to confirm or deny his suspicion, but had hinted he was on the right lines.

'Did my birthday present arrive?' he asked Hannah, switching the subject back to the personal and hopefully to less controversial grounds.

'I've got it here,' said Hannah, showing him a small, gift-wrapped parcel. 'I thought I would open it now.'

Raven held his breath as Hannah carefully peeled back the wrapping paper. Despite Becca's endorsement, he still didn't know if she'd like it. The wrapping paper came away to reveal a small box and Hannah's mouth formed a silent "O". 'Dad, is this what I think it is?'

'I don't know. Tell me what you're thinking.'

Her voice dropped to a whisper. 'I'm thinking jewellery.'

'Only one way to find out.'

Her eyes lit up as she lifted the lid of the box and saw what was inside. 'Oh, these are beautiful!'

He breathed a sigh of relief, pleased that Becca's choice of a teardrop pendant necklace with matching earrings had hit the mark. They had chosen it together from one of the jet jewellers on Church Street. Fortunately, there were plenty of other shops to pick from besides Alexander Rigby's.

'Thank you!' Hannah blew him a kiss over cyberspace.

The call was interrupted by the sound of hammering from the kitchen where Barry was finally installing the new taps. This was followed by a loud bark. The door inched open and a black snout poked its way inside, quickly followed by the rest of Quincey. The dog bounded onto the sofa beside Raven, nuzzled up to him and woofed a greeting at Hannah.

'Oh my God, you've kept the dog! I was going to ask what had happened to Quincey.'

Raven laid a hand on the dog's collar. A new purchase – the first of many, he suspected – and one that marked the end of Quincey's days as a stray and the beginning of his new life. 'I've agreed to foster him on a trial basis, otherwise he would have been sent to live in kennels.'

The arrangement was in principle a temporary one, to test how dog and owner got on together. If it didn't work out, Quincey would go to a more suitable home. But Raven was already thinking it might become a more permanent state of affairs. At first he'd dismissed the notion, protesting that his house was too small and he was out all day, but a chat with Barry had revealed that the builder's wife ran a doggy daycare centre from their home in Scalby Mills.

'Vicky would love to have a black Labrador to look after,' Barry had said. 'They're her favourite breed.'

After that, Raven hadn't had the heart to let the dog go into kennels. Quincey deserved better, considering the starring role he'd played in rescuing Lucille West from her grave. The arrangement suited everyone – Vicky Hardcastle would look after the dog during the daytime and Raven would collect him each evening. It would be company for him, and a reason to go for daily walks.

But not up a hundred and ninety-nine steps.

His leg had healed after the abuse it had been subjected to at Whitby, but he knew he had to go easy. Regular walking over firm and level ground would strengthen his muscles without subjecting them to damaging strain.

The hammering stopped and Barry called out. 'Raven? The job's all finished. Do you want to take a look?'

'I'd better let you go,' said Hannah.

Raven was reluctant to bid farewell, but couldn't risk Barry escaping without first checking that everything really was done properly. 'All right, but you'll come back and see me in the summer?'

'As soon as term finishes. Besides, now you've got Quincey, I'll definitely want to come and visit.'

'You prefer the dog to me?'

'He does look like a sweetie.'

The dog was staring at Hannah's face on the screen. He turned to Raven, his tongue hanging out. Drool slipped over Raven's trousers.

'Don't be fooled. He turns into a monster if I forget to take him out for a walk.'

'You'd better take him then,' said Hannah. 'Goodbye, Dad.'

'Goodbye.'

As Raven closed the laptop, Barry's broad form filled the doorway. 'All done, squire.'

'Have you really finished?' Raven asked him. 'No "bits and bobs" still left to do? No last-minute hitches?'

'Done and dusted. Come and have a look if you don't believe me.'

It hardly seemed possible. Barry and Reg had been a part of Raven's life almost since he'd returned to Scarborough the previous year. It had taken six months for them to demolish and rebuild his house. During that time, Raven had all but despaired that the project would ever reach completion. But it seemed that the wait was finally over.

He turned on the gleaming chrome taps that Barry had fitted, marvelling at the way water gushed out of them and gurgled down the drain. It seemed a miracle of engineering. A triumph of plumbing mastery. 'No leaks?' he queried.

Barry sighed. 'Leaks, he says. Hear that, Reggie? After all we've done, he still has doubts. What can you say to a man like that?'

Reggie shrugged, his arms spread wide in a well-practised move. He had nothing to suggest.

Barry clapped a large hand on Raven's shoulder. 'Any problems, Raven, you know who to call. And if you ever want something else doing, like a loft extension, you know where I am.'

'A loft extension?' Raven shuddered at the prospect. He'd be mad to take on any more building work after this. 'I think this house will suit me and Quincey just fine.'

VIGIL FOR THE DEAD
(TOM RAVEN #6)

**A desolate moor. A burned body. A deadly
conspiracy.**

DCI Tom Raven is enjoying the long summer days when
an encounter with an old army pal spouting conspiracy
theories reignites long-buried memories he would rather
forget.

A few days later, walkers crossing the North York Moors
discover the burnt remains of a body beside a stone cross
on a Bronze Age burial mound.

When the investigation leads to a top-secret military base,
Raven is drawn into a plot that threatens national security.
He must confront his mixed emotions about his own
military past while in a race against time to unravel the
conspiracy and catch the killer.

Set on the North Yorkshire coast, the Tom Raven series is
perfect for fans of David J Gatward, J M Dalgliesh, Simon
McCleave, and British crime fiction.

THANK YOU FOR READING

We hope you enjoyed this book. If you did, then we would be very grateful if you would please take a moment to leave a review online. Thank you.

THE TOM RAVEN SERIES

Tom Raven® is a registered trademark of Landmark Internet Ltd.
The Landscape of Death (Tom Raven #1)
Beneath Cold Earth (Tom Raven #2)
The Dying of the Year (Tom Raven #3)
Deep into that Darkness (Tom Raven #4)
Days Like Shadows Pass (Tom Raven #5)
Vigil for the Dead (Tom Raven #6)

THE BRIDGET HART SERIES

Bridget Hart® is a registered trademark of Landmark Internet Ltd.
Aspire to Die (Bridget Hart #1)
Killing by Numbers (Bridget Hart #2)
Do No Evil (Bridget Hart #3)
In Love and Murder (Bridget Hart #4)
A Darkly Shining Star (Bridget Hart #5)
Preface to Murder (Bridget Hart #6)
Toll for the Dead (Bridget Hart #7)

PSYCHOLOGICAL THRILLERS

The Red Room

ABOUT THE AUTHOR

M S Morris is the pseudonym for the writing
partnership of Margarita and Steve Morris. They both
studied at Oxford University, where they first met in
1990. Together they write psychological thrillers and
crime novels. They are married and live in Oxfordshire.

Find out more at msmorrisbooks.com where you can
join our mailing list, or follow us on Facebook at
facebook.com/msmorrisbooks.